GHOST RUNNERS

an Olympic Dream Betrayed

A novel by

ROBERT RUBENSTEIN

COPYRIGHTED MATERIAL

Ghost Runners: An Olympic Dream Betrayed

All rights reserved. Updated, fully revised.

2nd edition published by author.

No part of this book may be reproduced or transmitted in any form or by any means without written permission of the author.

Original copyright c 2010 by Robert Rubenstein.

2nd Edition copyright c 2015 by author.

Library of Congress Control Number: 2010913497.

ISBN-13: 978-0692534007

This is a work of fiction. Any resemblance to actual persons, living or dead, is purely coincidental

Printed 2015 by Create Space.

First published in 2010 as Ghost Runners

By All Things That Matter Press.

Cover Art by: www.anya.nyc   2015.

All rights reserved

AUTHOR'S NOTE

This is a work of historical fiction based on the actual events of August 9, 1936 in the Berlin Olympics. The characters portrayed, including well known sports and Olympic heroes, have also been fictionalized, including the participants of the 4x100 meter Olympic team, those who ran for the American squad, or those whom did not compete because they were Jewish.

DEDICATED TO
ALISTER AND SHAYA.

SPECIAL THANKS
SHAYA RUBENSTEIN

FOR ARIA AND ROSS

"WHY, SON OF PELEUS, DO YOU, WHO ARE BUT MAN, GIVE CHASE TO ME WHO AM IMMORTAL? HAVE YOU NOT YET FOUND OUT THAT IT IS A GOD WHOM YOU PURSUE SO FURIOUSLY?"

    The Iliad, Book 22.
        Homer.

PROLOGUE

The Indian tapped his cane inside the National Museum in downtown Washington. The way had been cleared for Native American recovery of artifacts: bones, headdresses, belts and buckles, and whole bodies that were stuffed and stacked, and neatly put on display. There were tools and weapons of the Great Plains hunters, housed in Washington, but belonging to the Native tribes. The federal government was beginning to see the light, paving the way for a rebirth of Native culture, despite violations to sacred objects, during and after the Indian Wars. It was beginning to be a new day, but the old was still in sight.

He was taking a tour, guided by a young woman who wore glasses. She was one of the Dine, the word used by the Navajo to describe her kind. The old one looked squarely into her eyes and knew her sad history. Alcohol made many Dine diabetic. They suffered the New World through the fog and dim light of the old. Opticians had come to Gallup, the Indian capital, for easy profits and federal money, and spread out in droves towards the neighboring Southwest Indians, even the youngest of whom wore glasses.

His cane had been a gift from his people, almost a replica of Ben Franklin's walking stick, but instead of gold-plaited, a turquoise stone graced the edge. The wood was carved from a downed oak that had survived well beyond the Indian Wars. The cane was larger than him. There was irony in that. Sometimes he had imagined himself like Moses with a walking staff that quickly turned into a serpent. He kept those images to himself for good reason. Outwardly, his dress was in the colorless light of the Navajo; blue shirt, jeans, drab dark jacket, and an L.A. Dodger cap. The gray hair hung like willows to hide his eyes, the window of a soul without vision. His were of a different hue. He was not as he seemed

But neither was the facade of The Smithsonian, a gift to the United States by a British born, illegitimate child, James Lewis Lace who had changed his name to James Smithson. The exhibits came from collectors from all over the world. Through the glass, his dim sight saw skeletal remains of dinosaurs and arthropods and a few that shone macabre, half-human faces.

There were murmurs and laughter erupting from some of the black youth that walked on the tour. Later on that same day, they were going outside the White House to see some of the athletes from the 1976 Olympic team who were invited there for the Medal of Freedom award. That year, it was to be presented to Jesse Owens. The old Indian listened with interest.

He was wrestling with himself, whether to, but knowing he would go. But dressed as he was, and for reasons known only to himself, he wavered among the old bones of the "others," those strange, cruel Indian remains.

"That's you," said one, jostling his friend.

"No, not me, man. It's your mother."

"Maybe that's Jesse Owens."

"Jesse ain't no Indian, N ...," said another friend.

"Jesse's an N ..." just like you and me."

The Indian whirled, the L.A. Dodger cap dropping to the floor. Therese Nightingale, the tour guide, squinted hard at his eyes. His gray hair flowing to the side had revealed a secret. "Your eyes, your eyes are blue," she whispered.

He ignored her, pointing his staff with dark anger towards the youth.

"What do you know about Jesse? What do you know about his suffering? You need a lesson," he said, lunging at them, his Moses staff suddenly shouldered for war.

Grabbing him from behind, security officers pushed him into the glass and smashed his stick under their heels. The macabre faces stared at him, but he never looked back. He had known restraints once or twice before. The past was palpable like yesterday.

Moving on, Therese Nightingale talked about another exhibit. It was from the "Bright Path," the Sac and Fox tribe. Old skeleton remains were displayed from a recent archeological dig.

"Many people don't know," she said, shaking from the tumult nearby, "that Jim Thorpe, a famous Native American, came from that tribe. In the 1912 Olympics in Stockholm, Sweden ..."

Her words were too much for the old Indian to bear. His hands and feet trembled, his breathing labored. "Ach," he said, visions of the past came on little fists that seemed to split his skull. Young Joshua Sellers, as he was known, had challenged Jesse Owens for six long years in foot races up and down the Midwest. In films of those races, Joshua was always second, eating Jesse's dust. Now he was handcuffed, the Indian under arrest, shamed by the stares of the museum goers and hauled away toward Pennsylvania Avenue.

"I must go to the White House," Joshua said. "Can you take me there?"

"Not today, old man."

"I need to find Jesse. It's been ... forty years. Can you take me there?"

"No, not today, chief."

"Jerry Ford, that old bear, knows me. He'll let me in."

And Joshua was crying. "I need to see Jesse. I have something to say to him."

"Oh, and you want to see *our* president too?"

One look toward his partner and the call was made.

"Well, what's your name?"

The old man thought. He smelled the dust that separated Owens and him in a foot race, the hugs of friends, the laughter and the tears among the heartache, the jokes, the singing aboard ship. Joshua remembered their rivalry again, those days and nights when his thoughts had darkly turned.

"I need to see Jesse to apologize."

"Not today."

An ambulance outside waited. He quietly stepped from the curb, but not inside. He knew his heart beat wildly. His face was smacked by cold, January winds that swirled toward The White House.

"Well, who are you, what's your name?"

He was hoisted inside the ambulance. To Saint Elizabeth's Hospital for observation. He had mentioned the president's name.

The name he went by didn't make any sense today. The guards stared. Tubes rolled round his chest. His head was pounding like little fists in his brain. "I don't know. I don't know my name ... anymore."

PART 1

1
Chicago World's Fair, August, 12, 1933.

Goodyear blimps flew over the fair and the lakefront, and disappeared in the blue haze. An aura of colored lights beamed across the corporate pavilions. Searchlights crisscrossed over the lighthouse, over the General Motors exhibit. Lights illuminated the fairway.

"Lights," barked the poor folk, huddled together outside the fair. The twenty-five cents admission price was too high. Only the privileged could stroll past the gleaming, white Ford pavilion. Floodlights bathed the nine hundred foot, ten stories high exhibition.

I.B.M. showcased an array of sorting, filing, tabulating, and typing business machines. It promised the future. Contributing to world business progress, it would serve the interests of clients both there and ...abroad.

At Rutledge Tavern, Anna Robinson did an exaggerated take of the southern mammy. Causing a nationwide sensation, her face would be on kitchen shelves throughout the country. Aunt Jemima pancakes were so good that sixty buses for Greyhound, built by General Motors, made her little stand in the midway a must-see attraction. She rolled her eyes and slapped her thighs, ogling for the white audience in a head rag promotion of General Exhibit flipped pancakes.

In the new age of skyscrapers, fairgoers climbed aboard the Otis elevator which took them to the top of the high towers.

Visitors marveled at the vertical operation, taking tours of the machine rooms from a hoist-way. On a clear day, they could see three states fifty miles away.

The Brother Crawford sky ride carried the crowd across beams of searchlights and through the fireworks that burst over the lagoon. The grounds were brightly lit. Through the aluminum window of one car, Joshua Sellers watched a panorama of water nymphs that tripped over the water in a light show of ovals and angles.

In its own way, that private car was special, honoring characters from the "Amos and Andy" radio show. The Chicago Tribune had the rights and a wide audience to the first sit-com in America. The fair also decided to include an exhibit about the progress of African-Americans.

"Whoa," said Joshua, seeing the posters put on the aluminum sidings of the Brother Crawford car. Black musicians, artists, war veterans and athletes were going to hold their own celebration. Joe Louis would be there. The Brown Bomber in a two fisted pose was sure to draw, but Joshua narrowed his focus on the image of the lanky athlete fate had made him pursue. Along with Ralph Metcalfe, the silver medalist at the 1932 Olympic Games, and Matt Robinson and his younger brother, Jackie, Joshua studied the face of the American champion. His ability seemed unearthly, the one who could not be beaten: Jesse Owens, the Brown Thunderbolt.

The blacks paid double the price to Soldier's Field. Not even to get to see the midway, outside the fair. It was an outrage worse than a racial slur. It was racism undisguised. The Century of Progress, the theme of the fair, served corporate interests. Neither women nor blacks were represented there. Blacks were not treated with respect, employed as porters, latrine cleaners, or exhibited as "freaks" or pygmies in midway spectacles. In Midget Village, The Old Plantation and Showboat attractions were coated with-washed and warped views of black history. In terms of lessening race prejudice, however, the world's fair could've been held just as well on the moon.

At present, Joshua's focus was racing, not racism. He was noticed by a few beauty contestants vying for Miss Bronze America. In his Michigan warm-up jersey, he had crashed the gates and fell in step with actors and musicians whom had gathered for another event, a spectacular pageant about Booker T. Washington and the progress of race relations since the slave revolts. When Joshua's blue eyes were spotted, he drew good-natured hoots, largely from the actors in The Epic of a Race.

"Hmm, didn't know we had white boys here," said a bronze-skinned girl, hands on hips.

Joshua smiled shyly. "I'm looking for the track, ma'am. I'm looking for Jesse Owens."

"Jesse Owens?" said one of the stragglers from the Knights of Python, "You just can't find Jesse. Don't you know he's the Brown Thunderbolt?"

"I've heard that, sir, but tell me where the race is going to be run."

The man took Joshua's full measure. It was not often a white boy would be a straight man for some colored humor. He looked up into the highest ranking of the tiers for seats that seemed to be located on another planet. "Jesse Owens is up there," he said, pointing, laughing at his own joke.

A family had gotten into a row with others upset about their southern plantation dress. The fair welcomed stereotypes, even "Uncle Tom's." It gave whites what they wanted and kept the blacks at bay. The sniping suddenly ended as the gathering saw a bigger threat.

Joshua and the Knight of Python froze as an ominous object appeared in the sky. A huge dirigible was flying above the last row of the amphitheater. Unlike the many small blimps that carried streams of small banners, that one dwarfed the others. It hovered menacingly over the fair, swirling the dust on the infield of Soldier's Field. The Knight of Python seemed to judge Joshua differently. He spoke directly, not for sport, smirk fading. "Jesse and the boys are over yonder," he said, pointing, his look still skyward.

His name was Jack Dawkins, a veteran of the World War, wounded in combat. He had also led a brigade of blacks who fought back in the streets of Chicago during the Red Scare episodes and the killing of blacks during the racial wars of 1919.

One of his war buddies had been shot dead in the south because some white boys objected to a black boy wearing an American uniform around town.

"Only clothes I own," the boy pleaded before he was murdered; killer, or killers, still unknown.

The infield of the great soldier's dome had a quarter mile oval, a red cinder path that kicked up dust in the crosswinds of Chicago. At that time of the day the winds blew unpredictably. The judges couldn't decide in which direction to run the race.

The contestants formed a circle, except for the one who was in a world apart. He had gone to Soldier's Field last May and shattered records. His school was East Technical High in Cleveland. Jesse Owens now wore the emblem of the buckeyes of The Ohio State. Though Owens had not competed in any Olympics, Ralph Metcalfe respected the high school champion. Metcalfe had come in second to Frank Wyckoff at the Olympic Games in Los Angeles last year.

Jesse's smooth brown skin glistened with strength and a graceful southern countenance. No matter the circumstance, the athlete would disarm his competitor with a soft ease, the same way he glided over the cinders. It didn't matter which event—the running broad jump, the two hundred meters, the hundred meter dash—first was his most of the time, and the others ate his dust.

Not everyone in that circle saw a color war when he approached. Jesse knew Joshua Sellers had earned the right to be there. In sixteen high school races, Joshua who had gone to Hughes High School in Cincinnati, had come in second fifteen times, but also beat him once.

"Well, look who's here? Hey Seconds," said Jesse, smiling.

Ralph Metcalfe looked up and bopped Joshua on the head. "You can't crash this race," he said.

"Says who? Sign says, 'all comers.'"

"Get out of here."

It was Matt Robinson who tried to tickle Joshua's ribs. Matt's younger brother, Jackie, laughed. The boy wore a baseball cap backwards and held an infielder's glove. He worked that brown mitt constantly trying to knead the perfect fit. Now he had a regulation ball tucked inside.

"That white boy wants to integrate us," said Matt.

"But this is Black's Day. That boy is white. Huh, more pink than white," said thirteen-year-old, Jackie Robinson.

"Oh, blacker than white or pink."

"Huh. You're not even brown."

Joshua's father had argued before that to be Jewish was to be more black than Caucasian. The old man said both Semites and blacks were oppressed. Joshua didn't see color when he saw Jesse. He only felt the desire to end that dusty streak of being an "also ran," someone who raced but never won. Joshua was eagle-eyed, face to face with Owens. A curve of the mouth, the dryness in the lips, and the stare down of rivals, the boys had no friends in the race to the tape.

By the luck of the draw, they went to the same conference, and The Big Ten Midwestern champion usually came from Ohio State or Michigan. Wherever Joshua was Jesse Owens seemed to be. Jesse had been given another nickname, "The Ohio Bullet."

But Joshua had an edge in the sixty meter dash. He was always first out of the hole, and held the national record for the short distance. He watched a judge in a black-frock coat and a few coaches with watches to measure time. Time meant records made or broken.

The crowd came down from the high rafters to the infield. They were there to see Jesse win. It would be from his strong, brown thighs that something miraculous was going to happen. Maybe if he ran enough times to prove the worth of a black man, the gates outside the fair would suddenly open wide. "Maybe," said Jack Dawkins, feeling a stab of left-over shrapnel in the dusty atmosphere.

"Let's go, Jesse."

"Go, J.C."

James Cleveland Owens became Jesse when his school teacher didn't understand the southern way he said, "J.C." Soon, everyone was calling him Jesse, the nickname that stuck.

Joshua removed his sweats and jacket. In an undershirt and shorts, his muscles were keen and rippled, and unbothered by swirling gnats. He got busy digging with his hands, finding a snug spot from which to leap. On one side of him there was Jesse Owens, tall and lanky; on the other, Metcalfe, the silver medalist. Joshua didn't know if they were going to have the sixty meters in the Olympic Games. Steely- eyed, he looked at Owens and smiled. Owens returned a sideways glance.

The airship waited to circle the lakefront. It had gone the entire length of Chicago before flying overhead. The Graf Zeppelin would travel a million miles. Chicago had seen it touch down, descending into its brown, gray haunches. By day it blotted out the sun, by night the stars. In times past it had been cheered on by fifty thousand. It made a half-turn to display the German flag of Weimar. But Joshua was not fooled — like everyone else, he knew what was on the other side. Flapping in the breeze, its mammoth banners carried a singular message on vertical streams.

Hidden from the folks at the fair; indeed, from all Chicagoans, the pilot had flown in a circuitous path to keep the new Reich government's accursed symbol facing lakeside. A symbol without real meaning, the giant swastikas heralded a new breed of Germans called Nazis. A chorus of boos greeted the hovering aircraft from inside the pavilions. There were skirmishes between German-Americans on opposite sides of the political spectrum, the black and red swastikas on the Graf Zeppelin's tail, inciting rage or adulation. But Joshua would have to run with cool detachment to beat Metcalfe and Owens.

His advantage — they could not propel toward a second gear in that race. Sixty meters cut short their thirst for top speed.

***

"Sixty meters for the Chicago championship," said a voice from a megaphone in the first row of stands.

"Ohh…enz," was a chorus, prayer, call to glory; anyone ever oppressed would bless that name.

"Ohh…enz," the voices shouted for their tower of hope, the poster boy of the dark quarters. On a cloud of cinder dust blazing with the feet of champions, his was the more hallowed name; the other, pretenders.

"Owens."

Even the ragtag children in the stands, wading on the infield beyond their parent's arms, knew that victory was the only way to beat the hangman's noose, the dirty jobs, and the double-priced admission they had to pay. Neither Jesse nor Joshua would bow to the other, but on that day, Mercury would prove to have the wings of a white boy.

"Better get used to the language of the next Olympic Games," the hearty voice on the megaphone said.

"*Auchtung,*

Auf die platz,

Fertig, Los."

Sixty Meter Dash, Soldier's Field, Chicago.
August 12, 1933.

The gun fired and five thousand Jesse Owens' fans came down from the rafters to urge him on. It was sports that would prove to be the equalizer to let them in the door, to break the yoke of race discrimination. No white man's legs could run faster. But this race was over in a heartbeat, and nobody on earth was faster than Joshua Sellers that day. He was off first, propelled by the tension in his thighs, grinding his feet into the soft earth and tripping over the cinders, moving in the dust with an internal engine. Soon he was thrust ahead an arm's length past the anguished breath of Metcalfe when Owens suddenly came leaping by — the gazelle nearly catching him, but Joshua pushed with his heart, his head imploding to lunge first over the tape, Owens bursting by too late. There was shock, tears in the eyes of his desperate army, the Brown Thunderbolt beaten.

"The race is mine," Joshua cried.

Except for some "harrumphs," nobody paid attention. He had proven that already, but suddenly red-faced, he fought back the tears. He saw Jesse Owens' hand out-stretched, walking towards him, "Oh, you'll have your days, Seconds."

"I just want to run like you."

Both looked skyward and saw the airship turn, swastikas now in full view. "We'll both get our chance," said Jesse.

Joshua nodded, admiring the grace of his rival. Neither would let the other's hand go, even when crosswinds erupted from the lake in a sudden gust, moving the airship skyward above the city of Chicago.

2
January, 1935, near Bakersfield, California.

Jesse Owens was in a world of trouble. The starlets were taking him for a ride, and he was so far from home that he didn't know where to hide. In California, a cotton picking contest interested him. He had known the backbreaking work of carrying cotton sacks in the sun drenched fields of Oakville and Danville, Alabama. At seven years old, he wanted to follow in his folk's footsteps. But nothing could ease the pain when his knees got sore. The fingers, torn and cut, felt crushed to the bone. But it was the work with plows and hoes that nearly did him in. The idea was to kill the weeds. The hot sun and the monotony wore him down. And during the wet season, he couldn't do the job. He'd go out into the fields with his father, and toiled with his brothers and sisters. Youngest of ten and sickly with pneumonia or boils that his mother lanced, Jesse learned to work through pain. His mother once lanced one, the size of an egg, close to his heart. His father took joy in watching young Jesse run. And Jesse knew the joys of freedom, win or lose, racing with friends.

In Kern County, near Bakersfield, California, where the contest was held, pickers were assigned rows, and had to pick the cotton clean. Strong, Mexican farm hands fought for the one hundred dollar prize. Jesse wanted to join them and jumped out the jalopy. The girls were horrified. In the cool frost, the temperature was thirty-three degrees, perfect for picking cotton. He took off his sports coat and rolled up his sleeves. The ladies pleaded and finally prevailed. It wouldn't be good to have an Olympic hopeful down on his knees except on the track.

But what was really bothering him that day were the ghosts that were chasing him, the ones he couldn't push back. His junior high school coach, Charles Riley, from Mauch Chunk, Pa., had often taken Jesse to racetracks where Jesse learned from horses never to look sideways, never to look back. There was always something in the shadows, and on that day it had a name.

Eulace Peacock, a young boy from his home state of Alabama, had beaten him in a foot race. Peacock's record, in the running broad jump, wouldn't be easy to erase. There were shadows in the cotton field and an inner voice that said, "You ain't nothing but a 'N.'" But Jesse smiled the more and flicked the voices and their racism away.

In April, in Ann Arbor, his dad watched while Jesse broke three world records in forty-five minutes at Ferry field. High with anticipation, he kissed his gal and two year old daughter and barnstormed around the country. He needed to get far away, but peacocks could also fly.

Spent on women and the night life, Jesse was humbled in Nebraska and on every American track. Peacock beat Owens seven races out of ten, humiliating him. Jesse became the "also ran." Peacock, not him, was the fastest human. Jesse had peaked too soon with the Olympic try-outs looming.

It was Ruth who changed his life. "Get yourself back here, and marry me now, or, I swear, I'm leaving you." It was the summer of 1935, the Olympic Games only a year away.

3
Coney Island, Brooklyn, New York, July 4, 1936.

The sand was cool under the boardwalk where the teens got together for the Fourth of July. It was the first time boys were allowed to take their tops off. But Bobby Gillman would rather die. He hid his ribs with a tank top under his Madison High School warm-up jacket. That summer he hit the beach early, but only his freckles got tan. They glowed like sun spots. He was also gangly and had to crouch down. Those wooden boards could zing. "Kiss me," he said, leaning down to his gal, Martha. He had practiced that art using a shower- steamed hand mirror. That would be their first kiss. Martha smacked her lips and chewed gum. She made clicking sounds drowning his words. Nearby, heads turned towards him. He heard the wooden boards creaking above. An army of heels and soles were marching by. Martha seemed to faint in his arms. But she was moved by the rumblings of the ironworks, not by the twinkle in his eyes.

The Cyclone roller-coaster ride had settled on its haunches and cast a dark gloom. It swayed from its shadow perch then leapt downward, carrying a cargo of screaming teens. Underneath the boardwalk, Martha held her ears tightly until the Cyclone rolled by. When the vibrations stopped someone kicked sand in Bobby's face. "Hey, punk."

Brooklynites liked to bring home sand. It meant they actually went somewhere that day. On the beach, the sand walked on a million soles near Coney Island's shore, but had never stepped once on a human face without all-out war. 'You don't like that?" Punk was looking at his gal.

"You're a 'nutter,'" Bobby said.

But punk answered in street and gutter talk. "Your gal's jelly belly. She's going to grow legs." Nobody made fun of your mother or your gal. Punk laughed. Martha would leave him, Punk implied.

Bobby went at him, but punks rarely traveled alone. That one had friends in high places who grabbed Bobby's hands and took his sneakers away. Then they tossed them back and forth, trapping him in the middle of a nasty game called *salugi*. He'd better not go home that night without his possessions.

His father whacked him with a belt buckle once when he came home without his hat. A learned man who even read *The New York Times*, Dad was no slouch. He liked tough guys like Bugsy Siegel and the Pitkin Avenue mob. A Jew's hat must be protected. He learned that on Amboy Street. Bobby scoured the back alleys and the rooftops, searching until evening fell. Defeated, he had walked home to face his father's belt that rained down many blows.

Now Bobby's sneakers mattered more than a hat. He could run hatless, but not without his running shoes. He didn't care that they gave him blisters. They were broken in like a baseball glove after a few nights under the bedspring. His mother had tried to wrestle them away from him. She even stitched the holes with pink mesh to shame him. She brought him the manlier Black Flash for a high school meet and threw the old ones in the trash. But Bobby pulled the old ones out and spoofed them up with some stickum.

A woman with curly hair looked for her son on the beach. She held a red, plastic fire truck in her hands. There was a lump on the back of her neck. "'Did'ja' see my boy?"

Bobby smiled said nothing. His running shoes were air born with the soles appearing as a pink helicopter. The other boys doubled up with laughter.

A copper came by, his badge shining in the sun. Bobby knew he couldn't tell him about his sneakers. Telling wasn't right no matter what wrong was done. "What's the tyke's name?" the copper said.

She thought a second. "Johnny, Johnny boy."

"That makes a hundred, ma'am; lost tykes, running loose."

Everyone was a runner in Brooklyn. Speed was the truth to tell kids apart. It was "pinky swears," a promise that could never be broken. Where kids played marbles, lies walked alone in the back alleys.

In the code of the gutters, speed alone was the stick measured by fists or feet. Those punks didn't know how to use muscles and limbs. Bobby, though, could burst through walls. That was the potential speed had, after all – to race beyond borders. He had done that to an old teacher of his Talmud Torah class that prepared him for Bar Mitzvah, the religious rites when a male Jewish child turned thirteen.

Bobby had fallen asleep from the drone of an overhead fan. He didn't hear what had crept by with a stick and a curse or muttered prayer. The teacher had sneaked up and whacked him behind the ears. But Bobby had learned to duck. He escaped more blows by running around the desks. His classmates roared. It was nothing like being hit with a belt by your dad, but his instincts were to run. He was fast and had the blessings of speed. Speed hid his clumsy footprints. Running was true democracy.

His running shoes were in the air, narrowly missing a swooping, laughing gull. Sounds of outrage now cawed from its black beak. Bobby pushed backwards, cart-wheeling against the sand. He had leaped to catch them. Putting the sneakers in the crook of his arm, he gave Martha a wink and was gone.

It was a race with the punks, but not a contest. He was the fastest kid on any block. In the fall, he was going to Syracuse University to play football. Bobby Gillman wasn't just a skinny dope. He laughed at the memory of his old teacher, the shocked stare; the feeble swinging of the rod with rage. He left the punks in the dust. Circling back he got his blanket and pulled Martha away.

Later on, they strolled arm and arm past the freak shows and laughed at the hawkers and shills. Bobby was a few months out of high school, yet everyone knew his name.

"Hey Bobby."

"What do you say?"

"Good luck at Randall's."

Bobby knew he'd need more than luck at Randall's Island. In two weeks he was going to run in the Olympic trials against the best dash men in America. He was told Jesse Owens knew how to fly.

In Bay Ridge, there were parades and outdoor celebrations near the churches where the crowds came to hear the sacred words: "We hold these truths to be self-evident, that all men are created equal …"

Elsewhere in Coney Island, guys and gals came to watch discus throwers toss pies into the air. For two hundred feet the apple pies hadn't crumbled, but the lemon meringues were worse for wear. Everyone was laughing when the sugar splattered, or when a seagull squawked and made off with the prize. There were Latin contests outside Erasmus and poster exhibits at the other local schools. S.J. Tilden and Brooklyn Tech held player's club shows. In Fort Hamilton and Kings County, drum majors twirled batons in the game of civics and parades and hysterical sporting events. Bobby was a Madison boy.

   Joseph Seuss made away with the grand prize for the fat man's race. He staggered in at two hundred and forty two pounds. Prospect Park had a new zoo with six baby elephants given by the German Reich in friendship and cooperation.

   Bobby and Martha walked down Mermaid Avenue past the hawkers, the bathhouses and some naughty salons. They didn't know where to go next- the barbeques or the bath houses- or for thirty-five cents, to steal a first kiss in the wide boats in the Tunnel of Love. Maybe, spend a nickel for a frank at Nathan's. With a buck left over they could see a flick. The Bride of Frankenstein was playing at the Albee. He was in the mood for monsters.

   Someone tossed a firecracker from a passing Buick, and it popped at the foot of a middle-aged gal. She was helped into the ambulance, and taken to a hospital. Luckily, she wasn't Jewish. Jews knew Beth-El Hospital, miles away in Canarsie.

   A firecracker also caught a cruising jalopy that careened into a flag pole. It was like that, like war. The same cracker landed and was tossed back out. Many autos near the tavern on Mermaid Avenue smoldered for hours. The injured were taken to the local hospital, Jewish or otherwise, to join the others- the lost children and burn victims.

   Later at the shore, Bobby and Martha saw people doing what patriots had done from the time of Ben Franklin and John Adams – light up the night sky with explosions, in honor of the birthday of the nation.

   The moon hung in the sky and the sun slithered away to the west. A small but rowdy group had come together. They were cordoned off from the rest. Their leader was a reverend, a man of the cloth. At least he looked like one, dressed in black. A firecracker rose in the air and exposed a crane that sat with a broken wing on the edge of the jetty. As the sparks drifted to shore, a pale light shone on brown shirts where their swastikas were patched. Stone-faced, they thrust their right arms outward and saluted, while the reverend planted the Nazi flag. It stood beside the American Stars and Stripes.

Someone threw a coke bottle. Soon a chorus of boos rattled from the sea. Another night swimmer drifted toward the maniacal lights. Another took aim and cursed their leader. The reverend was no man of the cloth nor a reverend, but a spellbound freak. Bobby watched the two flags making *"whoopee,"* a term of excitement, on the Coney Island beach.

In its last flight, the crane flew from the jetty to splatter its blood on the swastika that hung from the reverend's vest. And a crowd gray with fury came. Americans all: the Irish, Italian, and Poles; the Blacks, Latinos, and Pitkin Avenue Jews. They weaved a dark circle. A common enemy had brought them together. With chains and sticks, coke or beer bottles, they wanted to bust heads. Fists and curses rained down; a Grecian chorus in a sudden Brooklyn chill.

Some coppers crushed seashells, nearby. Others didn't know what to do. Those were friends from the neighborhood.

"Skully, you've no 'arse' in this."

"We're going to bust heads."

The copper frowned, but swung his club around. He had no love for Nazis either.

Bobby grabbed Martha's hand and ran. It wasn't right for an Olympic hopeful to be so close to that mob near the flag of the host city of the August Olympic games – Berlin.

"Shake a leg," he said.

***

Well, what next, Bobby thought. There was always what to do, but what to do? There was Bobby Sanford's show boat revue, but who needed that when he had an angel beside him and a movie calling him home?

And home was a ride on the trolley, through the rich neighborhoods of Bay Ridge and Flatbush. Home was the Lutherans and the Masons, schmoozing on the stoops of the Williamsburg tenements. Bobby and Martha left Coney Island on the B.M.T. trolley. He leaned toward her; now was the time, but a short circuit and sparks rained down. Soon smoke, then fire rose around them. "Gee Whiz," Martha said.

She had been thinking about getting a finger wave at one of the French salons downtown. When the fire started, she was dreaming. She would get two, maybe even three waves. Her hair would be oiled with lotions and combed into place. She'd test the warmth of the newest dryer and wait for her curls to hold.

"Fire," the man said, awakening her. He had the mustache of the gay nineties and three jeweled rings. "Oh darn," she said, opening another stick of Juicy Fruit gum.

Bobby and Martha, with eighty other passengers, climbed out through the windows. Bobby thought he'd never be kissed. The car ran through a private right of way along Eighteenth Avenue and Eighty-Fifth Street in Bath Beach. The motorman stopped the car and opened the doors.

"Everybody stay calm," he said. He was dressed in overalls.

After the day's tumult died down, two hundred and fifty children were lost and found. A thousand cases of firecracker injuries were reported. Yet that July 4th was the safest one ever recorded in modern New York City.

4

Michigan University, Delta Kappa Epsilon Fraternity, June 1936.

Among the wildlife and the great Huron River in the college town of Ann Arbor, there was a sprawling frat house at 1912 Geddes Avenue. That was the home of the Dekes, the fraternity, Delta Kappa Epsilon. Eighty percent of their brothers were lost to The Great Depression. Those who stayed struggled to scrape by. Not born of wealth, Joshua and Jerry cleaned house and washed dishes. They would be entering their senior year in September and were old hands at washing dishes by night and waiting tables by day. Between their work and studies, they played.

They played even as they worked, tossing dishes and cups into the air. Jerry cradled pots and pans and crashed about the kitchen. He was a footballer on campus, though the team had the worst won-lost record in the Midwest last year.

He barreled into the sludge with cups and gobblers, and heaved tin flasks into the pile. Wearing a white apron, his moon face was as friendly as a bear cub. On the gridiron, though, he had a reputation as a beast.

If Gerald R. Ford (Jerry) seemed like a bear, Joshua was a phantom. On the track in Michigan and in the Midwest, he was one of the best dash men that ever ran. He had just tied the indoor world record for the sixty meter sprint. Yet one kid made him second best, and gave him the cruel nickname that stuck: the "also ran." It was Jesse Owens, and the rest, just the others. The no names that also ran.

Joshua liked Jesse Owens, the boy they called the Brown Thunderbolt. But Jesse ran for arch-rival The Ohio State and set records even on the Michigan University track. Last March at Ferry Field in Ann Arbor, Jesse won three medals in forty minutes with a bad back that he had injured the day before. That was his bad luck, Joshua thought darkly. It was not certain what he meant.

Born in Cincinnati, he went to high school in the same state as Owens. Now, Owens beat him up and down the Midwestern tracks. When Joshua finally won a race against him, he wore a silly grin for a month. But once in high school wasn't enough. He had tasted Owens' dust much too much. It settled into his psyche of doubts and fears. He was the "also ran" except in the sixty meters. At that distance he owned the track. But the sixty was being phased out. The hundred was a different race. He was fast, but not fast enough. Yet he aimed to beat Jesse once more in a foot race. He knew he was only one short breath away from him.

Joshua was not yet twenty-one, his birthday a few months away. He welcomed the day when he could vote. Made of muscle with a rounded face, he looked plain scary when he ran. An unknown weight pressed his blue eyes downward. Carrying his gym bag, he thought about imaginary races that were yet to come. He thought about the one in Nazi Germany.

Lonesome at practice, Joshua burst into song to ease his duress. In the morning, and again at night, he sang like Al Jolson, like Eddie Cantor, he thought. He was going to become the singing cowboy from Cincinnati, when all this was done.

"Someday, when I'm awfully low,
When the world is cold,

I will feel a glow just thinking of you...
And the way you look tonight."

   "Shut up," said Jerry, or we'll never finish."
   "Tell me I can't sing," Joshua said.
   "Well you can't," said Jerry.
   "But I can out scrub you," Joshua said.

The two played in white smocks to the sound of glass steaming with soap, tinkling into bins. Sometimes the kitchen stank with leftovers. "Ha, Ha." Jerry had a wicked grin. He thought he worked faster, but the race had just begun. Joshua mocked the taller footballer by taking his towel and tossing Jerry's dishes into the air.

"The music goes round and around
 Whoa-ho-ho-ho-ho-ho
And it comes out here."

   "Ha, Ha to you, Henry Ford," he said.
   "Josh is second, even third," Jerry said, laughing.
   Both began crooning together.

"The music goes down and around
 Whoa-ho-ho-ho-ho-ho
And it comes out here."

And then Joshua did something with a cup and a saucer that left Jerry in stitches. That was the way they got through the night. Among the broken dishes, the talk never turned serious except once.

Jerry had talked about Willis Ward, the black boy who crossed the color line to play football against Georgia Tech. That year, the Engineers were a racist team. Lord knows, Jerry thought, those were rough times. Tech wouldn't play the Wolverines unless their 'N' left the Michigan squad.

"Willis could play ball, run like heck, throw a javelin a mile. The Michigan powers that be cut Willis from the team. Hospitality, not racism, was the reason, they said. When it happened, I almost quit the squad. He was going to try out for the decathlon before he was humiliated. Now, he sits at a table away from us, and I don't blame him."

"Not me. I'd never quit. How can you dash a boy's dream?"

"So, are you going to try-out for the Olympics?"

"Well, yes, of course, but, well, I wish ..," Joshua said, holding a dish close to his heart.

"I think you should."

"I wish I was one breath faster, Jerry."

Jerry grinned sincerely. "The team's bigger than one man. At least, that was what I had to accept."

"Thanks buddy, but I need to believe I can win. I need to feel I can beat Jesse Owens in a hundred meter foot race."

On Monday, it was hot and dry on the track. Around him an empty stadium; he found his spot and began to dig. He thought about the names they called him, growing up in Cincinnati.

They came with their fists and their lip, and their race hatred. Never had hate but kindness shone from his mother's face. His father said he was the proudest peddler in Cincinnati. He saved his money to take him by train to the Golden Gloves. Barney Ross was fighting to become the first Chicagoan and Jewish champion. They rode through the hills of Indiana with white clad clansmen. Their young women made a hangman's noose. During a fight in the racial turf wars of Cincinnati, Joshua lost a tooth from a blow to the head. They called him, "Kike." What was that European slur to him? "Jew." So what? What'd that have to do with him?

Joshua leaned forward and touched the cinders. The trick was to spring from the toes; to be airborne, never to feel the earth. He searched down the track. That heavy weight pressed his blue eyes again. His heart followed an imaginary crack on the cinder path. He'd have one dash to beat Hitler. That was the goal: one race in Berlin to smash the Nazis down.

It cost five hundred dollars to get to Berlin. That was the entry fee to be in the footrace of a lifetime. He'd have a following wind, and the foul breath of a Nazi crowd spring him to victory. Joshua dug the hole in the marsh near the river and smoothed the earth into his palms. He put dirt on the ridges of his forehead, sniffed the dust and cursed Hitler. Then he kneeled and took off, racing a bird that suddenly appeared. He whispered in German, with some knowledge of the language. He imagined a gray squadron and a poet's story.

Naught moves around him, save a swarm of cranes, who guide him on his way.

And Joshua on fire, ran out of body; out of his mind, through the woodlands past the marshes. Squealing sounds pushed him onward. All else was still but breath alone. He had been blessed with winged fury. At that moment, *he* was the fastest man on earth. He'd try-out in the regionals. Owens might win the glory, but he'd make the squad anyway. He'd be ready for Berlin. A perfect time for racing when the roses were in bloom.

He was chasing shadows that hated his kind. He'd show the world what the son of a Jewish peddler could do. That race would take place in New York on Randall's Island. Even Franklin Roosevelt would come.

5

University of Southern California, Pasadena, California, July, 1936.

He had a jowly face that couldn't hide the spite. His mouth was telling as he bared his teeth for the newsreels. Though he never went past sixth grade, he was known as The Dean. A coach of the Track and Field team of a small western college, he had brought victories on the cinders against all coast rivals. He had also a series of Olympic champions.

Southern California had the wave riders, those who came to surf and burn their shoulders on the ninety pound planks they carried down the sandstone bluffs. Betty Grable rode the gentle waves and the Santa Ana winds. The scent of orange groves was in her hair. She would be America's sweetheart in a few short years. It was sunrise in the intertidal fish communities. The film industry had brought young folks there to feed on the mussels. "How 'bout our darn Methodist school," the Coach would say.

He took pride in the young men who ran for him. The Trojans of the University of Southern California, dozens of whom set world records under his guidance, knew only victory. Dean got his young men ready, once more. His model T stashed somewhere up the cove, it was business with the tryouts just two weeks away. At the shore, he scowled despite the beauty of the waves and the blue of the skies. He thought Tom Grace was sleepwalking, and Davie Warren had some flu. The fish made him wheeze.

Dean knew he'd have to call his chief in Chicago. That call would take a half an hour to get through. He hated waiting for switchboards, and the strings of operators along the route who needed to find connections, through circuits and route books. He watched his two men gasping for air. Even with a cool breeze, Davie Warren was doubled over and Tom Grace spent. Golden haired, blue-eyed darlings, they were going to be chewed up and spit out early if they weren't able to run.

They ate too much of that damn fish. I can't stand the smell, myself, Dean thought.

The voice on the phone was sore. "Damn ...Damn ... expense…them…belly darn, damn … here," he said. "I … care … Warren ... dying. Get … over … for … race. Do hear. Get ... engineers … darn, dang, damn ...work. Do … hear?" he said.

Truth was the Dean had a bad connection. He heard static every other word. "Get … engineers ... .work ...you," the voice said.

Lawson Robertson would be the head coach of the American track and field team. He walked with a cane and a limp from old injuries loading hot lead into a shot put. The fiery ball suddenly burst on his body, permanently disfiguring him. Something of a scientist about sports, Lawson worked with the track engineers to help design the heavy cinders with layers of clay. Only insiders like him knew what it took to keep the cinders healthy, to let them drain, to keep them springy and resilient.

At the University of Southern California, his assistant, The Dean, checked to see if the track was swept and rolled before big races. It had to be smooth like a billiard table. He wished he could carry a piece of that California turf with him to the afterlife. He was sure Methodists kept house behind the pearly gates. Robertson taught Dean to use the men of the clubs, colleges and prep schools, the elite of the country. It was his business to know how to perfect, how to polish, how to improve the timing, the rhythm, the beat of the dash man. He studied graphs, movies, made measurements, used slide rules and diagrams. University sports, even in small colleges, were becoming big business.

"Sir," Dean said, "We'll get the maximum ... mum."

"What? You, about? Dean, *fakakta* ... be... swear, help me, nobody ... I mean, nobody *fakakta* me," he seemed to say.

"No sir," Dean said.

"Do ... Deannie?" the man on the phone said. "Do... unders ..."

The Dean didn't understand a word. "Yes sir, I understand. We're on our way."

"Yes sir," then, screaming at Grace and Warren down by the shore. "In my day, we ran the cinders with burning feet. Take your shoes off. Do it ...You are Trojans."

"What are Trojans?" asked Dave Warren.

"*We* are Trojans, son' of a gun.' ...!"

"Do they fly?"

"I don't know if they damn, dang fly."

Dave Warren was hacking for air with Grace there beside him. They would be champions, Dean thought, no matter what it would take. Nearby the scent of the orange groves, the warm sand, the shore where beachcombers were trying to ride a high wave. Above them, the sandstone cliffs and the sun, reflected off pocket mirrors. The teens left after causing a ruckus, or making "whoopee, "in secluded caves. But he liked the sounds he heard above the rest: the heaving breath of young athletes.

"Now go home and rest," he said, patting the sweat from their back. They had been oiled and already slicked from wintergreen.

The sweat glistened thick and manly. "My lads, tomorrow we go to New York. First we're going to show them a thing or two about what a Trojan horse can do. Maybe, Davie W., we can dang well fly.

"I think Hitler's a Methodist; would be swell to get your hot dogs back from those dang foreigners and Jews."

Dean, the maker of champions, was a man on a mission, who followed orders and the vision of that great man, Arian Bandage, the one who put sports above nations, the head of the Amateur Athletic Association, and the ferocious voice on the phone.

6

Randall's Island, New York, Saturday, July 11, 1936, 12 o'clock P.M.

It was noon, and the heat so bad he could see the dust rising from the horseshoe track below. Roosevelt was supported on a platform built upon a ramp of the new public works project, the Triborough Bridge. He could see three thousand heads in the new stadium, and from the sides of the bridges and from the seventeen miles of interconnected highways, he knew thousands more were on their way to see him.

For the overcast sun that bore down on the motorcade, Roosevelt wore a wide-brimmed, white hat, more elegant than the others; theirs, crunched like paper.

Even his entourage turned away as he was hoisted into the car seat. They didn't want to see their president's infirmities. The scene was staged for the speech and the merrymaking. Afterward, Governor Lehman, Mayor LaGuardia, and the master road builder, Robert Moses, would be first to cross the connecting bridge. They would go on toward the Connecticut border and eat lobster, never talking about the events that were taking place below.

Little did any of the would-be Olympians suspect that that moment would be the closest they would get to their president, no matter the race, no matter the glory.

From the cinders, underneath the supporting bridgework and the piles of ironworks, coiled like sagebrush on the sides of the tracks, Jesse Owens and Joshua Sellers strained to hear the words that filtered through the phonographs, the megaphones, and the static of the electrical stormed wires- to hear his words of inspiration and know he came for them; the horn rimmed glasses, the hand waved, the set jaw that gave the impression he was America's father. They, Jesse and Joshua, Ralph Metcalfe, and Bobby Gillman, were his sons handpicked for glory.

Roosevelt might come down from the platform to watch the contest of his children in a sporting event in the name of the country in a time of uncertainty. America was still the best hope for the human race.

But Roosevelt didn't mention lofty ideals when he spoke high above the athletes that would represent America. He talked about his grandfather, and a bygone world where bridges didn't matter. Would his grandfather see the need for connecting structures? Would people complain about the length of the work week or expect government to respond?

"It was not so long ago that no one used to protest against the dumping of sewage and garbage into our rivers and harbors. No one used to protest that our school houses were badly ventilated and lighted. No one used to protest against fire traps and factory smoke. In those days, government was not interested in helping to provide bathing beaches, swimming pools, and recreational areas.

"But, nowadays, government must respond to the growing and changing needs of the people. In order to survive, we must recognize change and meet the costly needs of a more complex life."

And then he finished, and the great bridge was opened for a twenty-five cents toll. The crowds began to trickle into the dust bowl horseshoe, under the electric clock, in the airless noonday sky. There was a threat of rain in the darkening clouds.

***

Governor Lehman stood beside the open limousine, shaking the president's hand. He watched the clouds soberly and anguished over the news from his own fair state.

Robert Elliot, the state executioner at Sing Sing, still was not done. Twenty-one more bodies would need burying. Who would pay when the toll of deaths by electrocution was calculated that month? And Mary Creighton wasn't going away without trouble. The state doctors needed to decide whether the Borgia murderer had a phony illness. What an act to starve herself to death just to get attention. Drat, but it still wasn't right to electrocute a woman, now in a coma.

The Mayor of the City, Fiorello LaGuardia, and his political rival for office, the Honorable Jeremiah Mahoney, had a brief moment with the president's entourage. The two had formed an alliance about the events that were going on below.

As Mahoney spoke, the president seemed to be drifting into his own thoughts. He shifted slightly between his leg- ironed fittings. He remembered those tranquil days in New York, growing up in Hyde Park with his grandfather. As the judge talked, LaGuardia wiped his brow. It was hot and humid.

"Everyone knows I'm Irish except those Nazis. They said I was nothing but a two bit Jewish financier."

"Mr. President," said the Mayor, "that's very funny. Mahoney, the Jew."

"We are not involved with the politics of sport."

"But race prejudice …"

"Mr. Bandage assures us Jews can compete for the German team. I don't foresee a problem, and that, I hope, is the last word on such a tiresome topic."

"Gentlemen, I am going on vacation. My sons and I will be sailing, so let us get off this damn bridge, please."

The President of the United States, leaving with his motorcade, waved to the crowd surrounding the bridge and along the highways, not looking down at the thousands waving back to him, nor give one glimpse toward his athletes, standing adoringly in the stadium below.

Gosh, thought Bobby Gillman, the president is here to see me. And Bobby tried to stay cool in the locker room. He could see the track outside pressed and manicured with a steam roller. He saw sweatpants and sweaters where the Californians did light calisthenics on the sides of the stands. Near the finish, the judges would stand in rows to make their decisions about who won, or who lost. The heats were already done, and he had come in third in his behind Jesse and Joshua. There was a second, then a third heat, given to Tom Grace only.

Grace hadn't qualified in the first two, and had a run-off in the third, but even that race was aborted. His coach, whom they called The Dean, yelled so loudly, dang this or that, which caused a ruckus and the starter's gun to go off accidentally in the middle of the race. "Do over," was the unwritten law of sandlot games, not Olympic try-outs, except for today. Grace won the next heat, making the finals by the skin of his teeth.

On a golf course in Carpentaria, one of Grace's backers, who helped provide three hundred dollars for the journey of the western squad, got a wire that said Tom was done. He went from misery to elation when the second wire came. It said that the curly haired Californian would be given another chance. And that was just swell.

***

"Swell," Bobby said aloud. He had the jitters. Suddenly his stomach was in his face. Walking around, pounding the lockers, he rubbed some wintergreen and oil over his body to try to keep his legs straight. Still, they wobbled apart. He heard a voice on the megaphone. "It's time."

"Gee," he said, but he knew he needed to place in the top three to make the squad. By tradition, the next four would run the four hundred meter relay. He burst out of the lockers and absorbed the heat rising from the dust. He raced toward his competitors grimacing. Newsreels thought they caught him smiling. The others kicked their legs high, heaving their chests out to say, "Hi," to one another.

The crowd of six thousand fanned themselves with straw hats. The people under the hats sat in rows of perspiration, breathing the humid air. The champion was taller than the rest, even Mack Robinson. Robinson was another black champion, out of California, but not Dean's man. Davie Warren paled between the two black men. "Joshua, I know you'll be on my heels." Jesse said.

"I think I'll take you today. I'm tired of eating your dust, J.C."

"Got a song for me?"

"Gentlemen, please go to the starting line to draw your pill," said a voice on the acoustical device that sputtered into the windless, electrical sky.

Black pills, the size of marbles, were given randomly to choose starting positions. It's definitely going to rain, Grace thought, watching the haze through a blackening sky. He smelled the paint that wafted off the new bridge that Roosevelt had just dedicated. Grace drew the third position.

With a slight sneer, Joshua walked over to the champion chest out and circled him. He didn't want anyone else to hear. But, of course, all eyes were on Jesse anyway.

"So you met someone who set you back on your heels – goody goody."

Owens understood the menace in Joshua's tone, and Jesse's smile held both wisdom and fear. There was always someone ready to take a poke at him. Thank G-d, Eulace Peacock would not be there.

Joshua's eyes had turned inward. Jesse drew 'four.' Tom Grace was to his right, with Dave Warren in the second post near his California buddy.

Bobby didn't know how he felt. He hadn't slept too soundly the week before. Despite extra fluids, he was lightheaded. The crowd seemed farther away than usual. He thought he was still home, or running from the monsters on the movie screen. It was so hot, he thought, half walking, and half jogging to his starting position. He grazed Jesse Owens who was digging into the cinders. Bobby drew the fifth post. He had the champion on his right and Metcalfe in sixth. Metcalfe was the silver medalist in the 1932 Los Angeles games.

Oh, if I spring on my legs, I know I can win this race, he thought. He saw Joshua at the far post. Joshua was looking toward the sky. He seemed upset by the lightning and the cracklings of thunder. A barnyard of birds suddenly swooped about. Joshua held the seventh position.

Bobby began digging a starting hole. The others already were crouched in position and told to go to their marks. He tried to put his left leg down, but it wouldn't go. His leg shook so much that his foot couldn't find the spot. The starter, Johnny McHugh, saw the trouble the eighteen-year old was having. "Wait," he said, raising his hands, an unofficial 'timeout' signal. He watched Bobby's left leg shake. "Jog it off," he said, and Bobby did.

Bobby came back to his spot more relaxed, talking to himself for courage on the hot, humid and dusty track. Seeping into his brain, he heard his coach from the athletic club. "Don't run on the ground; run over it. Lift and lengthen the stride, and reach for the ground in front to pull over, instead of pushing over the ground."

He tried not to see the competitors alongside him, the silver medalist and the strapping thunderbolt, the national champion. The ground, the hot cinders, the blinding dust, the airlessness of an electrical storm that was already rumbling in the tepid air, and the six thousand who were sweltering there at Randall's Island, on the opening day of the connecting bridge, were held captive for one purpose only: to be Jesse Owens' own cheering squad.

And Jesse was ready to oblige. He waited to push his taut legs out over the cinders. He saw the gun raised from the corner of the fourth position. He thought he was looking back into his childhood, and he was going to race to make his father proud. The footsteps were far behind him. Eulace Peacock had shattered his hamstring just before the trials. Bad luck for him, but maybe an act of G-d, for Jesse Owens wanted to race for the American team. That was his day to realize a dream.

"Get set," said the starter, and Bobby drew air and settled into the regimen that he had learned in training. He stood as tall as he could between Owens and Metcalfe, and thought about last winter in the Syracuse gymnasium, lifting the knee ever higher. He'd throw his feet as far in advance of himself as he could to use the body muscles and increase the stride; the fewer steps, the faster the race. He went over it again. Run over, but not on the ground. Make his strides longer to shorten the track.

Only the curious sat in the stands to watch the race. Despite the gravity that would pick the American Olympians, the megaphones and the acoustical system broke down. The *Saturday Evening Post* described the "action" as a pantomime of sport. For the spectator, it said that event was no more than "potato races at a church bazaar."

But what did they know? The stadium was surrounded by bales of tin cans and metal works and lumber, sitting in distant slumber to what happened when the dust settled, and the race won or lost, or, as was the case in the one hundred meter finals, left open to questions about how it was judged on the sizzling cinders that day.

***

July 11, 1936, 100 Meter Qualifying Finals, Randall's Island, New York.

Breathless the takeoff, go, on the cinders-push, push, cough the dust, push, he never heard the starter's gun, dead even for thirty, thirty-five meters, forty, Owens and Metcalfe take long strides on either side of poor Bobby Gillman with Joshua far behind, having a bad start, push, the fight still in him despite the running that was done, the roar of the crowd settling into the lungs, push, push, what have they done to leave him at the station? Tom Grace must have caught a following wind, sizzling in on Owens' right, one step behind, but only one breath back, Metcalfe, as the crowd chants the name that matters, sucking him into the dust, the breath pushed farther, it is only the heart that matters, the face flush. Warren behind him done, Joshua nowhere in sight, Mack too, fighting for last, push. Owens turns urges Joshua on with a hand.

"Come on, come on," he says.

Newsmen with umbrellas and pencils, straw hats flying, the judges sit one head on top the other at the finish where Bobby is closing in on Grace, one last push makes up the distance, and Joshua hears Owens' call again and now feels the swirling dust of desire, his legs finally catching fire, not too late to push, one final burst to qualify across the tape, the crush of the crowd, the dust that is eaten, push, at the finish the lunge that is taken, the race settled breathless gasping for air; there's nothing but dust and the death of air. A final burst, Bobby may have caught Grace, but certainly Warren; Joshua now, an eagle soaring past Mack, but all are "also ran's," a blur in the pack, hands high to the harkening crowd, heaving in the heat for Metcalf second, Tom Grace, third, Warren right there and placed fourth, not Gillman who was declared fifth, Sellers and Mack Robinson, sixth and seventh, but the stands are on fire for whom they desire to cheer; only for the Brown Thunderbolt, thunder across the skies, the only Olympian, only for Owens the champion, always the fastest alone with the glory at the throne of history.

7
Prospect Park, Brooklyn, N.Y. July 12, 1936.

Casey Stengel and his bunch were dawdling in seventh place, and some rookie named Joe DiMaggio was tearing up the Bronx. Bobby spent the morning with Martha. She was his girlfriend officially. She had kissed him without cracking her gum. It didn't seem like she'd ever grow legs. Then he rambled out the door to meet Joshua Sellers, the Michigan champion.

The two walked along Prospect Heights, Crown Heights, and Prospect Park, ducking the subways before dusk when the knifings seemed to spike. The pair turned on Bedford Avenue for a view of the matchbox baseball field where the Brooklyn Dodgers played. They headed past the new zoo and the botanical gardens north of the park. Bountiful fields of freshly planted oak brought them towards the only wooded area in Brooklyn. The chirpings of cardinals and songbirds burst through the noonday air. Glacial rocks, eroded by rose gardens, came in view.

Along the footpaths and through the spacious meadow, they talked about boxing. One third of the fighters in America were Jews. Joshua liked Benny Leonard. He told about the fights he had seen with his father. Memories arose in the fragrance of the woods. Along the maples and oaks, his heart stopped. He imagined his father punching the sky in a Chicago arena the day Barney Ross became the first Jewish Golden Gloves champion. "Hey what do you say, what do you know?" said a bunch of Jewish thunderbirds, many with yarmulkes covering their heads.

"Want to race me?" said one. No more than fourteen years old, they took part in clubs that pounded the pavement from the footpaths of Williamsburg to Gravesend.

"Give Hitler the' boid.' It was Brooklyn speak for "bird.' "Yeah, beat him." "Give 'em a Bronx cheer."

"Yeah, knock his mudda's, or mother's, socks off."

But the young runners weren't all Jews. Freckle-faced, red-haired Irish kids, sons of the most vocal anti-Nazis, ran around the meadow. Those were men like Jeremiah Mahoney who said race prejudice was not an Olympic ideal. Joshua and he never talked about race hatred, or the politics of the day. "When this is over I'm going on stage. Jolson, Cantor, Joshua Sellers. I'll bring home the gold medal, and America will say, 'that's the Olympic champ, the singing cowboy from Cincinnati.' "

Bobby popped Joshua on the shoulder. "You almost didn't make the Manhattan."

The Manhattan was an old steamer, scheduled to leave in three days from the twentieth street pier.

"I know." Joshua says. "J.C. pushed me on. I swear I don't know if I can race anywhere, but behind him. I don't know what happened. I must've froze at the start."

"I was nervous too. Gee."

"No, that's not what I meant. I was just thinking about what it all meant. I couldn't run while thinking about running. I was caught in a circle. I wanted to race, but my spikes were stuck to my head, and my feet burned clear through the cinders."

"Hey, you were in the clouds."

"Gosh, I was," says Joshua, "I didn't hear the gun pop. I thought I'd run a thousand races just to eat J's dust. Oh, that's me in the newsreels. That's Josh, the "also ran." Before I knew what had happened, it was already too late. Jesse screamed, 'Come on, Josh. Come on,' that woke me up.

We're strange bedfellows, him and me. I need him, but I think he also needs me. He's the wind that I get caught between, and he feels me whether I'm there, or not. So many races with J., I don't know which feet are mine or his. Even birds can't tell us apart. They hit us both with one poop."

'Where was Josh?' J.C. told me, later, 'if he weren't going to be second?'"

As if the world would change for him and me if I weren't closing in. We had a date for singing, and he knows my yodeling,' my western twang, and wants to saddle up with me. I wouldn't miss that for the world. Had I more time, though, I'd have run through him."

Bobby stopped in his path, shaking his head. "I didn't hear the gun, either. But I swear I beat Dave by at least a yard and caught Tom at the tape.

"Even the judges walked towards me, their hands over my head. One pointed with the white card: First was Jesse, second, Ralph Metcalfe, and in third, the card raised over me.

A newsman said, 'Bobby, Bobby Gillman, how does it feel to come in third and race the one hundred meters in Berlin?'

"And The Dean came between us, waving his hand in the reporter's face. 'Wait, wait, wait a darn minute, if you please, that's Owens first, Metcalfe, second, Tom Grace, third,' so, I was thinking, Tom got me, but The Dean wasn't finished, 'and Davie Warren, fourth.'

"Well, Dean, I wanted to say, that's not the way it went down, but he didn't turn around, and I really didn't care. You and I buddy grabbed the last spots for the 4x100 meter relay race. We made the Olympic team."

With a break in the heat, the pair became silent. They began jogging naturally. Bobby the 'Orangeman,' in his orange Syracuse track jersey, and Joshua in the fierce, Michigan's wolverine. Jostling with the other they sparred lightly, picking up speed. Then the two came running through the meadow.

Joshua found a stick and played his own game of "fetch," as Bobby flexed and came towards him. He reached behind Joshua's hip and with a firm grip grabbed it tightly. The trick was not to look back. They ran into the meadow where children knew them, knew whom those Olympians were, and what they were going to do. They were going to stick it to Hitler.

The children of the neighborhood strained to keep up as word spread of the Olympians who were running there. Soon the park was cluttered with children in caps, with balls and bats, or just their G-d given legs.

The children came racing into the meadows and across the lake from Flatbush Avenue to Eastern Parkway. Bobby and Joshua shared common thoughts about the race. Their hands would pass the wand, firm of grip. And they'd remember the scores of kids that gathered on the hills of the meadow where the lilacs and roses bloomed with the heady pungent smells of summer. They knew they'd be racing for them as well. The Olympians weaved like pied pipers. The children draped about them.

"Shake a leg men," said a little kid on the side of the swarms.

He was in a wheelchair, his legs bound in an iron brace. Joshua stopped running, lowered the stick. He kneeled down to the kid's chair. Looking up at his mother for permission, he handed the stick to the boy and kissed his brace. "We will," he said, "just for you."

"Promise?" the kid said.

"Scout's honor," Joshua said, and took off his Michigan jersey and gave it into the kid's sure hands.

"Gosh, mom," the boy said.

"We saw your picture in *The Eagle*," she said, "both of you. You're Jewish boys, they say. Jewish boys are going to run to beat Hitler."

"Oh, who's he anyways, ma'am?" said Bobby Gillman. The woman blanched.

"He may be some devil," she said, as Joshua hummed a song on his knees. A nearby group of girls, bounced balls and crossed their legs. "A, my name is Alice," one said. "B, my name is Bobby," said another, laughing. She was flirting with him. They turned to the singer and the boy in the wheelchair.

"One of these mornings
You're gonna rise up singing
Then you'll spread your wings
And you'll take to the sky."

Bobby Gilman heard Joshua's voice, then an anguished cry. The singing cowboy from Cincinnati, that's what Joshua wanted to be. But that sad melody took him to another place. Gershwin's tune haunted him.

"I don't think there's a devil, ma'am, and I don't think you want the boy to believe there's one," Bobby said, turning to his friend.

Her eyes, though, had crossed with the lonesome eyes of the singing cowboy. Without his sweatshirt, the muscles of his biceps were gleaming. In that moment, they needed no further introductions.

"Mommy, is there a devil?" the kid wanted to know.

"Devil could be closer than we ever knowed," the woman said. She held Joshua's hard stare, and didn't let go.

The sun left its lonely path along the western sky. They walked the woman and the boy to the side of the park toward the beautiful beaux-art museum and down another path to the heights. The woman asked Bobby to stay with the child downstairs. She said she wanted to show Joshua something, and something she must have given him upstairs, as well, because he was gone a half hour.

Then he came down the stoop, his jersey slung over his shoulder. "I'm the devil, and Hitler's just another mug. When he sees me, I'm going to punch his lights out. That's what an American cowboy can do."

Bobby Gillman stood arms on hips. He was smiling as was his blue-eyed companion. Together they walked down the side streets adjacent to the park, the last of the day's bouncing balls careening off the stoops.

It was an art to hit the edge of the step, to launch the ball in a high arc to the gutter. Like sparklers, like bullets, it made a great sound. Rubber balls that shattered windows, or got lost on tenement roofs, or pinkies bursting between five boxes, bouncing on concrete or in back alleys between peewees and waxed soda tops. Hundreds of games were played. A bouncing pinky popping the walls, but it took a strong arm to punch one between the sewers, or smack it with a broomstick, or slap the concrete with the palms stinging from the smack.

Kids played with heart, or showed off for the gals. The gals chewed Juicy Fruit beside them. They got together in beauty parlors for hours, miming Rochelle Hudson or Joan Crawford, the icons surrounding their dreams between the curling contraptions.

"O.K., teammate-for G-d and country," Bobby said, as night engulfed them. He would remember the last time Joshua was happy to be on American soil.

8
Manhattan (United States Lines,)
Sails noon from 20th Street.
July 15, 1936.

Not a sound of protest, not in print in *The New York Times*, or on the docks at Twentieth Street pier. Twenty five hundred people came to sing along with the Coney Island Nazi who had waved the swastika flag. He came with his Yorktown gang to give a rousing send-off to the American team.

"Ray. Ray. U.S.A. A.M.E.R.I.C.A."

The fans wanted to touch their heroes, but the athletes crowded the Olympic rings on the deck. Five Olympians unfurled the white, five ringed banner, and hoisted it to the mast. The Manhattan was ready to sail. *The New York Times* reported that the Olympians were a worthy group of athletes who would "carry aloft in this fine hour ideals of sportsmanship on a mission of international goodwill."

"Bon Voyage," said the nation. *The New York Times* was on board, as it was for the Calvert Guinea Expedition. The company had just gone to Guinea to prove how whiskey actually cooled the body by refrigerating the blood. On the crowded sundeck, the chant picked up.

"*Ray. Ray. U.S.A.*," and the crowd was ordered to back off as a cordon of cops rushed the deck.

The athletes and the coaches had arrived the night before their departure at the Hotel Lincoln to deal with passports and visas, foreign money and other purchases.

Eleanor Holm Jarrett, the reigning one hundred meter backstroke champion, weighed her luggage down with whiskey and champagne. Eleanor liked partying. With her white Stetson, a bathing suit and a posed smile, the leggy champion was ready to have a good time. She said she wanted champagne for breakfast and lunch, and some gambling for after dinner fun.

But Emily May Socket was in charge of entertainment and the chaperone of the women's swimming team. She had to set a good example for Marjorie Gestring, a thirteen year old high diver who was the youngest woman ever on any American Olympic team. Socket had taken one math course at Princeton University. She had been taught there were simply good, or invalid examples. She prepared vocal, musical, terpsichorean, and dramatic interludes that demanded proper decorum. To cure homesickness, she would give the girls deck tennis, shuffleboard, chess and checker tournaments, mock trials and debates.

A culture war was brewing the moment Eleanor came aboard. Photographers fawned over her from every angle. Bouquets of orchids were tossed at her feet; autograph books, begged to be signed. All the while, Eleanor posed for photos and dazzled the crowd. The reigning queen of the Olympic Games, Eleanor didn't know she had made a fatal error. She'd caused a commotion during the introduction of *his* name. Arian Bandage had insisted on the French pronunciation: 'Ban dauge,' the man who had fought his opponents to make possible the Berlin Games. He mustn't be ignored.

In his white suit but hatless, the square jaw was set in an iron mask. Bandage peered through his glasses, watching the women's team with disdain. Women were built to procreate, not compete. Bandage said they lacked discipline. Eleanor Holm Jarrett was a distraction to real sports and productive men.

He was the able engineer- the fearless and agile builder of duplexes and apartment houses. He erected and sub-divided- from the Illinois Central Railroad to the Chicago Loop. After the Games, he'd take his greatest prize. He'd construct *that* building, the new German embassy in Washington. That was his secret alone.

Then was the time for diplomacy. On the verge of his greatest acquisition, if Mahoney resigned from the committee, he'd be the voice of American sports. Mahoney said he would resign in protest to race hatred if the Americans sailed. Bandage had been to Garmisch during the Winter Games when Goebbels and Von Ribbentrop assured him race prejudice against the Jews simply did not exist. It wasn't necessary to talk to *them* to know Goebbels spoke the truth. If only Mahoney thought about sports, not the Jew-Nazi political problem.

His athletes cared less anyway about politics. They wanted to know what the port side was, and how to tell time by the bells? The athletes heard the cheers and speeches, and all the farewells. William Dalton, the President of the New York Athletic Club, and Black Mike, manager of the Detroit Tigers baseball team, smiled squarely at his "*moxy*," or swagger, but Bandage knew they mocked his name. So what should he be called?

'Avery Brundage?'

He hated the sound, and the memories of that name. When Bandage was given power of attorney over his mother's affairs, he took all family photographs and threw them into the fireplace and watched them burn. His mother had written a diary of the history of father's drunkenness. He watched that burn, as well. He became a smooth sober slate. "We have the strongest athletes in the world, but the world is getting stronger. In order for us to win in Germany, we must be ready in mind, heart, and soul. Let the arguments of the past stay buried. We're Americans first, and we represent the will of the majority, and the majority is all," he said.

No sooner had he stopped talking than members of the crew jostled the crowd. "Ray. Ray. U.S.A," was drowned out by martial music that came from a little, brown-shirted fringe quartet. The phony reverend waved his wand. A tugboat washed away the sounds with little toots of its own American horns. The Dean told a story while Bandage posed for photos nearby. Straw hats were tossed in the air.

But Bandage stopped paying attention. His face had undergone a sickly metamorphosis. He listened flushed then quickly paled.

"There were peddlers up by 134th Street. They at least go for junk- the metal, wire, electrical stuff- union men-out of work plumbers, carpenters, and the salt of the earth. They sell junk and get by. I have no damn problem with them buds. But down there's a different story. Peddlers with beards smelling of that dang fish and cheese, and talk like foreigners. How'd they get here anyway? Cheating poor women of their damn dole, pushing real Americans around; one in a black coat blocked me like a horse between the pushcarts. It was ... dang, dumb, and disgusting."

"LaGuardia is changing that. He's rounding them up and going to put them in the retail market. The day of the peddlers is over," said a reporter, his sharpened pencil ready to write.

Leaning over the rail, Joshua heard the conversation. His eyes suddenly felt heavy. He imagined his father's happy eyes, the hairy knuckles handing out free apples to those who couldn't pay.

Bandage turned with a frozen smile. A collector of many things, Bandage learned faces and hidden thoughts. He glowered as if he knew what Dean was about to say.

"So, I said to the Jew, I think Hitler has the right idea about you people."

Bandage grabbed the short man's throat. Dean wilted but didn't whine, while the bowler hat fell off his head. A small crowd saw that and rushed in; but by then intervening angels had prevailed. Dropping him like a sack, Bandage picked up and dusted off his hat, and turned with a pasty grin to the newshound next to him.

"We have the best athletes in the world, assembled here for the glory of sport, and I want you to print that."

"No problem, Mr. Bandage, sorry, 'Ban dauge'."

Arian Bandage leered at The Dean. "Get your men in shape, all of them. We're all Americans, aboard this ship, at least."

One was Marjorie Gestring, a thirteen year old diving hopeful. She was photographed in white, with Alice Arden standing beside her. On the foredeck, Glenn Morris, the decathlon champion, lugged his spears and smiled broadly for the cameras.

"Ray. Ray. U.S.A.," he shouted, and the crowd spelled each letter.

"A. M. E. R. I. C. A."

But the nation wasn't cheering. In editorials, *The Commonweal*, a Church newspaper, condemned the games. The American Jewish Congress and the Jewish Labor Committee staged counter-Olympics in Barcelona, Spain.

In sunny weather, Abraham Alfred Chick Chaikin and a large group of American athletes arrived for the *Olimpíada Popular*. The games with six thousand athletes were to begin there on the nineteenth. With one voice, trade unions, worker's clubs and unions, socialist and communist, Jewish and Christian associations, denounced the Nazi Games as racist. *The New York Times* was silent on the day the Manhattan sailed. Protest lost its purpose, but Bobby Gillman didn't care. He was young, and the Olympics, a dream come true. Berlin, the city, not the Nazi Games would be remembered. There was a difference, he thought.

Joshua also thought about Berlin. His eyes defiant his thoughts aflame. He listened and wanted to believe; together, Bandage and he would triumph. Sports, indeed, was above politics.

Bobby Gillman enjoyed the send-off like a celluloid, a good, silent film. In the theaters that day there were many double features. Two flicks for the price of one. Could you beat that?

Joshua was clairvoyant; he invaded Bobby's thoughts. Bobby suddenly saw Joshua Seller's name on the marquee.

"I'm not playing, pal. Ever hear of Johnny Mack Brown, Tex Ritter, or even Gene Autry? I can ride a horse into town. Me, the singing cowboy from Cincinnati."

Joshua lit up laughing, but often fell toward darker moods – the songs he sang, the way he watched the birds swoop down. He prepared for the coming races like war, but shared a moment with the grimacer god who held his stare under his glasses. That hard jaw and muscular mien had called Joshua to a more serious purpose.

"U.S.A. U.S.A.," he said, his heart about to burst.

Bandage acknowledged the men of the track team, and Joshua with a nod of the head.

"A. M. E. R. I. C. A."

North of the steamship, off the coast of Maine, on a fifty-six-foot schooner on their way to Campobello, the President of the United States sailed and practiced the art of "loafing." And on the Manhattan, all visitors ashore, the steamer cast off from its moorings to the sounds of tugboat's whistles and symphonies of martial sounds galore.

Charles Lindbergh was going to Berlin at the invitation of Air Minister Hermann Goering. Helene Mayer, the German half-Jew, was photographed with Rachel Brach as proof that the Reich let Jews compete. But the headlines were fearsome and the news bleak.

Canton declared its independence in defiance of Nanking.

Father Coughlin cursed the President as a great betrayer.

King Edward escaped assassination.

There were wholesale arrests of socialists in Austria. Linen dresses cost six dollars and ninety-five cents from Best & Company.

Nuns in Berlin were arrested for immoral behavior. Mrs. Creighton, G-d rest her sad soul, suffered only from hysteria, the post mortem revealed no evidence of organic disease.

Republicans railed about the new Social Security system, born at a time when the parent government had gone broke. Twenty-six ships on a training cruise moored into Pearl Harbor: the battleships Tennessee, Pennsylvania, New Mexico, Texas, Maryland, and the Arizona.

Becalmed by the wind in the flapping of the white flags, in the mournful salute of a gathering of small crafts and the screeching of wild gulls, Joshua's spirits rose. Despite the hoot and catcalls of grown men and the steam lifting down the harbor, he was sailing undaunted by the immensity of the seas he was about to traverse. He was getting ready for war.

It would take eight days to embark at midnight in Hamburg Harbor, another day by train to *Lerhter* Station and to the bus along the Triumphal Way. Then toward the festive stadium in the city of chariots above Brandenburg Gate; in Berlin, Germany, in a race he wouldn't lose, he'd seize the American Dream.

9

The air was fresh, the weather calm, the strapping sons and daughters eager to please, but the mood was wrong. In the athletes' rooms, subversive pamphlets were found, and Bandage was furious about that when he was alone with his face mirror in his concrete private bunker. But a gentleman must control himself, even under the watchful gaze of Arthur Daley. Daley had the honor of being the first newsman to report for *The New York Times* in foreign seas.

Arian placed his glasses on the bed. He knew that protest demanded a response. Abandoned by his father and raised by an uncle, he had made his way in the construction trade by hard work and an iron will. His buildings were never of inferior concrete. He gave an honest product for an honest price. A man among men at the University of Illinois, Bandage grew to love the purity of sports.

He remade himself in the image of an Olympian ideal. Tormented by school-mates, Bandage developed strengths of physical prowess. He was shamed because he wore glasses. When "four eyes" was invited to join the Olympic team in 1912, he may have been the first athlete to compete with them. He put the pamphlet on the bed near the glasses. The hysterical words seemed to leap into the blur.

ATHLETES: REJECT NAZI GAMES.HITLER IS THE ENEMY. DON'T BE USED FOR PROPAGANDA. DON'T SHAME AMERICA.

***

The Princess Matoika was bound for Antwerp in 1920 with mutinous Olympians on board. The athletes thought they were poisoned by the water and retched overboard. Attacking the American Olympic Committee, they brought them in chains from the boiler room to walk the plank.

Horatio Townsend, now the committee treasurer, saved their lives. There was little to be done with the food or water, he said. But he'd share his supply of port wine. That seemed to soothe the athletes who began an orgy of drinking that went on until the wine kegs were gone. When they reached Tripoli, one of the official's wives ran through the port, and gathered chickens and goats from pirates and thieves, and prepared a feast onboard for the mutinous young men.

Bandage learned about the breakdown of discipline. Rules and regulations brought order to chaos. In order there was beauty; in beauty, perfection. He traveled freely to spread his ideals, and made business and social connections. He bought and hoarded vast storehouses of Oriental art. Desperate to leave the house and his wife's loathsome touch, he dashed for the mountains, traveling by auto with Joseph Goebbels to Bavaria for orgies, wine, and young German chorus girls.

In the newsreels, his wife always beside him, he fed the public with lies to build his Olympic dreams. The man was ruled, however, by something else: spite, and the need for revenge. Behind closed doors, he plotted. He had to get even for real or imagined slights. Jim Thorpe was the one name he carried in secret. Arian knew he was the one who turned him in. Thorpe had played a few games for money. That was enough to have him stripped of his medals. Bandage had been beaten so badly by him that he refused to compete anymore. That 'damn' Indian humiliated him, he thought.

In the mirror, the face that Bandage hid had bloodshot eyes. His jaw dropped sideways, and the sneer of the straight aristocratic nose smelled a malodorous conspiracy. Mahoney finally resigned but Bandage survived. Lee Jahncke also refused to set foot in the new Germany. Arian Bandage was left alone at the top.

In the American Press, Jahncke condemned the World Olympic Committee. He said Bandage was a "stick on dupe," a stooge of the Nazis. Joseph Goebbels, head of the new Ministry of Enlightenment and Propaganda, worked tirelessly to showcase the peaceful nation. Germany wanted world domination, Jahncke warned. The Olympic Games was our "mark of shame."

Well, good-bye, he sneered. Public displays of lewdness or intoxication, or protest had to be avenged.

"*Verboten*," he said to his contemptuous reflection. It was forbidden by civilized men. But what he couldn't understand were the Jews. Where did they fit in? They whined and made the world weary of them. What was their problem?

Last winter, the foreign minister, gave him a copy of *Der Sturmer* at the winter games. Von Ribbentrop showed him proof, in print, of the rape of young, flowering German girls. "The Jews and Communists in America were raping the whole 'damn' capitalist system like steers in the Chicago stockyards. Rosefield was their fuehrer with his rotten New Deal. Someone had to solve the Jewish problem."

Someone had to solve the Jewish problem. A minor German S.S. official asked Arian Bandage if he could come aboard at Cuxhaven. He told Bill Brogan he'd be dressed as a reporter. A quiet, nondescript man with the laugh of a hyena, he wanted to see American Jews. It was said that summer the little man, Adolf Eichmann, had fallen in love.

Bandage didn't understand the need for Eichmann's civilian clothes. None of the athletes knew the difference anyway between black or brown shirts, or flashy lettered insignias – S.S. or S.D. They had the same silly names. Tongue twisters like *Gestapo*. It was funny how the Germans called Eichmann "the little Jew." They said he spoke Yiddish.

Bandage looked into the mirror. "Mein own Kampf," he laughed, imagining his meeting with der fuehrer; how he would greet the man of the hour. Of course the smart Nazi salute by the American team was out of the question. Pity he would not be able to stem the stink of that protest.

"To mein own kampf be true," he laughed. He would be greeted by Herr Hitler no matter the salutation. He alone had delivered that precious cargo of American concrete and dust. 'Ban dauge,' despite the protests had preserved the purity of sports.

Sporting a finger over the tight upper lip and tossing his hair down to one side, Arian Bandage knew what he alone had accomplished. "So where are my damn glasses," he said, "I must be the sober image of amateur sports." Then he raised his right arm level to the chest, or should he use the left with a powerful fist? "*Sieg Heil*," he said, nonetheless. He was surprised to see an alcohol flask in his iron grip.

10

Bobby Gillman made his way to the tourist dining room. He wobbled toward the swimming pool, besides which stood a monstrous machine buoyed to an anchor. It was supposed to help steady swimmers from the turbulent sea. As the sun beat down, he paused. There was always the danger of sunstroke. With the games less than two weeks away, he had to be careful. Bandage wanted to know everything. A slight cold could upset the delicate balance of muscle and bones. Stay fit, or be dropped from the team.

The floating gym was equipped with new gadgets. Oarsmen replaced their long shells with a new invention trussed overhead on the Touring A Deck. Half of the eight-oared team were seasick. Mal de Mer attacked the American squad. Jack Torrence, the shot putter, couldn't eat and had lost twenty pounds. The wrestlers retched over the far deck of the port bow.

Olympians swarmed below to the infirmary. A nurse in white stood-by with two large attendants. The ship's doctor scaled the high shelves for the compound that cured the malaise. Mrs. Socket sat outside in the little alcove opposite sick bay. She fanned herself, the sweat pouring down her ruffled dress as the first of the athletes retched on the smooth, white deck. Marjorie Gestring who wore a cotton blouse and smart sailor hat came down to sick bay.

When it was her turn, Marjorie said, "Ma'am, I need something for seasickness."

"In here, dearie," the nurse said. Inside the cabin, a small vial and a glass of water were readied at the table. Marjorie took the compound and turned to leave. Mrs. Socket held her in a bony vice.

"Miss Margie there can be none of that. We need your violin at the recital in Cuxhaven. Mr. Ban dauge' will be having important guests."

"No," Marjorie pleaded. The attendants bore down as the nurse opened her mouth. "Now be a good girl and swallow."

Marjorie gagged and clutched her chest.

"All better?" said Mrs. Socket, but the young Olympian was red-faced.

"I just wanted something for my mother. *She's* the one threw up all over the cabin bed."

"Now run along, sweeties," Mrs. Socket said, not hearing, will young Marjorie gagged and wheezed. At the same time, Bobby Gillman came down the stairs. He'd made a terrible mistake, and knew he needed to get out of his sweats. The dress code for dinner, a white and blue uniform, was mandatory. He was disrespecting the five rings.

He moved unsteadily toward his compartment and saw Eleanor Holm Jarrett drinking from a flask with an entourage of muscle-bound men. Suddenly, she leaned over the ship and hurled a series of curses toward the sea. The ladies had been falling into the pool with champagne glasses. Jarrett, the reigning gold medalist and captain of the women's Olympic team was warned not to drink or miss curfew, or training sessions again. She was heard saying, "What are they talking about? I'm bored to death. I *train* on champagne and caviar."

Mrs. Socket's fan drifted over one eye, and she appeared to shrink into vapor and to levitate suddenly out the door.

After he dressed, Bobby Gillman walked up the narrow stairs to the first deck. He was given the choice to train on the two hundred meter track. But the interim coaches, The Dean and Robbie Lawson –the head coach who hadn't been named officially–warned the athletes not to be there without supervision. They must be cautious to avoid shin splints. Only one athlete could do as he wished. Bobby Gillman watched him without a competitor's eye. Jesse Owens jogged towards him.

"Gillman, the last time I saw you, you were scared to death."

"You tore down my track." Bobby smiled from ear to ear. He so admired his captain.

"It was hotter than mustard. I just lifted my legs," Jesse said.

"Yeah, but yours didn't touch the ground."

Bobby forced another grin, but had something on his mind. He knew that Owens had more than just muscle and limbs. What made Owens a fraction faster?

Fencers dueled in the afternoon sun on three strips of the massive deck on the "floating gym." A crowd gathered by a twenty by twenty-two foot mat to see huge hulks wrestle for the last spot on the Olympic team. But *mal de mer* had weakened them both. Whoever won or lost would be mute in the stiff winds of the Olympic air.

The Manhattan was both a floating gym and craps, or dice game, as well. Betting parlors sprang up in the athletes' quarters. Newshounds met them there. The committee had reserved the entire tourist section. Bandage had his quarters in a secret concrete bunker. He never forgot the mutiny on the *Matoilka*.

Along the sundeck, a great roar erupted when the winner was crowned at the wrestling pit. Head down the loser wept. It hurt to see a big man cry.

"I've been thinking about Randall's Island, you know? It was a good day for Southern California. When was the last time someone was given three, four chances?"

The captain saw unease in Bobby's smile. "You mean, Tom?"

"How does he get to run again?"

Can't help you there, Bobby. I don't know. I "jus'" knows what "*massa,*" tells me."

"Come on, gosh, be serious."

"Look, talk is that Grace and Warren are teachers' pets and what Robertson says goes. He'll be head coach."

"But something's going on. He wants us to race against each other at the village. We need to practice handing off the baton. That's what we need."

"It's already decided: Tom, Davie, Josh, and you are running the relay."

"Then why the extra work?"

Jesse laughed. "Maybe to help you boys stay in shape. No slip-ups. Hitler's not lying down for a few blacks and Jews to just pick up, and walk away with his gold.

"Look, Bobby, I don't have a copper penny. Ruth will kill me if I don't come back with something. This is it for me. My chance to cash in. I have a family, and I'm the breadwinner without a crumb of bread. I've no job, no prospects, and come home smelling of dust and sweat. Sometimes I feel I'm running like a fugitive slave. Back bent, running out of the cotton fields on a wet day. You know what the New Deal did? It took my daddy's farm away and put him on the dole. I want gold sure, but nothing's certain. I know the feeling of what it is to lose. To have everything taken from you. My picture's in the papers my family can't afford to buy."

"Well, here's an easy one. You're a cinch to win, and your name never to be forgotten."

Jesse was the taller of the two. He slapped Bobby on the back. The two liked each other.

"Better hurry if you want some food. It's Sunday. Almost time for church. The Bandage wants everyone to come," Jesse Owens said, curious how Bobby Gillman's look darkened, how his mouth opened wide enough to catch flies.

11

The Manhattan was on the last leg of its journey, its smokestack belching out black smoke into the salty vaporous air. They passed the coast of Newfoundland and St. Pierre, the ship churning briskly through the North Atlantic. Somewhere near the wreckage of the doomed Titanic, they saw the flapping and heard the low flying cacophony of black and white puffins, and the seagulls hovering over the hump-backed whales. Starry-eyed, and huddled with army surplus jackets, they watched slithers of Belgium and the Netherlands disappear.

Rough seas and wind-swept hail pelted the Olympians, past the coast of Ireland, and through the English Channel into the North Sea. They grew weary from the voyage. The athletes couldn't train properly, the floating gym was a debacle that had to be abandoned. During a fourteen-hour stopover at *Le Havre*, in France, Arian Bandage forced them to march on the sundeck. He wanted them prepared for the opening ceremonies. With his face flushed, he went over the breaches of curfew and training, gambling, and, 'ahem,' drinking violations. Bandage would root out that unpatriotic fervor, if it were the last thing he did.

Before the ship reached Cuxhaven, but already into German seas, he stood under the awning of the navigator's platform, while his athletes were pelted by fog, wind, and a slight, horizontal rain. He bellowed into the bullhorn with bravado, but was barely heard.

"American athletes walk proudly

 Hear the roar of the wind.

"Reviewing stand,

Awaken the lonesome foghorns of ships passing into the night.

"Merely,

Rain smacking the face.

"Doff straw hats....and...Extend …

Cracking contraptions screaming from the ironworks,

"Forward and ever upward, but parallel, not raised, more rain pelting the necks and the ears that can't hear a word.

"Never use the Nazi word. Their salute is *verbot*...forbidden,

There are distractions on the foredeck. Now, the whispering grows louder.

"Eleanor, no," the voices scream, "That's so unfair."

"Walk smartly, our host, Herr Hitler."

The news spread on deck about Eleanor Holm. The night before, Socket had told her to go below to the athletes' quarters. Eleanor had already been warned in the sportscaster's lounge for after-hours drinking. But it was only nine o'clock, too early to go down to that stuffy room.

"Who won gold medals," she asked the matron, "Bandage, you, or me?"

Socket told him what she had said, and the next day, summoned by the committee, she was told the grim news. For conduct unbecoming a "water queen," and for breaking the rules, the reigning Olympic champion would face charges, and be dropped from the American team.

Despite the goings-on, the Olympians were excited when the ship stopped at Cuxhaven. Curfew was lifted at the first glimpse of German soil. Joshua Sellers clustered with other athletes and gazed at the lovely Elbe, and the happy crowd that came to the pier. Rosy-cheeked girls sang sad German folk songs throughout the night. Under a pale, crescent moon, the Americans picked up the tunes and hummed them softly. Jesse Owens and little Marjorie Gestring came to say, good-night.

At the starboard side, Joshua leaned his arms against the railing with an ever-cautious eye, listening to the cherubic voices and hearing the crackling of bonfires nearby. It occurred to him that he was one of a handful of free Jews on German soil. The recent Nuremberg Laws had stripped German Jews of their citizenship, forbade work in many industries, and caused half to lose their jobs.

The politics of the day, though, didn't really bother him. He was taught to stand behind in the shadows and wait for a favorable wind. When the athletes bandied about, talking about Eleanor Holm Jarrett, Joshua wasn't there.

He did the bidding of the coaches one hundred percent. Physically he was ready to run. In light workouts and the extra competition, he was better than the rest. He bested Warren twice around the two hundred meter shipboard track, and beat Grace, two out of three. The Dean held a stopwatch and chewed on a cigar that dripped from his mouth each time he won. "Son of a gun."

Joshua was ready to race Jesse Owens again. It wasn't just a physical sensation that put him alone at the end of the Cuxhaven pier, but something closer. He thought of the gathering of land animals, even before the arrival of cranes, or their scurrying about in the onset of a summer storm. Last night, Owens played trombone and Joshua sang. Everyone had a good time but him.

"Yodelede, yodelede, yodelede oh, yodelede, yodelede, yodelede dee."

The song brought peals of laughter when Jesse appeared on a raised platform, singing the white man's yodel while Joshua wore "blackface" make-up, and had a white cowboy hat on his head. But Joshua stopped singing, and was about to lay an egg. Jesse noticed something peculiar with his friend. That same smile he had given to bring Joshua to urge him along on the cinders, now urged him on again. He wanted to smack Joshua, to wake him, to call him into the fields for some hard morning toil. All the while, he cracked a smile for the cracked-up Olympians. But something wasn't right. Something dreaded like fog that crept into the skin. It was there gnawing at Joshua. It was stifling, a stink in the German air.

Down from the raised platform, Jesse was near. He hammed it up for laughs and twirled Joshua around, whispering. "What's up, bro?" He wanted to say how much he needed him. How much he needed Joshua to be, o.k. Then, he gave Joshua a bear hug, and squeals of laughter came when the black paint smeared on Jesse's clean white sport coat. He touched Joshua's cheek and held it there.

On that ship, black and white weren't segregated. The Jew and the black were one and the same. That was the message of the Manhattan. An integrated group was going to tame the Master Race.

But it wasn't the crowd that had caused the presentiment, the thought that doom had followed him to that place. It was something else besides.

The athletes cheered the farce wildly. It was slapstick, a two-bit vaudevillian prank. But before taking off the blackface make-up, alone in his cabin, Joshua looked into his face mirror and broke down.

Without understanding the emotion that had confounded what he thought was his sense of well-being, he removed the mask and lost that feeling that had overwhelmed him until then. But on the pier serenaded by simple folk tunes, he soon forgot his own dark visions.

In the morning, a boat pulled alongside the Manhattan from shore. During a slight drizzle, the athletes stood until the five ring Olympic flag was raised. The adoring crowd came closer; a little pixie held a bouquet of fresh orchids in her tiny hands. She sang in a shrill piercing voice.

"*Sieg Heil.*"

"*Sieg Heil.*"

"*Seig Heil.*"

Tossing the lovely bouquet to Joshua, she raised her arm in the Nazi salute. "*Sieg Heil, Sieg Heil,*" she said. Her tiny hand thrust outward as she fixed her gaze keenly on Joshua's eyes.

Was it her he had dreaded, in blackface, alone in his cabin, about a thought yet to be voiced, a presence unseen? It was not the present that terrified him but the future. That future was coming now as a demon in a pretty, little girl's, ferocious face.

Joshua looked into the menacing eyes of the child, her shrill voice hailing gaily, until he dropped the orchids like a baton at his side.

Squads of foreign photographers and newsmen, who had boarded at *Le Havre*, and at earlier ports of call, now left the ship hurriedly. A fresh group came aboard. They told Bill Brogan that all Germany was "agog" at the arrival of the American team.

A German pilot arrived. During a game of shuffleboard, he joked with the American athletes. He wanted to fly with Lindbergh in Berlin. Charles Lindbergh was scheduled to speak that afternoon at a luncheon honoring him. He would caution the Luftwaffe against the deadly use of the airplane. Hermann Goering would take notes, and cheer wildly at the end of the speech.

German customs inspectors, in spanking white uniforms, came aboard, earlier. They told the committee that the athletes' luggage would have only a slight inspection. When the ship reached Hamburg, the Americans could declare their money and change cash into Reich marks. Only non-Olympic luggage would be inspected more closely.

Bandage alerted the news media for an important announcement. With no exceptions, he wanted everyone on deck. All athletes, even those in the infirmary, were to report in fifteen minutes, or less, to the dining room. A Waterways customs official, wearing a smart navy Blue uniform and gold insignias, walked beside the press secretary, Bill Brogan. He was followed by a member of the *Wasserschutpolizei*, waterways protection police. That man had a casual air, his great coat with gold plaited buttons bobbing as he strolled on deck. Bill Brogan pointed out some of the features of the floating gym. The official feigned mild interest.

By then, the athletes had filed into cramped quarters towards the dining room. The customs officer asked Bill Brogan if he had read the German bestseller, The Sixth Ring. Bill had an unusually pale face so that when the color rose in his cheeks, it was obvious he hadn't. He was taught to use caution when talking to even minor officials of The Third Reich. One slip of the tongue and his job was...*kaput.*

The *Wasserschutzpolizei* came to his rescue. He said The Sixth Ring told the story about an American athlete falling in love with a German girl. In Deutschland, the romance was selling second only to *Mein Kampf*, My Struggle. The new novel was written by the boys of The Ministry of Enlightenment and Propaganda. Brogan overplayed his hand. "Imagine a book selling more copies than d*er fuehrer's*," he said.

"That, of course, is not possible," said a voice, not yet heard. A dour-faced man with non-descript eyes, wearing civilian clothes, a drab suit, brown tie, with a pad and pencil, had joined the conversation. Like walls of a ship, painted in dull shades, or flickering pale light in dark corners, or shadows of faceless men under umbrellas, he walked into the mist that had slowly crept away.

Brogan was taught to warm-up the press. But Eichmann was dull, distracted; even when he seemed to be note-taking, he was lost in thoughts. His pencil uselessly skyward, he never wrote a word. He was abstracted, purposeless, asking questions, not caring for answers.

Usually, it was Jesse Owens who fielded the worst: where he came from, what foods he ate, how did he learn to run? Jesse answered without a trace of anger, even when the questions were insulting. Had he many relatives in the jungle? Jesse softly hurled the answers back. He fielded racism cleanly. He was taught to do that and an early age. It was their problem, not his.

Brogan thought Owens hardly seemed phased. For Jesse, those were background noise, a droning sound under the surface, not real enough to disturb his visible calm. Brogan was talking to the great coat of the customs officer, but wanted to be excused. Arian Bandage wanted everyone together in the dining room. "America was a Christian nation," he said.

"If you don't mind accompanying me," Brogan said, not seeing the vapor left by his noxious guest. Eichmann had posed a question, the effects not yet certain. "Do you have any Jews aboard this ship?" the vapor had asked, very quietly.

"I don't know anything about Jews," said Brogan sincerely. "Everyone's in the dining room, sir."

"Let us see," the customs official said. It was unclear what he wanted to see.

Brogan beckoned for the two to walk behind him, but as he did, he was jarred by the sound of gold buttons and the insignias that jingled the great waistcoat along. He didn't hear the footsteps that had left. The other, like morning mist, had already gone.

12

Joshua Sellers had breakfast in the dining room. He was happy to be alone to enjoy the scenic Elbe River. How certain was the sea, not so much of tides, but of men. Germany didn't fit the reports of savagery and persecution. The young folks at the pier serenaded him from the heart. Their youth needed to connect to us. Americans were simply adored. The thought that Nazi Germany persecuted any race must be exaggerated, as Bandage said.

Then why couldn't he sing with a glad heart; he who loved to sing? Why did his heart pound when that "Sieg Heil," shat out of the mouth of that little German babe?

Really, he could trust only his limbs; speed bursting with courage, his creed to win. Purpose broke through in the muscles and fibers that were tuned to the dual gift of strength and speed. More than any other, he was ready to reach the highest peaks. That was where the athlete gazed, and the Olympian's vision rose even higher.

The heart of the dash man was indescribable, born to rise and fall with twice the mortal beat. By heart alone, he couldn't race a moment without that surge. It wasn't just the body, but the thoughts and emotions that were enslaved. At a gathering, he would take out his papa's old pocket watch and count to ten. But what happened in the next ten seconds, his soul transformed into a rage that would smash the orchids out of little Nazi girls and crush the fingers that held them?

As Jesse said, it was a lifetime of training for that ten-second run. Running at full speed came much later into the race. Joshua had often tried to think as a clock. He set his feet and hands in the sure stance of a millisecond. Testing the jerk of a wrist could be measured in laboratories. At the track, the relay so fast, the running starts and the hand-off must be perfect, for speed alone was but one factor to win a race between men.

There were two bodies, one running at top speed at the finish of his run, the other set to begin inert as the baton. How must the body be waiting, rigid or relaxed? How would the legs break free? He knew the number of strides from start to finish, but not what happened between the strides-the gray areas where death may have also come for the ride –when the body was bursting to unnatural limits, and the mind had gone beyond whatever had made one a human being.

A great wind outside the dining room stopped his thoughts. His breathing measured in the moist sea air, his thoughts had been serene. The scrambled eggs on his plate turned cold. By instinct, Joshua touched the dishes on the table. He thought about Jerry Ford, and the games they played at midnight in Michigan. He'd be going back for his senior year after the games. "Jerry Ford," he said aloud, and had a clear vision of that man's future. He trusted him, that clumsy bear, would hem and haw and barrel his way to the future.

The doors of the dining room swung wide open. Horatio Townsend stormed in, carrying a large wooden cross. He was followed by an entourage of Olympic officials. Then a muscle-bound athlete cleared the dais of chairs and benches, and the smorgasbord table that had been used for breakfast.

"Give us a hand," said Greg Morris, bursting with muscle and bones. The blonde-haired decathlon champion seemed to be posing, each move of his muscular body meant to be seen.

"What's up?" said Joshua.

"Church," chimed an official.

Good grief, thought Joshua, helping to arrange rows of benches, while Horatio Townsend made an altar from a garland of roses that he placed around the speaker's podium, at the rear of the dining hall.

Solemn ceremony in the dining room, Joshua was only an observer, protected by his invisible dream. Nothing really mattered there anyway except the gold medal. Joshua helped the others lift the planks, as Horatio Townsend stuck religious symbols on the walls. With little reverence, the athletes filed in.

Joshua watched the blacks on the port side of the dining room. Theirs was a special bond. Owens kneeled among them, shepherding his flock. No matter the outcome, they would be the victors. A splash of blonde, southern Californians, stood in the center of the room relaxed, their manners serene, The Dean chewed on an unlit cigar and watched their every move. Robbie tapped his cane before taking off his cap. The Californians circled him with great respect.

Joshua saw Tom Grace. He'd grown gaunter than he was at Randall's Island. But his curly hair shocked the senses with a wild and brazen look. The two-time Olympian, and California's favorite son, Tom had known glory in the '32 Games. Glory was already taken and received. Joshua's view was blocked when the women athletes arrived.

A few of the swimmers vied for the Californians' attention. They swooned when Greg Morris walked by. Eleanor Holm Jarrett, her back arched in stately comportment, sat alone near the door. Thin-skinned Emily Mae Socket pounced with the heavy weight of authority.

"Mrs. Jarrett," she said loudly, although Eleanor had already turned towards her. "Mrs. Jarrett," she repeated, "You are to accompany me to the stateroom of the American Olympic Committee."

Even the Southern Californians stopped talking. Dean said, "Son of a gun."

Tom Grace, who had shared the glory with Eleanor in nineteen thirty-two, bit his lower lip. He watched while the Olympic champion quickly left the dining room.

Arian Bandage appeared below deck, even before Eleanor began to cry. He was mauled by a careful selection of news hounds. Patting his hair, he clenched another thin strand falling from his crown. He'd ignore that for he had news to tell. "Eleanor Holm Jarrett has been dropped from the American team. She was twice warned about her condition and behavior in public after drinking many glasses of champagne. Our physician couldn't revive her in the room she shared with two other young female athletes. Our course is clear. Mrs. Jarrett will return home on the next boat. She'll return her Olympic uniform, and be lodged until the Bremen's departure, at the committee's expense, in Berlin. She can lodge an appeal that we'll hear on the train."

As his words spread, the athletes groaned. Outrage followed Eleanor's retreat below deck. Afterwards, she was seen red-faced and crying. Some shouted obscenities, or banged on the committee room. Bandage skulked below, hidden in a corner of his bunker, and put another iron bolt on the door.

Nevertheless, after the Manhattan docked at Hamburg, Eleanor Holm left the ship. If only Americans had self-discipline like the Nazis, Bandage told reporters when it was safe to leave his stateroom. His words were quoted roundly in Deutschland.

But discipline had improved. Under the eyes of the Olympic officials, the captain's dinner was held with the utmost decorum. The athletes excused themselves courteously at curfew. They walked quietly back to their quarters. A petition, written by a West Virginian newsman, and signed by two hundred athletes to reinstate Eleanor, was passed around, put under the door of the committee, but was ignored.

But soon morale improved. The end of the voyage was in sight. The Manhattan steamed steadily through perfect weather and calm seas.

13

Joshua and Bobby found themselves in a makeshift dining room. Bobby squirmed, and couldn't sit still, his eyes darting toward the portholes. He was beside Joshua, poking him in the ribs, when Tom Grace came by.

Joshua locked eyes with his competitor. Tom's gaze suddenly softened. Bobby would never forget that the man facing him had connived to make the team. But what did he want from him now? Both would be running the 4x100 meter relay run. Still, the coach made them compete.

The dining room began filling to capacity. Olympic officials came through the doors. Foreign press steamed along the sides, hoping for the best advantage. There wasn't an exit. Had they left then, the newsmen would circle, sharpen their pencils: Jews refuse to attend church services. …, what are we to do about them? Thousands of Americans would read that at breakfast. Arthur Daley, correspondent for *The New York Times*, already had his pad out, his eyes squinting toward the platform.

Joshua thought about the wind and its effect on speed. Sometimes, when cornered like that, he would count the number of flaps of a gull's flight. Sometimes, he dreamed cranes had flown by. But if Joshua stayed, he could be considered to be a Christianized Jew. There were three hundred thousand in Germany alone, married Germans hoping to be Aryans. Many were baptized, and had the documents to prove it. He'd seem to be very much like them, he thought.

Bobby Gillman was even more uneasy. Under his breath, he said, "My father's going to say the prayer for the dead, *Kaddish*, for me." It was Tom Grace who locked into their thoughts. On a doomed crossing, he helped them over. "Bandage is watching you. He suspects you handed out the anti-Nazi leaflets. I don't care if you did. They make us race you because they don't want you here. They want to find out how much you can take. Smile, Gillman, do you see the one near him?"

Bobby raised his eyes slowly. He saw Bandage seated among the glitter of the platform, all right, but not who sat at his side. From the lights, and a steady stream of dust, he saw a gray-haired, little fat man, then, like mist, a kind of cloud; a hat, a suit, the cuffs. His pencil seemed to hover above him, untouched.

"They were drinking last night," Tom said, "and that one told Bandage his idea. He said, "If Jews wouldn't leave Germany, or go to Palestine, he'd propose sending them to Madagascar. Either way, they must go.'"

"So, what?" said Bobby, "We're Americans, not Germans? Who cares about him? We're just going to run. This is only about a ...who gives a hoot for a forty second race?"

Joshua wasn't listening to the conversation, but his eyes never left Grace. If he wanted to stay on Robertson's good side, he'd have to beat Tom Grace every day. But Robertson loved Grace as well. It was a very delicate situation. Grace turned to the steely blue eyes.

"I'm Protestant, Joshua. Germany is a land of Protestants fighting for their lives. Pastors put in prison. The church obeys Dr. Hans Kerr, an atheist in charge of church affairs. He forces the pastors to hang swastika flags above their parishes, then takes their youth away. Baldur von Schirach has put seven hundred thousand of the evangelicals into his pagan youth. Last May, the confessionals wrote to Hitler. I want you to read this."

Tom tried to give him two small pieces of paper. "That doesn't concern us, buddy, and...," said Joshua, tight-lipped.

"Why are you busting our chops?" asked Bobby Gillman.

"Because you're in church, and we're not Shirley Temple."

"Your '*mudda*,'" said Bobby.

"You're cursing me?" asked Tom, politely.

"So what?"

"O.K., your '*mudda*,' too."

Suddenly, for no apparent reason, they both started laughing. Joshua found Tom Grace unsettling. He felt he needed to dislike him, but his manner was disarming. He was actually likeable. He took the paper from Grace's hand, and read:

"When blood, race, nationality, and honor receive the status of eternal values, the Evangelical Christian is obliged by the First Commandment to reject this scale of values. When the Aryan man is exalted, G-d's word testifies to the sinfulness of all men. When, in the framework of National Socialist ideology anti-Semitism is imposed on the Christian, telling him to hate Jews, for him the Christian commandment of brotherly love remains binding."

"I just want you to know, I'll beat any man that runs against me, but gosh, know you're also my brother," said Tom.

Joshua turned from Tom to the stage, and the booming voice.

"Ok, ok," said Bobby Gillman, "but can you get us out of here?"

"Sure, follow me, rabbis."

He led the pair to the rear of the dining room where with a slight push an unlit emergency exit door opened.

"Thanks," Joshua said. It would be hard to hate this guy.

"Just remember, when I beat you, the race will be fair."

The pious scowls bellowed from the platform. "Hallowed be Thy Name ..." It was the stentorian voice of the sportsman, then preacher, Arian Bandage.

Bobby smiled, "This is a race for heaven's sake, isn't it?"

Joshua was smiling too. "I hope your man wears running shoes," he challenged, leaving Tom Grace with a puzzled look by the door, before heading into the fog and mist that waited for them in the pale Nazi dawn.

14

The Manhattan swept into the pier at midnight in Hamburg harbor. The athletes stayed aboard because of the lateness of the hour. They were tired and exhausted from the long journey. But they awoke to a celebration. A crowd had gathered at the Hamburg pier for a rousing reception. Even parents came, despite the hour, carrying sleepy-eyed toddlers who held American flags. Bobby wondered what he could tell his father who was fearful about the New Germany.

"Don't be flashy; just *shlump, or shuffle* along, but don't look happy. Remember, maybe, there are some happy Jews somewhere, maybe, but none in Germany," his father had said.

On deck, Bobby Gillman tried to quell his broad smile, but Jesse Owens was jubilant, and waved to the crowd. Could he write his father about that? About how the Nazis that just loved blacks and Jews?

Jesse had emerged from below deck. He couldn't sleep, but awoke to a dream. Before, it had only been at the track where he was truly free. Gathering his followers like a shepherd gathering his flock, nobody saw color, nor did he have to stay at the back of the bus, or live off campus, or crouch behind the servant quarters. He connected with the Germans as an equal. Going to take that for a ride, he thought, maybe to Hollywood. Eddie Cantor told him just win, and the doors would open for him. But the gnawing came with the delirium of his admirers. Peacocks were out there, even in the worshipping crowd, ready to knock him down.

"We want to see the American heroes who came to der fatherland," the crowd cheered, in a steady chant of halting English.

And the Americans obliged. Throughout the night, and toward dawn, the Olympians came aloft. The German *frauleins* whistled when Glenn Morris appeared in shorts. Morris' eye caught a beam of light just off the pier. Leni Riefenstahl was filming behind a tripod there, but when she saw Morris, fell into a swoon. Her dark eyes followed him with such urgent intensity that the decathlon hopeful shied away.

A group of German athletes came on board to chat with the Americans. Long-legged German girls in white shorts with garlands in their hair, compared training programs. Weather and food were common topics. So were the athlete's regimen, the hours of training– the lineaments used when the joints got sore. A few of the Americans were too forward. They stayed away from the banal, and made time with the German girls. The *frauleins* laughed, and the American boys did the same. But two were not playing that game, at least, not with words.

Joshua had been unable to sleep. He walked the foredeck alone and watched with only passing interest the goings-on. The German girls had sidled toward some of the black athletes. They seemed to admire them. One of the girls, however, stood apart. She hadn't tried to join the others. The others disdained her kind.

She was dressed like the other girls, and wore shorts, and had an athletic build. Her hair, though, was unlike the others there, nor was she of jovial spirit. She saw Joshua who paused by the railing for a moment to breathe the mist and watch the pale moon in the awakening sky. He noticed her green eyes, and it seemed the crowd parted, as she walked towards him.

Her fingers were long and feminine, but she had strong features besides. She had developed biceps, a thin frame and curves from exercise. Her complexion was dark, her lips full. She gave Joshua a firm hand, her green eyes seeking his.

"You are Joshua Sellers," she said.

The precise English, the way she said his name with halting expression, the voice insistent, but quiet like a songbird, brought him to attention. He thought, somewhat madly, of surrounding her, of having wings to fan her blush, to moisten the lips that parted; made him dizzy enough to blush. Joshua didn't even care how she knew him. "You are Jewish," she said.

It was a statement, not the one question every blind date had asked him in Cincinnati, in Ann Arbor, in every corner of every Jewish neighborhood in Ohio and Michigan, he thought. His muscles tensed, and his brow reflected that he needn't be reminded of that.

"I am also Jewish," she said. She seemed the saddest woman ever to say those words.

"I'm sorry; we don't care much about such things in America."

"That is why I wanted to meet you. I am Rachel Brach, a runner like you. I have been following you this year. I wanted to meet you while I still can," she said, turning in the direction of her companions with an anxious face.

He wouldn't wonder how he came to be known as a Jew among the three hundred and thirty four athletes aboard that ship, feeling a vague presence, lingering in shadows, behind the light of the pier and the gaiety of the crowd.

He thought only about her, a Jewish athlete in Germany. She was like Helene Mayer. Another German-Jewish athlete Bandage used as proof of Nazi racial tolerance. "Yes," he said, finally, "I'm happy to meet you, too. You're also quite beautiful."

After a quick blush, she turned, suddenly a more serious face. "I wanted to see how it felt to be Jewish and free," she said, her green eyes swelling with tears. More cheerfully, "Tell me about America."

Joshua told her about Hollywood and Shirley Temple, baseball and Coney Island, Michigan and washing dishes, birds in flight, and being free. He made her laugh, imitating Charlie Chaplin. He was walking the way of the comedian when he saw the other German girls begin to depart from the pier. Rachel leaned towards him. She was almost Joshua's height. Her eyes told him to bend down. She didn't want to be heard. "You and I ... I think we are *'Bashert.'*" Before he could ask her the meaning of that word, she was gone.

15

By morning, some of the stars of the American team caught laryngitis. The change of climate brought cold, damp air. As expected, the coaches had been selected the day before. Lawson Robertson was named the overall coach, and given the job of handling the sprinters and the relay team. The Dean, from his own alma mater, the University of Southern California, would coach his former students, Tom Grace and Davie Warren.

Passing through a whirlwind Customs inspection, the Americans were given keys to the city. They boarded a train for Berlin, but held their own feelings. Most were uncomplimentary towards Arian Bandage.

Another petition, protesting the dismissal of Eleanor Holm, circulated on the train. The petition demanded her reinstatement, but Bandage was unmoved. Appearing in a plain, white tunic, the beautiful Olympian faced the committee one more time. The old men ogled her, let her stand while she spoke, and watched her every move. Arian Bandage, with his packaged pose, practiced in his stateroom mirror, let her go on. He wondered how deep the knife could go.

"Do you have something else to say to us?" he said, his words measured, the tone, though, a giveaway.

"I'll never touch another drop of liquor. All I want is one more chance to show I can take it, and make good. But you don't like me because I'm a woman and an athlete."

Dr. Raycroft, a committeeman, talked for Arian Bandage in a measured tone. "You were warned twice. Young athletes admire you. They follow you. You led them toward drunkenness."

"You know I like to have a good time. I only had eight or nine glasses of champagne on the whole voyage. It would've taken a hell of a lot more liquor than that to make me drunk."

Bandage rose, but she wasn't finished.

"There's no general rule against athletes drinking. The bars were open daily and nightly in two sections where the athletes were quartered. The bars were open well past midnight."

"Thank you, Mrs. Jarrett. We've heard you, and will render a final decision."

An hour later, she was brought back. There was nothing more to be done. The facts were clear, the decision unanimous to drop Eleanor Holm from the American team.

Outside the compartment almost fainting, Eleanor told reporters her career was ruined. She'd never forgive Arian Bandage for persecuting and humiliating her in public, but would stay in Berlin, at her own expense. She walked toward the drawing room followed by a nurse, and tried to compose a letter to her husband. After three tries, she gave up, and tossed the paper on the floor.

For others the train ride was endless. Bobby was antsy. It had been a while since he ran. The track on the deck of the ship had made him move gingerly. With the ship swaying, he jogged lightly.

"Gosh, I got to run," he said.

He was talking to a sympathetic ear.

"I better run," said Jesse.

From the windows of the train, through splotches of rain, they waved to peasant girls that held tiny American flags. Despite the weather, the Germans were smiling. By the ministry's decree, it was time to be happy. The beginning of the week of laughter had begun.

In Berlin, a dentist pulled the wrong tooth, but his patient left the office laughing, and the dentist doubled-up in stitches. Doing back-breaking work with concrete at the Air Ministry, a few Gypsies that swore were carted away. Goebbels arrested anyone who seemed unhappy during that time.

Bobby fumbled with an English newspaper. "Hey, the Bomber is going to get another chance."

"That's real good," said Jesse, his eyes closed. He didn't want Bobby to see how important that news was for him. Max Schmeling, Hitler's showcase fighter, knocked Joe Louis out in the twelfth round on American soil. It put extra pressure to win squarely on him.

The Nazi papers say the Aryan is better than the blacks. "We are jungle creatures," Jesse said.

Jesse aimed to prove he belonged to the human race. It was a big problem for those who were forced to hate. His father had taught him early on survival skills in the south. A smile went a long way, a tip of the cap, eyes down, never to challenge the white man in his place.

Bobby looked at the headlines and read the other news: the Nazi 'cold' putsch in the free city of Danzig. The Nazis abolished the democratic constitution guaranteed by the League of Nations.

The Nazis ignored the League of Nations to take over Danzig for the 'maintenance of security and order.'

The Luftwaffe began strafing Spanish cities.

War had broken out and the athletes of the counter-Olympics were stranded in a war zone. Some had taken up arms against the invaders. Two U.S. aides were killed in Spain. One hundred U.S. citizens sought refuge on a British rescue ship that reached Barcelona. Spaniards who wouldn't make the Leftist salute to autos with red flags were mowed down by machine guns, in the town of Malaga.

Five hundred aristocrats faced death as Madrid's liberalist defenders flung eight thousand militiamen into a mountain battle with fascist armies, twenty miles from the capital.

San Sebastian was captured, and recaptured by two thousand miners.

But nothing in the papers, not even the Spanish Civil War, rivaled the war that waged when Brooklyn's own Eleanor Holm was dismissed from the American team. Hers was the story in both *The Brooklyn Eagle* and *The New York Times*.

He read on. The President of the United States sailed through a fog bank which he navigated, and dropped anchor in a Nova Scotia inlet after a run from Cape Sable with a few of his sons, aboard the Sewanna.

"Ah, here's a good one," he said, "*Das Angriff* says, 'Hitler is infallible.'"

He didn't read the next one. In Kentucky, a crowd of fifteen thousand would come to watch the hanging of a black man next month.

"Go ahead," said Jesse Owens, though his eyes were closed, and he was half asleep, "I read that paper before. What aren't you saying?"

"Oh, the news is pretty bad."

"Yeah, thanks, Bobby for not telling me about my race. The one that's a long way from winning."

Later, Bobby dreamed about taking Martha to Maison Foffe on Montague Street. They served French food and the choicest wines. Lunch grub was forty cents; dinners, fifteen cents more. He'd make that happen when he'd move to Brooklyn Heights. He could work somewhere in the city. After winning the race, there'd be real opportunity for him. Winning was the key, he thought, drifting off to sleep, his legs churning into a dream.

Before the train pulled into Lerhter Station, Tom Grace wrote to Pastor Paul Schneider. After leading a funeral service in June 1934, Pastor Schneider was arrested. The Nazi *Kreisleter* stopped the service to say that the dead boy had gone to heaven to join the Horst-Wessel brigade. The Pastor denounced the *Kreisleter*, saying there was no evidence that Saint Peter would give Hitler Youth a ticket into heaven.

He wrote a letter when he came out of prison. When ninety-nine percent of the German electorate affirmed Hitler's policies, Pastor Schneider wouldn't affirm. A swastika flag was hung from his church steeple, his house almost burned. But on his motor bike to help the needy, he carried on as before.

Tom Grace wanted to talk to the pastor about American and Protestant cooperation. But where was he? He fell asleep, the question on his mind.

Davie Warren held a tiny metal airplane above his bed. He had traded his spare sweatpants for the glistening swastika toy bomber. It was a good deal, he thought, mouthing sounds of guns, and making hand dives at angles that were impossible, except for the most skillful pilot. Davie's little plane scattered from the best enemy fighters. He had heard about the new Luftwaffe that was practicing bomb raids on defenseless Spanish cities. Life was simple for the flying Trojan, clear and certain, for now he knew his enemy's name.

The plane shaking,
His grip strangling twin swastikas.
Black soot rising. That's a Messerschmitt there;
His enemy, the Luftwaffe, his enemy,
Falling in the screams of Davie's night.

By himself, in a compartment, Joshua couldn't sleep. Singing old songs didn't help. Counting birds numbed him, but didn't bring relief. He tossed about on a straw-filled seat. An emotion he loathed crept into his veins, and made his muscles flex, the breathing labored, and the thoughts insane.

It involved the old neighborhood. It happened when they called him those names in Cincinnati; that name, "*kike*," in particular. That one bothered his father who had to sell door to door. He pounded those streets with holes in his boots, but the sounds of a tinkle of bells were so irresistible it brought the people to the windows, as he struggled to keep the pushcart from falling down.

His father had a special skill to solder pans. He could fix them as new. At first he worked with pride. Jewish people wanted to do an honest day's work. It's good for customers; good when the family breaks bread to know their money came from clean hands. But soon, he couldn't work without the bullying. In grammar school, gossip passed along the walls. They thought his old man was dirt. Joshua had to take the fight to the streets.

Even before he learned to duck, the ragamuffins came with fists. At first, he let them humiliate him. He walked in back alleys and side streets under their heels. By the time he was twelve, he knew that he could out run them. He made a plan. Through Reading Road and Plum Street, it was not only the '*goyim*' the Jew had to watch, but the settled German Jews. Trying to fit in, to make their own mark, they joined the racist, intermingling mob. Race and race hatred knows no borders, no shame. So, whether Joshua was chased by Jew or gentile, it was really the same. But that time, he sang his songs and waited for them.

In the neighborhood, fists were an armed curse that drove him to hide behind the stones in Walnut Cemetery. By the time his tormentors climbed the hill, he was running safely east. With speed and a sudden burst, he retraced his path and came upon their weakest foe- he would be the first to go-, and Joshua pelted him with fists and fury, and awful kicks, and he wouldn't let go until the boy cried 'uncle.'

The pack grew smaller the next day. Joshua crept behind the slowest, and beat him badly. By the third day, they knew the must surround him. When the school bell rang at three o'clock and the school day was over, they waited for him in the playground.

That's when he challenged them. Beat him all they wanted, but he'd get up and get them, one by one. That's when the gauntlet scattered, and he walked away, singing an old song about Jewish girls who dreamed of living in the upper crust of Avondale.

Tossing in his compartment, Joshua thought about Rachel. Meeting her was not his doing. It was an act of chance, not, *bashert*, or fate. But beauty alone wasn't enough for him to forget what he had set out to do. Breathing heavily, he tried to relax his muscles. At the heart of a ten second burst, in a race without end, anger often came upon him. His was the rage of a silent enemy that speed couldn't control. As he thought about her, his hand was shaking. He had the same foreboding before when he ran from taunts in the cruel streets of Cincinnati. The anticipation was real. It never let him go.

What had happened to him then when he must control his thoughts? He tried to sleep, but he could ignore, neither his torment, nor the awakening of a great desire. Joshua said her name again until he fell asleep. "Rachel." But he was awake the more in slumber.

Alone again on deck, trying to hear the laughter, the intermingling breath of athletes, dawn had broken into another round of gulls and morning birds, and foghorns. The sky was visible now. The noises of vessels in the harbor, of children awakening from their mother's arms, the smell of fresh air and gardens, the wide expanse of the seas and the mountains on the horizon, the welcoming cries of the host nation, and the faint promise that, beyond that splash of blue above, the sights he'd always ever after see, in the rivers, in the fields, and high atop the mountains, and in the woods, in between, would be her green eyes, bathed in light and tears without borders, but sacred; her eyes that saw such misery, but also hope, glittering green in the gray light, singing in the rising dawn; that still held the promise of tomorrow, and the world that tore at her today would only take away the fabric, maybe even the body, but never her soul away.

But how could he tell her, in a moment that he'd come to see only much later in dreams, of her and him in the square under the swastikas in love, that although he'd never heard that word, "*Bashert,*" before, he wanted to say, through the embrace of immortal souls, that he had always known its meaning.

PART 2

16

    Berliners hailed the arrival of the 'wonder men' and lined the streets through the giant, semicircular dome inside Lerhter Station. High on their parent's shoulders, little Nazi *kinder* were laughing, from *Unter den Linden* to *Tiergartenstrasse.*

    Dressed in white, a band of policemen, welcomed traffic with a wave of harmless, white truncheons. Defying their depiction in news stories, the youthful blue- eyed brigade of the S.S. were courteous and well- mannered. Even the S.D., bobbed and weaved like porcelain figurines, or dolls strung together for a beer fest.

    From the Lustgarten to the Brandenburg Gate, the crowd grew gaily, surrounding the shanties and the sand piles on the concrete dunes construction site. The Statue of Victory, to alert her chariots, raised her glistening sword at the apex of the Hohenzollern Palace. Berlin was reeling from forced laughter. A few slave laborers, shackled into service by Germany, guffawed in chains. As soon as the Americans arrived, even Goebbels giggled.

    The athletes, roused from sleep, stepped off the train to a band playing "The Star Spangled Banner." Delirious Nazis stampeded the platform.

In the excitement, Reich hosts read the wrong proclamation, welcoming the camp army, rather than the Americans. The Nazi hosts were confused by the myriad of badges that were designed for the Berlin Games. Colored badges were made to identify the campers, an extra twelve thousand more, or so, for the huge Olympic ensemble. Since foreign guests bought emblems and pins from the badge makers, Nazi officials weren't able to identify a high dignitary from a lowly beggar. They bowed to janitorial staff in the formal European way. Helter-skelter, they ran around, holding up their pants. They had forgotten to wear their suspenders. Obliged by the formal public decree, they remained jovial, even as the summer sun bore down, and the sweat turned their smiles to deadly glee.

Only the International Olympic Committee was easy to recognize. They came off the train wearing heavy chains of office, like rectors and chancellors of ancient universities that carried their authority with literal weight to the high platforms.

Walter Lemcke designed their chains. Taking his cue from originals in the old Berlin museum, Lemcke made heavy emblems of office in brilliant, colored enamels with lower plaques linked by the five rings, and a larger plaque suspended to those with a heavy weighted chain configuration of ancient Greek deities. He was a sculptor, not a medal maker, and the chains began to strangle its wearers.

Committeemen had badges. Members of subcommittees, and committees without portfolio, wore ones to show their office, as did the secretaries to the committees, the judges, coaches and their assistants, athletes, press correspondents, film and radio correspondents, and their secretaries, honor courts, sub-committees of the various International Olympic committees, and their special guests, and others whom, by complex formulas, were allowed to wear badges and ribbons. Everyone in Germany wore badges-everyone but the Jews.

No longer were Jews citizens of the Reich. Reduced to spectators, but denied entrance to the stadium, they remained silent and invisible. Houses in Berlin displayed the five ring Olympic flag alongside the Nazi swastika banner. The Olympic rings, and the electrically charged crooked cross, flapped side by side. It was a draped message of propaganda that went across the seas. Even the poor house had these. The Stars and Stripes were visible in pretty Nazi rose gardens.

Yet, in Berlin, Jews were not allowed to wear badges, even of lowly honor, nor hoist the Olympic rings. To visitors and common folk, it seemed to be by their own choice that Jews had defied the popular will, ostracizing themselves from the popular zeal.

Riding on drab gray buses from Lerhter Station to City Hall, Bobby Gillman glanced at the unadorned houses with the shutters closed. The residents must have simply gone away.

"Humph," said a member of the International Olympic Committee.

"Quite right," said an Englishman. "You'd think they would try harder to conform."

The committee thought Jews were snubbing Olympic ideals by complaining, and causing disturbances around the world. Count Henri de Baillet-Latour, silenced them with a slight lift of his eyebrow.

"No mention of politics, please," he said, reclining in a specially made cushioned seat before falling back asleep.

"That's Jew-Nazi business. It's not our concern," beamed Bandage. He was elated about the way his athletes were treated in Germany.

***

In the crowd of faceless men, one was blander than the rest. He could have lied among the stones, another brick of the concrete dunes, except for his *S.S. Hauptscharfuhrer* uniform. After that dull ocean voyage, it was nice to be back in Berlin. Strangely, as he sang, his Nazi boots began tapping to ten. He was practicing the unmistaken language of the Jews:

"*Eeyns, tsvey, dray, fir, finef …*"

In Unter den Linden two months before, he had encountered a feeble wasteland of ripped pavement, vast mud piles, and unfinished construction. The beautification project changed the area by rolling the broad center pathway with a landscape that could illuminate the way. By now, it could hold a hundred thousand storm troops, a special elite guard on parade, or the German children with their proud, little fists raised, who goose-stepped for Leni Riefenstahl.

He was happy to see that the young trees had survived the late planting. He loved the old lindens that sadly were sacrificed to the new subway lines. They had withered because of the paucity of the roots.

City police took great care with the roots of the new trees. With the strength of gentle hands, they carried them in firm baskets, filled with the finest fertilized soil. A large battalion of workers helped in the transportation process from the nursery. The trees had grown, and Berlin was bursting with the fresh odors of blossoms and mature leaves.

At Potsdamer Platz, he turned toward the new subway. Workers built arc lights, and tidied up the surface there. Walking along a freshly rolled path, he thought about Vera, his lovely new bride. It had taken some strings to pull to marry a Christian.

The crowd walked faster to the new air ministry, a three-block structure surrounded by reams of scaffolds that workmen were still cementing. He walked faster, too. Busy legions of tireless workers noticed him briefly. Fumes of the new prosperity belched out of the sewers.

Odd fellow, on duty, but humming Horst Wessel, a nationalist song, they thought. That martyr had died by the hands of communist conspirators, not as Jews had said, at the hands of the exploiters of the gutter grifters. He noticed the attention with an odd expression, melding invisibly into the passing parade. After all, he was a little functionary, a bureaucrat who followed orders, compiled and sent information to places, there and abroad. How many were there, and where did they hide? It was the facts he was gathering; hard to get, their names even harder to say.

Mist and a constant light rain, washed away their strange names. Only addresses were certain. Those were firmly planted in the sparse gardens. Without friends or companions, Jews were buried alive, waiting to be identified by him. But, yes, he was really their friend, Adolf Eichmann, the man from 8 *Prinz Albrecht Strasse*, who tabulated and categorized, and wrote lists of the names that were already filed away, in Department, 11/112-3. His was just a little cluttered office that compiled them, and thought of a solution in a place of lists and names, to help him with that problem: like dust that keeps forming on the pavement under the lindens, he wanted only to sweep the Jews away.

17

Weird sounds came from under the gray bus. "Open the buses. Open the tops. Open the damn tops of the buses," said Arian Bandage, "now roll them back."

The Americans were able to stand waist high to return the cheers of the crowd. The blue clad wonder men smiled while Nazis banked solidly along the curbs.

Traffic stopped in all directions and trolleys ground to a halt. The people's cars, the Volkswagens, were backed up for kilometers. Only officials of the Olympic committee could pass with a wave of a genuine Olympic flag. With Hitler salutes, smiling police waved them on in white gloves. As the buses pulled alongside City Hall, white clad escorts from the Olympic Village rushed toward the Americans in squadron formation and cleared a path of honor on the red-carpeted marble steps.

After the Reich Commissar for the city of Berlin formally introduced them, they walked inside to a spacious, elegant reception room. Arian Bandage got his gold medal by thrusting both arms to the rafters that glistened with a thirty foot gleaming, crooked cross. "No nation…since ancient Greece…has captured…the true…Olympic spirit…as Germany," he said to thunderous applause. His words echoed along the walls. Goebbels knew how to amplify that message around the world.

Bobby Gillman couldn't stop from straining his neck. "Will you look at that?"

Beside him, in a frozen posture, sat his square-jawed, blue-eyed companion. Bobby found Joshua under a grandfather clock at the far end of the platform. He talked to him in a frenzied undertone. "I'm going to get some real kosher food," he said. Then, he turned serious, "I don't like the setup here, Joshua. Did you see how they stripped the Jewish homes along the way? What goes?"

Joshua faced Bobby askew. His was a spirit dressed only outwardly in the blue and white Olympic dress. Inside, Joshua was unknown, even to himself. More comfortable in black face than his own skin, he was also the young man who sang silly songs on the deck of the Manhattan. Hidden behind a mask and a grin, ambiguities took hold of him. He was both a man of compassion, and unsettled thoughts. Without shame, he hadn't memory of what he did in moments of great and small distractions.

In the hall, Joshua sat as if he were hearing the fury of the wind. He'd gone to the Michigan arboretum to hear the sounds of nature, but swore he heard the whooping cries of cranes. And Joshua kept a strange smile to the last of the speechmakers. He loved them now, their narrow vision, those Nazis. He loved them for what he'd do when he raced in the Olympic Games.

Later on, the Americans climbed aboard the buses to their final destination. Eager hands reached to touch him. Joshua moved away to the rear of the bus. The large, white columns of the Hohenzollern Palace spoke volumes. The one word he grasped, the concept he worshipped- in the statue and the message, the meaning was the same:

"**Victory**."

The bus passed the streets of blossoms and old lindens, and once luxurious homes. On Gregorstrasse, Olympic, American, and Nazi flags rose above specious gardens and Gothic designs. One of the homes on the street looked bare, and out of sorts without an Olympic, or Nazi flag. A beautiful, dark-haired woman with a faraway gaze graced that porch.

She wore a simple black dress with no sign of Olympic ornamentation. Indeed, when the bus drove by and the athletes waved, she seemed frightened by the attention. Bobby noticed the girl with an anxious heart. He hadn't written to his own girl, Martha, in a long time. He wondered if she'd be waiting for him. That girl was taller than his, and more athletic. She had a graceful presence, but under the fluttering Nazi cross was out of place, out of sorts on her own porch, under the landscape of the lindens.

He was watching Joshua, too. His countenance hadn't changed since Bandage left the platform to a thunderous ovation. Joshua's crooked smile had transformed his own features in an unnatural way. He seemed like a deaf person, straining to hear the way of the wind, the sounds of the sea. When that woman came down from the porch, Bobby saw that Joshua made no pretense of smiling.

Joshua saw the girl in the passing of an eye. But she really never left him since their eyes met on the ship. In the quiet of his thoughts, during the speeches and the sounds of celebration, he saw only her. Now that he passed the drab, almost invisible houses without Olympic, or Nazi ostentation, he'd thought about her again. But seeing her in the flesh, touching her hair, embarrassed not to be waving a swastika, or an Olympic flag, he knew she was in danger now, especially in her own home.

Joshua raised his hand toward the gothic roof, the overhanging lindens that lingered in the garden and the darkening sky. A squadron of black, movable things, raced in solitary formation, squealing through the woods and diving over the lindens, over the houses, with fleshless wings.

***

The gray bus carried the Americans to its destination, along the five-mile Triumphal Way. From the *Charlotteburger Chaussee* to the *Tiergarten*, rows of sycamores graced the wide avenues. In the lead bus, the white-haired Count Henri de Baillet- Latour awoke from a short nap and marveled at the beautiful Berlin landscape. In unison, the International Olympic Committee agreed. Germany was wonderful.

"Just see the beauty of the sycamores," Said Baillet-Latour.

"That's what I meant to say," said Arian Bandage. "No nation has captured the true Olympic spirit as has Germany, and I'll be damned if we let the likes of Lee Jahncke spoil their good name."

The white, domed oval aroused the senses as a model of totalitarian design. It was something to worship- the Olympians said the stadium defied description. They gasped as clean, white tiers of concrete rose over the sycamores at the far end of the hundred yard wide avenue.

The athletes were awed by the new German stadium. Mack Robinson, Metcalfe, and Tom Grace had competed in the colossus of Los Angeles in 1932. The Nazi stadium was simply above the rest. The bus rolled up to the gleaming, high towers, and swerved along a lesser road where the Olympic swimming stadium came into view.

Greeted by gymnasia, clay, grass, and other fields, they passed the swimming pool and twenty thousand empty seats, yearning to be filled. The bus slowed for one more glimpse of paradise; a permanent open-air theater, a polo field, football fields, and an indoor swimming hall, illuminated by stone towers and gates of honor, and at the apex of that grand stadium–the Marathon Gate.

Finally, the bus creaked to rural surroundings. Fog rose steadily from a winding, superficial lake. The two-mile stretch had brought them to meadows and woods, inhabited by wildlife and game. Soon, they arrived quietly in a community of solid houses and attached dining quarters. White barracks formed drably row by row.

As the bus halted, white-clad messengers raced to the four corners of the Olympic world. It was a clarion call to the nations to embrace a miracle; the arrival, not only of athletes, but the elevation of the fascist state. Hoisting the flag of the fifty-fourth nation alongside the banners already raised, the Nazis were delirious. The entire village erupted into pandemonium that spilled into the streets and along the avenues. The crowd came to celebrate a miracle. *Deutschland* had wooed the last hold-out of the Olympic Games. When the Americans arrived, the Nazis knew they had seized their greatest prize. The crown jewel of nations, The United States of America, had finally kneeled down to the master race.

18

Kindled by the sun through magnifying lenses at the ancient site of Olympus, on the ruined altar of Zeus, through the sacred wood, fourteen young women, wearing antiquated costumes of priestesses, carried the blue, fiery torch.

Near the square on the outskirts of the woods, in the stillness of the forest, the first runner waited to light the Olympic flame. In Athens, a national holiday was declared. King George led the speech-makers that included the white haired father of the modern Olympic Games, Baron Pierre de Coubertin-Latour. He was joined on the dais by the Greek Secretary of State, George Georgakopoulos and the amiable German Charge d'Affaires whom nobody seemed to know.

At exactly twelve noon, the Greek national anthem was sung amidst the blasts of trumpets that resounded among nations through which the torch would pass. In the spirit of the universal brotherhood of nations, those invisible boundaries which had divided people were then scorched with the passage of fire.

A clear sky and hot sun saw the first runner race his kilometer on barren roads that had been cleared of autos and pedestrian traffic an hour before he was scheduled to arrive. Wanting to prevent incidences on the Grecian highways across Athens, Delphi, and Salonika, the International Olympic authorities followed the runners in special cars, guarded with the pomp of German movie and radio trucks.

"That was exactly Herr Goebbels idea," he said, shifting from a turn in the ever-winding road. He liked to talk like that, about himself, in third person. She kept her focus on her dancers through the smoke filled tele-photo lens that her projectionist tried to steady.

"Thank you, Joseph, for that self-serving piece of information," she said. Leni Riefenstahl was taller than Goebbels whose lame body made him seem the more shriveled beside her.

Then drooling, now writhing, the Minister of Enlightenment and Propaganda, as he came near her, began to sweat. "I can help you with film, dear Leni," he said with piercing black eyes, and a leering gaze. She was disgusted by his manner and repelled by his deformity.

"I know you can, Joseph. You are a very powerful man," she said, with enough humility to make Goebbels blush, and fall to his knees.

"Stop this mad drama, and be a *mensch*," she said.

"What, what are you saying?" he said.

"You are a Nazi. For goodness sake, act like one."

Goebbels could barely contain his desire for the statuesque, dark-haired beauty. An actress, dancer, and photographer, Leni Riefenstahl found a home behind the camera and a partnership with the Third Reich. She'd been seduced by the strength of the crooked cross, and the power of the fuehrer.

To escape the rabid minister, Leni left the truck, took off her work clothes, and put on a flimsy dress. Then, she ran away to dance with her pagan priestesses.

Through the Balkan Peninsula, and halfway across Europe, local police scanned the highways, stopping any would-be troublemaker from marring the parade. Solemn, choreographed ceremonies, greeted the arrival of the carriers of the flame. While he never forgot Leni's allure, Goebbels attended to the task at hand. He made tens of thousands of youth from every European nation line the roads, at attention. They gave the Olympic salutation by raising their arms level with their shoulders, or thrust out and up in the Hitler salute, much to the delight of the trailing German press corps.

The three thousand runners who passed the flaming torch were prepared with twice enough fuel for their kilometer run. Every detail had been provided for, including the vast network of security, planned with the help of the Olympic and the German organizing committees.

Proclaiming the Eleventh Olympiad a youth pageant and festival of the world, the Germans waited in the towns and villages along the Czech-German border for a glimpse of the last non-Aryan runner to appear. Peasants assembled into Hollendorf in Saxony where the living flame brought out the best and worst delirium, fainting fits, and wild behavior. One woman tried to douse her hands in the flame.

Marching onward, with a paroxysm of the spirit, the blessed blue trail of smoke lingered in the wild, agitated air, as the flame passed into the sure hands of the first Reich runner. Pandemonium broke the last tentative chord of restraint.

"This is the moment in the history of the world that Germany rises again," said the men with their cheers, said the nation with fireworks and drums, said the hysterical faces of an impassioned Aryan race.

Gone was the humiliation of Versailles, the odious treaty, the reparations of world war. Germany grew silent in gratitude and prayer. A midnight candle vigil was held along the route of the processional. The nation came to bear witness. Deutschland wept and wept.

Peasants assembled in silent, communal displays across the German border. Joyous peasants and strength through joy excursionists watched the solemn flight, as the living flame breathed its firestorm through Dresden, into the roused night.

In the morning, the traffic police moved traffic and masses of people with an air of friendly authority, through the Triumphal Way, leading to the great, domed stadium in Berlin. White gloves flickered and waved, and the crowd responded, perfectly behaved on the streets, at the shops, and along the bustling boulevards that led to the Olympic stadium. The police were admired for directing traffic without incident, twirling their clubs with white gloved panache, and smiling to their visitors with genuine German affection.

The transformation was apparent in the uniforms. Two weeks before, they had high military boots and black trousers tucked into them, a glistening black shako, and bayonet with a rubber truncheon that hung ominously at the belt. For the Games, the colors had changed into the national color of the Reich: snow white. Shiny, white shakos, white blouses, cream-colored caps and soft, white gloves gaily moved the crowd of millions along.

On every street, a peaceful authority greeted guests with respect and humor. The S.S. Storm troopers begged the people not to spit cheery pits or saliva on the immaculate sidewalk. A capital offense two weeks ago, the crime had been reduced to a gentle glance and a kindly warning. The S.S. allowed the often untidy Americans to leave their trash wherever they liked. They left lovers to lie on the green infields, on the grass fields surrounding Olympic Gate.

"*Verboten,*" i.e.,' forbidden,' was a concept alien to the American guests. Gruff businessmen, with hearty moon-sized faces, peered through wisps of cigar smoke and flicked ashes on the clean, white pavement. S.S. smiled through barred teeth.

"What a set-up!"

Indeed, what was there not to like? The Reichswehr conscripts and labor camp youths were disciplined. The call for world hatred of the Jew had stopped. Even the slogans of hate over the booths that contained *Der Strumer* were given a coat of whitewash, and the newspaper absent from places most foreigners were likely to go.

There wasn't one disturbance. The dissidents, gutter goons, and gypsies had already been hauled away for six months rehabilitation at *Sachsenhausen*, the new state-of-the-art concentration camp. The waiters, bar girls, streetwalkers, taxi drivers, and assorted types spoke English with uncanny accuracy. The cafes and pubs of the West End could've been mistaken for the quaint, cosmopolitan side streets of Greenwich Village. Berlin was a replica of America, an ally whose needs were serviced at once.

Nobody was happier in Berlin, however, than the Japanese. That morning, head to head among the sea of swastikas, the International Olympic Committee awarded the Nipponese the coveted prize of hosting the Olympic Games to be held four years later in 1940.

After Lee Jahncke's expulsion, William May Garland became the prime mover in gathering support for the Nipponese. He had a solid block of north and south American support along with the British Empire, impressed by the generous Japanese offer of a half million dollars to help defray costs of sending athletes to the Far East. A stunning turn of events, the Japanese public awakened at dawn, and the Mayor of Tokyo ordered municipal festivities to express their citizens' joy.

"Banzai!"

A crowd of Japanese youth took to the streets with discus and hammers and swords, preparing, at once, for the next

Games. General Juichi Terauchi, the War Minister, said the Twelfth Olympiad would be dignified. Their girls purified spiritually as well as physically trained, and in the Japanese spirit of friendship, international hospitality would be its highest aim. "Japan," he said, "would use the time to make ready for peace and the Olympic spirit."

"We will be delighted to go to Japan because we know the Japanese are fine sportsmen," said Arian Bandage. In private, he thought, what greater allies for America, for business and sports, than Germany and Japan. The Nazis felt the same. Their spirit would spread joy, their message the world's own. What Jew protest would dare compete with what the eye then saw?

Down the Triumphal Way, nations paid homage to the joy of the Third Reich. They would give Germany the time it would need … in the spirit of friendship…time to grow, time to be whole again, time to plan. Goebbels, the architect of enlightenment, knew planning was everything. In pre-Olympic ceremonies, his voice translated into French and English, Goebbels said,

"World opinion is excited by the sentiments expressed. Hear the exalted ideas of the German nation (to the Olympians):You are entering an arena of peaceful combat whose preparation rested on the totality of the nationalist art of government, and its fundamental idea of the community of the whole people. The world stands in honest admiration before this work because it has totalitarian character. Without unitary will that which today will astonish the world, would have been impossible. You are witness to the supreme achievement of the totalitarian state."

The Oriental sportsmen led the procession through the tall columns of the Brandenburg Gate. The watchful eye of Victory looked on, above the streams and pennants of Nazi and Olympic and American flags. Vienna waltzes and snappy, marching tunes interrupted the sounds blasting from the loudspeakers. Goebbels' bulletins pounded away with a steady stream of National Socialist enlightenment and propaganda.

That morning, hundreds of thousands of Berlin youth assembled at *Olympiastadion* to hear long- winded speeches from members of the International Olympic Committee. With frenzied applause, the youth embraced the most banal, monotonous speech. Protestant Cathedral and St. Hedwig's Catholic Church held divine services, and exhorted the international populace to stand ready to dedicate their forces to the friendly pursuit of sports for the betterment of man. With much weeping, the Germans paid homage at the tomb of the Unknown Soldier. During an open air Volkspark festival, a woman disappeared into the arms of Arminius.

Yet, nothing could rival the march into Berlin of German runners carrying the flaming Olympic torch. Arriving in the *Lustgarten*, a proud Army officer saluted the Hitler Youth whom had come to line a pathway for the torchbearers. As the sacred fire entered the city, the runner suddenly began weaving in a snakelike procession, among the youth that had gathered to honor the guardians of the flame.

Without a sound, in choreographed precision, they marched in quick procession behind him for his standard thousand meter run. Angling the torch to the next German, he joined the procession, as the next runner took off with fresher limbs. Following the youth, sound orgies of Wagner piped through the clatter of Goebbels' loudspeakers, and the staccato clapping of the crowd.

Gathering about the fire, fickle in its frenzy, the youth of the Nazi nation, awakened the Woten gods. The gods of fire, and the symbols they conjured, licked up, without mercy, the fringes of the pennants and the flags of the countries, scorched the souls of the people through the little towns and shops they passed, and brought them under the banners of forty -five foot swastikas, with the strength of their joyous, untamed hearts.

The march of the fifty-four nations had begun. A staggering array of color and pageantry preceded the very last German runner into the stadium. At a cost of twenty-four millions, the sports plant was ready to make history its Reich mark. In the rain and the dampness and overcast gray surroundings, the German folk screamed the loudest to those who would pay homage, while parading past the throne-like dais of the host of the Games.

Sound waves, in a wind cave, ricocheted around the arena, the French passed the vacant stands, rendering to an absent Caesar, the Nazi salute. Around the spanking clean concrete, the crowd suddenly broke into rhythmic clapping. Caesar was coming. Hitler would appear at the rim on the top platform of Marathon Gate at 4 P.M.

Until then, the crowd thrilled to the goose-stepping attempts of the friendlier nations. By a quarter to four, Bulgaria tripped over its feet. Costa Rica and Haiti each represented by one athlete who were both delegate and flag bearer, lowered their flags past the dais. The Japanese women stayed behind their male teammates, while the Hungarians marched with heads poised high. The Germans at Reich sport field believed every nation bowed to the Fatherland, whether it did or not.

"We did not Heil Hitler," said a Frenchman. "It was our salute, and it is different."

No matter. Even when a Swiss flag juggler merely juggled his flags, the audience broke into applause. Next came the United States, followed by Germany.

The "wonder men" marched past the dais, white straw hats bobbed like a swaying carpet, until they reached the square, gigantic platform where the dignitaries and special envoys sat. Huge microphones amplified the sound of a crowd that suddenly turned carnivorous. Americans had walked with arms extended, but pointedly not raised. Whistling wound around the great oval.

"Americans do not praise der fuehrer," a woman whispered.

"That is a mistake," said her paramour.

"Their flag does not dip."

"A disgrace."

Then a great roar erupted, bursting upon the stadium like gale winds on a tranquil sea. The sound resonated around the stone oval in an ever narrowing circular swirl, gathering energy with the energy from deep within, renewing itself, over again like hurricane winds. Toward the center of the huge infield, the Third Reich, goose-stepped smartly to the last spot of brilliant, green turf. Six thousand athletes waited in the murmur as the noise subsided, and the last German came to fill to capacity the awaiting stadium.

Out of the desolate, gray skies, Zeppelin Hindenburg arrived, looming low over the entire arena, its crew waving to the crowd that never recovered from the shock of seeing so gigantic a specter that made the Olympians duck in awe.

Nobody needed to cue the crowd, but, suddenly, all voices lowered to whispers, and became quieter still. Air sucked in, but not out, and a murmuring rose from some thousand caged white doves that were attended to at the far end of the stadium, while sixty trumpeters ceremoniously climbed the high Olympic towers. In the arena below, at both sides of the oval, across the red cinder track which sheltered the awaiting athletes in a giant circle, a wide granite stairway seemed to arise into the heavens, broken only by the tall clock towers and the bare outlines of flagpoles.

Motion of every sort ceased, save for the frenzied movement of a large, snow- white choir, and a few drummers and buglers of the military bands. While they surrounded the German Philharmonic Orchestra at the eastern end of the stadium, beneath the wide steps of Marathon Gate, Riefenstahl and her company filled the space underneath the platform for a close-up of the master of the master race.

Promptly, at Four P.M., he arrived, at first sight, a blemish in the sky, small, even slight in form. Wearing khaki, he could have passed for one of the many campers who had come to pay homage. Nothing in his appearance was remarkable. In a startled manner of a man suddenly roused from sleep, he paused, then walked down from the ceremonial hall located in *Fuehrer* Tower. That was Adolf Hitler, a mere mortal, mindless of the adoration as he circled the parade field before walking through a lane of honor to the stadium.

As he entered the arena, walking between Count Henri de Baillet-Latour and Dr. Theodor Lewald, head of the German Organizing Committee, he looked lost among the gray and white haired gentlemen around him.

A beaming little pixy gave him a bouquet of orchids. Count Henrie Baillet- Latour took her hand, and whisked her away, his white hair weaving in the wind. Then Hitler stood alone atop Marathon Gate.

"One wonders what he thought and whether his thoughts traveled back for just a moment to his modest beginnings … It was little more than a decade since Adolph Hitler was a humble workman …the man who has now wrought a miracle," wrote Frederick Birchall, *New York Times* correspondent who loved his work in Berlin.

"Adolph Hitler was receiving the plaudits of a league far removed from politics, a league of peaceful sport in which he had become the proud host," wrote Arthur Daley, *The New York Times* correspondent.

The crowd grew gruesome. Standing on their seats, "*Sieg*, (their arms thrust out,) *Heil*," in adoration. "*Sieg*, *Heil*," of unquestioned devotion. "*Sieg Heil*, *Sieg*," to the leader, the 'proud' man, the 'humble servant,' the 'workman,' Adolf Hitler.

Hitler spoke to six thousand athletes, one of whom broke into a Brooklyn grin. His words exhorted the athletes from medieval times. Hitler, gave a celestial benediction to the honored guests of the Third Reich.

" ... Compete in knightly spirit for the honor of our Fatherland and the glory of the sport."

The trumpeters appeared amidst the blasting of sirens and the grinding of six simultaneous bands that played the dual anthems: *Deutschland Ueber Alles*, and the *Host Wessel Song*.

A thousand white doves suddenly rose into the air, scattering over the arena before coming together and soaring away for home, in perfect formation above the tall towers. The spectacle ended with the breathtaking appearance of a lone, blonde athlete who appeared, as if from a cloud, at the top stairs of Eastern Gate.

He was striking in appearance. The torch he carried sent wisps of blue flame behind and skyward. Stopping at the top of Eastern Gate, the graceful marathon runner, and carrier of the flame, paused as his fuehrer had done moments before. The response from the crowd was ecstatic when they saw what he was about to do. Turning, as if sculptured, he shot his free arm out in a wayward, crooked path. The torch took off in the opposite way that, while he turned, sent blue wisps of flame, and revealed the future in a holographic message. Turning on a moveable platform, Hermes, itself, had arisen in the exact replication of the swastika.

Running down the steps and across the stadium, the blonde haired runner swiftly made his way to the distant platform –his sacred torch now set blazing upon the altar which, together with the rolling of drums and sounds of overhead trumpets, signaled the beginning of the Eleventh Olympic Games.

19

Dawn crept with morning mist, into the grass and woodlands, where a lone runner brushed past the delicately planted foliage that rolled away from the American quarters to the village gates. He wore sweatpants and running shoes with a blue top, upon which the flag of his country was embroidered at the side. On his back, emblazoned in white, the initials, U.S.A., fit between his small, but powerful arms.

Altering the run from fast to slow to help relax his muscles, he was aware of the tension and the exact tuning he needed to get his body into maximum stride. Lifting off one leg, he visualized the effects to his limbs. In the thickets, he was able to relax the calves, and then the thighs. Jesse Owens always said,

"Don't run with fury –tension unbalances the delicate physical machinery. You need to burst from the start and gain maximum speed, and maintain it across the finish."

If that race were today, he knew he could beat almost anyone on earth. He knew that because something in the Nazi air had changed him, and he ran through the woodlands, no longer feeling the undergrowth beneath his feet. He ran without effort toward a place he had never been before. His feet lifted with ease of motion, carrying him speedily through the woodlands. He thought he was jogging slowly, but he was really bolting past squirrels, rabbits, and the deer of the forest.

Then, on grass, he saw storks overhead, and flamingoes following a rising arc in flocks of morning sky worship. He ran forward to hear sudden yelping sounds thrust from the surrounding sky. Cranes reeling upright and defiant were close by. He didn't know from where they came, or why they bothered with him.

He was a half mile from Olympic Gate and the American quarters. Most of the athletes hadn't yet risen from their double beds, under the sloping roofs, in their simple white- framed cottages. Last night, they had had their outdoor get together sing on the porch with Jesse and Ralph Metcalfe. That was a lot of fun. Joshua heard footsteps racing toward him on the grass. That runner matched Joshua's strides with acrobatics that barely lingered on the short cut blades. The steady, rhythmic breathing of the two were then as one- their arms sallying in slow synchronized motion along the sides. With heads raised in the same relaxed expression, they knew by scent, in the veins of natural rivals, that a race was on.

Tom Grace had seen Joshua running through the woodlands before the others of the American team were out of bed. He knew Joshua liked to take early practice, and be up with the birds. Joshua had told someone about that. The night before, through cigar smoke and overcast haze, outside the coaches' quarters, separated by fog and a flashlight, The Dean and Lawson Robertson told them what everybody else had already known.

Lawson told Tom and Dave they must do their best in the four man competition up, and until the beginning of the four hundred meter relay race. "I'm not saying that I know how the chancellor will feel about … say … the… eastern runners. I'm just saying the situation is very grim."

Grace pleaded. "Coach I want to win in a fair race. We all know Josh is very fast, and so …"

"I'm not saying …"

"The four of us are going to run. We don't have to beat them."

"What I'm saying is that anything is possible. Now, Joshua rises early in the morning ..."

Joshua expected to beat his foe from the very first steps on the grass. The unspoken, but obvious finish lines were between the two towers of the Olympic Gate. The Nazi insignia there propelled the wolverine to run with a burst of hate.

Soon, a small crowd gathered at the finish. Early morning risers watched at the village gates. By the pillars between the swastikas, a woman in white shorts and a snow white jacket was crying. A black suited, brown gloved driver of a Gruber Mercedes, the large, luxury State car, carried her luggage to the gate where the Olympians were running, near the finish line.

Joshua didn't recognize the man; the woman was *her*, but he was in a dogfight to the end. There wasn't right of way taken or given. Tom stayed with him stride for stride. Their elbows interlocked for a moment that made Joshua careen slightly, and almost break stride. In that instant, Tom Grace took off. A specter of witnesses, under the village gate, beamed with clear, frenzied pride as the pair raced toward the imaginary finish line. When Joshua was elbowed, his body tensed. He felt his muscles veer from the narrow course that he had set. Pulled to the side, there was no avoiding injury. He ran in anguished shortened strides.

Did he do that on purpose? The question not really framed in the words it took to say them. He had time only to feel rage rise, and chased the speedy Californian with a vengeful burst. Tom Grace accommodated, moving toward Joshua with a slight turn of the ankles, as if he were taking the curve of the track. Giving his foe a weak smile, he slowed down when he saw Joshua's invisible rage begin to claw near his back. Tom knew in that instant that Joshua would race, even if there were no competition. If there were no finish line, no clock to time his run, no time, no distance to be measured, that something within him was driving him beyond his endurance. Joshua, it seemed to him, wanted no less than to burst from the finite enclosures of the flesh, and enter the world of a death run. Gee, he thought, Joshua is running at me. *He aims to run through me.*

Joshua was reminded of his tormentors in Cincinnati, the delirium of the chase, and the knowledge that nothing on earth could stop him from driving hard into his foes. Upon the staggering Californian, then a breath away, he knew he could run through him, and his competitor turned around. It was enough to make Joshua want to grab the hand that was guarding his face in a defensive pose, and dance with him to the village gate.

"Don't you know you fool you never can win

Use your mentality, wake up to reality."

He became lightheaded, letting Tom Grace race across the imaginary finish to an imaginary first place prize. Beaming, his muscles finally relaxed, Joshua greeted the stunned Californian.

"Thanks for the exercise," he said.

"Don't mention it," heaved Tom. He was well- spent, opening his mouth to say more.

"It's not your style to be up early. Is this a church day?"

Tom Grace was the one then with the tortured gaze, the eyes, darkened.

"Don't play fair, rabbi. The cards are being stacked against you."

"Don't you know you fool they never can win."

"What?"

But Joshua didn't answer. A silent stoning was taking place around the luxury car. Summer rain now pelted the dark windows, not so gently. Athletes with haughty stares peeked inside for one last glimpse of the fallen champion. The Germans said she hadn't qualified for the team, and gave her a standing room only ticket to watch the Games.

Her driver, grim-faced, opened the window and handed Joshua a note from his wet, gloved hand. Joshua searched the limousine for her, but Rachel shuddered and looked away.

"The young lady wants to meet with you. She says she will find a way. Oh yes, she says it's a matter of life and death."

20

Bobby Gillman came to Joshua with a thousand odds and ends. Today, it was the culinary statistics from August 1 through August 16: thirty tons of meat and poultry, seven- and-a- half tons of fish, one hundred twenty tons of vegetables, fifty tons of flour, seventeen tons of butter, thirty-four thousand gallons of milk, a quarter of a million eggs, three hundred thousand oranges, and one hundred thousand lemons would be on hand for the American Olympians. Several thousand pounds of turkey had been shipped over from Philadelphia, and an equal number of Long Island ducks from New York. In the refrigerator were two hundred and forty-four melons.

"Along with one thousand pounds of eggplant, and two thousand pounds of potatoes, our kind hosts ordered two hundred thousand oranges…two hundred thousand more oranges than they ever really needed from…California."

"Business is booming," said Joshua. Apparently, many hands were beneath the surface, he thought.

Bobby stayed up one night and watched three trailer sized trucks from America that delivered a quarter of a million packs of chewing gum to the American quarters directly. "That's a thousand packs of chewing gum for each of us. I have to tell Martha about this." Another two trucks rumbled by with a million Aunt Jemima pancakes. "They're already battered and guaranteed to be digestible."

There was a lot of laughter in the American barracks. When the German butler assigned to them came for their orders, Bobby imitated Peter Lorre. "Yes, Hans, we've been expecting you."

It was easy to be in good humor because the team had such high hopes, especially in track and field. Only the relay runners fought extra hard during forced competition. Alone, they scratched and pawed for advantage with Robbie, and The Dean kept tallies and changed the rules.

Joshua had winning trial runs. Afterwards, Tom kept his head down, and Davie went by without a word. By Thursday, with three wins and a second, Joshua was certain he had finally sewn up his position for the relay race. Bobby also beat Davie Warren and lost only once to Tom Grace.

Yet, the American coaches hailed that lone victory by the Californian as a stunning win. Lawson Robertson was both head coach and track and field coach of the American team. Timing the race, he said that Tom had tied the world's record for the hundred meters. Joshua and Bobby, and even Jesse, raised their eyebrows. Tom didn't run that fast. But Robbie had the stopwatch, and that was that.

Leaving the track on Thursday, and again on Friday, Robertson told newsmen that the time trials were dead even. He lauded Jesse and Ralph for great runs, and said the twice crowned Olympian, Tom Grace, was racing better than he did in Los Angeles, and Davie Warren was 'right there at the finish.'

He said little about Bobby, or Joshua Sellers. Only an article by the 'cub' reporter…Eleanor Holm Jarrett spoke the truth. The disgraced American champion had accepted an offer to report the games with William L. Shirer and other correspondents assigned to Berlin. Eleanor was bitter about the Olympics, and the open admiration of the International Olympic Committee for the Nazi regime.

During lunch, under the lindens at an outdoor café, she spied on them, taking note of the whiskey they consumed in one meal alone. She interviewed Tom Grace about the Evangelicals, and the fate of Pastor Schneider. When that was printed, Lawson Robertson rushed him. The newspaper twisted in his hands, Robbie told Grace not to make statements of any "political" kind. During that interview, Tom said that the American track and field team could beat anyone in the world. He cited Joshua Seller's lightning speed out of the start.

Eleanor smelled a rat. She had heard Robertson didn't talk about the "Jewish runners." Wanting to interview him, she was stopped by security, under the high towers of Olympic Gate.

Still, she wrote an indictment about the newly elected President of the American Olympic Committee. She questioned Bandage's integrity, and private business deals with the Nazis. With beer bottles exploding on the tranquil scenic roads, Bandage drove publicly with Goebbels and two German girls. She wrote, "Does a concerted anti-Semitic network exist in the sanctified Olympics of 1936?"

After that article, she was banned from Olympic Stadium, and the *Gestapo* searched her hotel room. She was politely asked to leave Germany. It was merely a suggestion, they said, but one she took gladly. Furious and sober, she left Germany the next day.

But Joshua was buoyed by his practice. On Friday, he was tested in preliminary runs of the 4 x 100 meter relay time trials. He bolted into the lead in four different races, winning three events. He had also mastered the key hand-off of the baton.

The handoff was essential in the relay run: to turn the head the instant before the baton was put downwards into the palm, and to hold the stick securely with clenched, sure fists, from the time one left the check mark crease, until it was passed to the next runner.

One time, Davie had almost fallen, his unsteady hands lifted the baton a fraction in the air too high. Joshua seized the stick, made sure of the passing, and darted past with such a burst that from the rear sidelines, Jesse Owens applauded.

"You're not going to be 'seconds' much longer," Jesse yelled. "You can darn near beat me now. One more 200 meters for me, and I'm done."

Owens and Metcalfe watched the races and the trial runs. They never practiced the passing of the baton. Obviously, they weren't going to run. Afterwards, newsmen gathered around Head Coach Lawson Robertson and sharpened their pencils.

They asked Robbie to confirm that Warren, Grace, Sellers, and Gillman, would round out the foursome for the relay race. Robertson raised his eyes. Shifting his weight on his cane, he seemed old. His tongue wet the corners of his mouth as he turned to his grimacing companion, the little man with the bowler hat and cigar in his mouth. "Well, by gee, we're not, at this point, saying that'll be or this'll be that. We want our horses ready to go. That's just the way it's darn well done."

By then, Joshua had taken his gym bag and headed back to the Olympic village. A bus took him into the woodlands and left him off on the American side. He had time for a quick shower and to relax his muscles. He was pleased with his performance.

Waiting expectantly by the window, his heart jumped when he saw the face of the stiff necked chauffeur, and the Mercedes rolling on the gravel, moving slowly toward the Olympian's quarters and coming straight for him.

21

Captain Fuerster should have been the happiest man in Germany. Having built the Olympic Village, he was awarded a gold medal from the Department of City Planning, and a silver medal in architecture. The special medals in sculpture, painting, literature, and music were already 'won' by Germans.

There was little competition from other nations. Indeed, the sole judge, who was German, closed nominations soon after the host nation submitted theirs. The Nationalist Press reported that the Germans were leading with five gold, five silver, and two bronze medals, even before the first sporting event.

The gifts from a grateful nation brought Fuerster to the pinnacle of glory, and to a seat on the balcony beside the fuehrer. Photographed with the Chancellor of Germany, his picture appeared in Das Angriff above the inscription,

'Heroes of Der Fatherland.'

During a reception in his honor, his lovely wife, Lisa, received a bouquet of roses from Frau Goering. Reich dignitaries stood and applauded his work.

On Sunday, the first day of competition, he sat in the fuehrer's box and engaged the nervous Count Umberto of Italy. Umberto was a nervous wreck who fawned over the fuehrer. The closer the Count came, the farther the fuehrer festered. Umberto tried to find common ground. He talked about French wine and women's fashion. Hitler whirled toward him with a wild look, then turned away. Both crawled out of their skins.

His banker, Schroeder, arrived with Avery Rockefeller. Hitler waved them away. Stumbling in, his head shaped like a Planter's Peanut, Harry Laughlin walked in, lopsided, with

Charles Davenport, director of research at Cold Springs Harbor, New York. With two hands Hitler acknowledged them both furtively.

He didn't like to be reminded of his days in prison. While incarcerated, he wrote to Laughlin about his eugenics work. Hitler wanted statistics for the book he was writing about inferior races. It was to be entitled *Mein Kampf*.

Fuerster stood with the crowd when Hans Woellke won the gold medal. It was the first by a German athlete in a field sporting event since the beginning of the modern Games. Woelke was a simple policeman, made a Woten god after he dug into his circle, whirled and thrust the shot put into an overcast sky to shatter the world's record.

Even Leni Riefenstahl stopped filming, nearly damaging her movie and delicate projection equipment, and fell into another swoon. Promoted immediately to lieutenant, the policeman met Hitler, with medal and oak tree, and laurel wreath in hand. Fuerster listened to the sound of Wolke's name.

"Woellke," in ecstasy, "Woellke," echoing along the tiers.

At that very moment, Fuerster was at the pinnacle of his career. Standing beside his fuehrer, keeping the desolate Count Umberto at bay, he wept for joy and the Fatherland.

When the names of the American blacks were announced, The fuehrer was bothered by cross current winds. As Hitler honored Woellke, Jesse Owens began shattering other myths. While Tillie Fleischer, an American Olympic champion of the javelin throw, joined Woellke for a brief audience, the name of The Ohio State champion was being piped into the stadium.

"Eh zee Oh Enz."

As the very air was erupting into the combined screams of a nationalistic orgiastic chorus, the name of the American transformed that mass expulsion into one collective breath. The eyes of the stadium saw the Brown Thunderbolt, as he tore his competition to shreds. Owens shattered the one hundred yard dash world record, leaving Hitler stunned. The Aryans had suddenly been upstaged by black men.

Leni Riefenstahl was joking with Goering and Goebbels. Hitler had told her he envied her freedom, and whom she was, and what she was doing.

"Suppose I was really a Jew?" she asked.

"Not very funny," said Goebbels, knowing Hitler wouldn't laugh, though Goebbels contradicted himself and laughed spasmodically. He liked to see Hitler irked.

But the brief Teutonic moment had passed. When Jesse tore down the track, Riefenstahl realized she needed more cameras, and that the story was not the blonde gods, nor Germany, but the black usurpers. She rose and walked away, oblivious to the slimy hands that groped her from behind. While history was unfolding, her eyes stayed on the track.

Cornelius Johnson hadn't removed his sweats until the bar was raised to a height only he could reach. He waited for Dave Albritton who had to win a separate run-off for the silver medal. Hitler saw his own reflection fade to frowns.

The international press corps was watching. Would Hitler nuzzle up to Cornelius Johnson the way he had to his buttercups of Deutschland? Well, it was already too late, by then. Der Fuhrer rose with his entourage and left the Fuhrer's loge. He couldn't wait in traffic with the common folk, could he? In the eyes of the world, Hitler had snubbed the black Americans.

By the second day of competition, upon entering The Fuehrer's box, Captain Fuerster was stopped by a white clad policeman who had the day before ushered him in with *heils* and fanfare. Fuerster was commanded to sit further back along with the crowd on the gray, stone benches. He entertained Charles Lindbergh and Adolf Menjou, the American actor. Both wanted an audience with the Fuehrer. That was, of course, impossible.

The German, Blask, tossed the hammer, and his countryman, Hein, bested him. Captain Fuerster rose from the stone benches. He cried, "German eagle fly to victory." But he had been goaded by unease caused by the change in the seating arrangements, and his proud heart beat little less wildly than before.

During the noon recess, he joined other spectators at the busy concession stands. Passing among them, he wanted to seem happy. He talked about Hein's record one hundred and eighty-five foot hammer throw, and heartily agreed that Hein would be promoted to the rank of lieutenant.

Someone saw the bars on his uniform and said that Hein might even make Captain. Fuerster shrank away from that casual comment. In the damp chilly air, he walked back toward his seat, sulking within his glistening, white uniform.

At the top of the gray stone benches of the lower tiers, he watched the high hanging television screens. A new medium, displayed at the Berlin Games for the first time, showed athletes warming up, who seemed to glide into strange, white muck, during the race for the fastest human.

Walking briskly down the steps to his seat, he heard a shrill, deafening roar. A collective explosion burst with such terrible intensity that threatened to shake the sturdy foundations of the stadium he had helped to design. He thought he was in an arena of a hideous apocalyptic dream. Even the clouds seemed horrified at the sights below. A desolately cold rain began to fall. Fuerster felt he was crawling between the layers of a dream. A black- uniformed security officer sat in his seat.

   Raising his arm skyward, Fuerster brought his arm down without the obligatory *'heils.'* He thought a farewell would be more in order, studying his hand with sudden, but resigned alarm. He looked beside him where guards were waiting. So much for the designs of man, he thought, being led away by many hands. They know I am a Jew.

22

Monday, August 3, 1936.
The One Hundred Meter Olympic Final.

"Auf die platze."

The starter with the long, white butcher's frock bids the athletes to take their marks. The crowd is silent. Metcalfe kneels and prays. Yesterday's record 10.2 seconds has been washed away. Scorers said there were winds. It is five P.M., one and a-half hours since the semi-final heats. Jesse shakes every hand but stays beside Metcalfe. The coaches worry he won't have the stamina, but Owens knows better. On the track, he knows what he needs.

The gun is raised, *"fertig,"* the shot heard, *"los,"* and with a billowing puff of smoke, he is gone, running on burning coals, so hot, his feet don't seem to touch the cinders. When his foot rises, it's like a cool breeze just for him.

Jesse Owens, racing from the hands of the starter, leaving Osendarp, his challenger, far behind- smoothly he glides along. The race is his only the time unknown.

For Ralph Metcalfe, racing in third place, behind the Netherlander and the Ohio Thunderbolt, the hundred meters is an adventure. Four years before, under the epistyles of Los Angeles, in a close race with Tom Grace, the title eluded him. But now, Tom Grace fades into history.

As the Trojan falters, Metcalfe runs ahead with tired legs. He grinds through the milk muck television prototypes through whitish scum. His eyes are ghostly, and he glares into streams of crippling snow. With one last burst at the finish, within one yard of Owens, by passing Osendarf, Metcalfe grabs the silver, but not the gold.

***

But what of the breath to glory, when the air is sucked out of the stadium, when the sounds reach a crescendo that bounces around the oval with a scream across a Grecian chorus?

'Uhh' becomes the sound of beating hearts, made wild by the very confines of the arena, arising from hellish, gleeful beasts, thrown into a hellish tempest of world end. An awful sound crashing down in a terrible wind, the bitter 'enz,' the last syllable of recorded time, ticking as the world ends. His name, set upon the altars, exhort the demon gods, whose winged feet atop the red cinders are now ablaze, though his feet really never even touch the ground. Who is he? What is he?

"Enz..:Uhh..Venz..Uh venz."

Jesse has the tape, the glory, and the crowd. In the future, his would be the only story, the glory just for him: the story of the times when a black man rose to touch the stars, in a galaxy preserved only for immortals, in a time even above history.

Nazi scientists calculated his speed at seven horsepower. The great thrust of that human engine only confirmed a private suspicion. Nazis believed his speed could be traced to the odd-shaped configuration of the blacks' bones.

Jesse had heard that tale, but his was a story about dreams on an Alabama road. On the platform, his name exalted in the illuminations of the message board, flanked by Ralph Metcalfe, Jesse Owens led the grand, one, two, the gold and silver, for the Stars and Stripes. The German band played 'The Star Spangled Banner,' and as Jesse heard the faint sounds, he turned toward his flag. Now that hymn was resounding, and the American flag risen for him. He was lifted to the banners, beyond the glare of swastikas, an American black man had come to claim the victory on the red cinders that day. He knew he had raised, not only the banner, but brought America's anthem to a new day. He seized the small English oak, the crown of laurels, and the cherished gold medal on that day. Ruth would pass them onto his daughters, and into history. It was the memory of a lifetime.

Hitler was seated in his raised platform, among the one hundred and ten thousand in the sporting arena. Yesterday, he had walked out of the stadium after Cornelius Johnson, won the high jump. Today, the Fuehrer exited through a private stairwell under his loge. He had met Nazi's and Finnish athletes, and Stella Stevens, the small Caucasian runner from the state of Missouri who had won the women's hundred meter trials in record time. But not one black man.

Still, after the race when Jesse bolted to the radio booth, his eyes interlocked with his. For one moment, Jesse felt the admiration of the leader of the German nation who waved to him in salute. He thought about how his father never really looked a white man in the eye. And there he was, face to face with bigotry and race hatred, and he was smiling into the face of the worst of them.

For Jesse Owens on the happiest day of his life, Hitler, the racist, had recognized him in a way his own president, and many others to follow, never would. That day in history was a breakthrough to many at home in Harlem, or in the old fields of the rural south. Though lynching still would conspire with the silence of President Roosevelt, much of America rejoiced at the victory of a black man for the glory of his country, and for the glory of his name.

23

The slow ride in the Mercedes disturbed him. With his leather gloves and an air of casual disdain, the chauffeur held the wheel without moving a muscle, or saying a word. Only when they arrived at the house on *Gregorstrasse* did he tell Joshua that his host would be late.

In the morning room left alone, Joshua considered a walled bookcase with German titles. Between hardcover, leather-bound books separated by expensive looking gold-plated bookends, a slight indentation indicated that a few classics had been removed. He was skimming The Protocols of the Elders of Zion that had heavily penciled marks. Joshua's German was passable, learned in the gutters of Cincinnati, and at Michigan language classes. He was able to pick-up the hate that man had for the Jew. And with a Jewish name like Alfred Rosenberg, Joshua thought.

That Nazi said Jewish wise men planned to conquer the world. There was nobody wiser than the Marx brothers, Joshua laughed, putting the book back on the shelf. The book with the black, crooked cross, came into his hands. It was the nation's number-one best seller.

He read:

"It is the Jew and still is the Jew who brings the Negro to the Rhine with the object of destroying the hated, white pure race by the resultant mingling of bloods, to cast the white man down from his political and cultural preeminence and to make of himself the master."

Joshua picked up a third book, the name unknown; the picture, strangely of a runner. It could even have been him. The book was The Sixth Ring; the author, anonymous. He read:

"Tom Marcy held the gold medal in his hands. He was proud to be honored by the Fuehrer. He went to sit with him in his majestic balcony. The crowd stood at attention. White doves flew around the stadium. America and Germany were now joined forever. The fuehrer looked at him with his fatherly blue eyes.

"The city is yours," the fuehrer said, "I will grant you a wish."

"'Go my son and marry,' said Hitler." The voice was Rachel's. "For honor and love the American would gladly lay down his life, is that not true?"

Through the wide open oak doors that led from the parlor into the morning room, Rachel had entered, wearing a chic, white dress with a fashionable high collar, illuminating her strong, dark features and glowing green eyes. She was no longer embarrassed as she was when she stood beside some of the leering American athletes who had passed her on the excursion bus. There, in the privacy of soft lights, her flowing black hair and long, thin hands spoke of a vital presence under the works of the German masters.

To Joshua, even Goethe and Kleist seemed to stand erect when she strode into the room. She wasn't sad as she was the day she was forced out of Olympic Village. Today, she was proud and happy to see him.

She had a slight military bearing. It showed in the way she carried herself. Her gait, erect, her shoulders straight. She was from a military family. Her father fought beside Ludendorff and was decorated by Von Hindenburg during the campaign in the Ardennes. Although Jewish, Rachel's father still considered himself a patriot of the Fatherland despite the Nuremburg Laws which had stripped him of his citizenship. He'd been allowed to keep his small clothing shop on the *Potzdamer Strasse*, but had to pay the transfer tax of twenty-five percent in order to stay in business. Yet, doggedly he stayed open and continued to sell cheaply to old friends and familiar Aryan patrons who considered him, for the moment, an exception to the rule.

He'd always dressed in the modern fashion with shaven face, unlike the orthodox eastern Europeans. He believed he was as German as the next man, with shrapnel from the enemy as proof. Allied fire was his reminder of his devotion to Der Fatherland. He attended veterans meetings, stood on podiums, and delivered eulogies to Aryan comrades who had fallen in battle. He had even sent his daughter to the fashionable *Victoria-Oberlyceum* School in Berlin.

His wife, Esther, until 1933, was a secretary of the National Women Teachers League. Like her father, she had helped Dr. Heyn, superintendent of Berlin High Schools, to develop the *Fachlassen* and Block system method of arranging time and space within school buildings. She received commendations for her work in clustering classes into blocks of at least two consecutive lessons, helping students with German, history, and geography, the *'DeutschKundliche Facher,'* subjects dealing with patriotic studies.

He often thought about his daughter, her wild spirit, her independent way. Her gifts as an athlete were unparalleled, though he thought her ideas strange and a trifle rude, owing to her stubborn Jewish nature and her prideful behavior, which he often apologized for. During a Christmas gathering, for example, which itself was frowned upon by the new government, Rachel placed a Chanukah menorah near the Christmas tree.

Rachel's father was enraged by his daughter's tendencies toward what he knew to be dangerous ideals. He wanted to assimilate her, but she was a devout Zionist.

"You are German, first and last," he said, drinking glass after a glass of sherry, as he waited for better times.

Joshua was puzzled by the girl whom he spoke to on the Manhattan. She didn't appear to be in distress. She was in command of her words and her actions.

What does she want from me? Joshua thought. He wanted to make the visit brief. With the rigors of Olympic training, he knew girls must be sacrificed to the running gods and the gold medal. Meanwhile, he was still holding *Mein Kampf*.

For a time, they were wordless in the morning room under the books of the German masters. She was beguiling; her eyes didn't waver. She spoke first, and to the point.

"You seem to be a man of divided allegiance, Herr Sellers, or would you prefer "Mr.?" Before he could answer, she pointed delicately to the book at hand.

"Hitler's book is not exactly literature; you know, merely, required reading. It rivals the Christian bible as the number one bestselling book in the world. But what do we know about the tastes of the reading public, or the editors and publishers, for that matter? Perhaps life offers only that kind of joke, the dribble that is bought, the brilliance that is tossed away, though I expected you would find something else more entertaining. Forgive me. I never had the chance to introduce myself to you, again, more formally. I am Rachel Brach."

"Joshua. I'd like you to call me, Joshua."

"Then, Joshua."

"Good. It's a start. So, what happened to you?"

"My word, Joshua, no informalities, and you are still a stranger," she said, blushing after the word 'still,' as she hoped that Joshua already knew she had intentions to be much closer to him than that, despite her formal tone.

"I don't understand. How do they allow you a private car?"

"Oh, I am Cinderella for a day. The foreign press wants to know I am treated with dignity since my country disqualified me from the German team," she said, with a bitter turn of her lips.

"I'm sorry. You had poor training?"

Rachel laughed gaily. "Oh Joshua, I tied the world's record in my training"

"I don't understand."

"You don't understand," she teased. "There are no Jews on the German team. No real Jews. Just that traitor, Helene Mayer, the half- Jew who thinks she is Aryan, and doesn't care about how they use her. She would see her father's side of her family hanged."

Politics, he would have to stay away from politics, he thought. "You said seeing you were a matter of life or death."

"It is," she said, then quietly, "yours."

"Go on. I have to get back to the village. So, please, Rachel, say what you want, and let me go," said Joshua, though he already knew he was captivated, and wouldn't let go. But, Life or death--just what did he have to fear?

"No, no, you do not understand. I have something to give you. You, dear Olympian have come to Germany with the sole purpose, not only in seeking the gold emblem," she said.

"Medal," corrected Joshua, a little more sweetly, putting *Mein Kampf* on the sofa.

"Oh yes, medal," she said, very softly this time. "My goodness, there are so many medals inside my house. My father, you see, but that is beside the point, as you say. I often wondered what 'point' and what was 'beside' it. Do you know?"

Joshua turned away. Her eyes were a paradox. They were intent and glowing with passion, if not desperation. But her words were bandied about without rhyme or reason. He stood to go. He had to go before he would be agitated, not only by the words, but by her feminine allure.

He saw her, suddenly, in a different way. She returned his stare with a slight quivering of her nostrils. She penetrated him with her concern, not for his dreams, but for him, the essence of the man.

Little by little, she would bring him to an unguarded passageway at the heart of the matter where an ultimate war of the spirit and the flesh was about to be waged. "I want you to understand the danger to you, and to world Jewry," she began.

Joshua shifted nervously. He was an American Olympian.

"We are told not to talk politics. Where's the mug with the red neck. I have to get back."

"Five more minutes, please. Hans is ready, Joshua." How she breathed his name, he thought.

"Go on, then."

As she talked, Joshua thought of a sales pitch about running shoes. There was money to be made by selling stuff, especially from an Olympian. "Frankly, you are not welcome here," she said.

"How did you get permission to bring me here? Was it Bandage?" he said. Inside, he was feeling cramped.

"I know nothing about that. As far as I know, it is a courtesy they are extending me. It was purely my idea."

"What, what idea are you talking about?"

He came closer to her. She smelled of fresh scents from a world he hadn't known. Nearer still, he came to a different realm. He thought he saw her lips quiver, and took them. Her face blushed, her lips pressed his, and wouldn't part for more words. She spoke her eyes ablaze. Her voice urgent, obvious in the breath, in the passion of her words.

"Joshua, there are millions of American dollars ready to give Germany the time it needs. Germany needs time to be accepted in the economic markets. A Jew, winning an athletic contest, is not possible here. Not for me, and, maybe not for you. It may upset their timetable."

"I don't understand you. What are you talking about? Your eyes are so beautiful." He was holding her about the waist, breathing in her scent from her hair, her neck.

She moved him away. "A Jew cannot compete here. Forget the medal."

"I don't understand what one or two Jews winning here means, one way or the other. Rachel, the 'emblem' is everything. Reaching the peaks of the mountain, one doesn't pause to consider the climb. Thanks for reminding me why I run. When I do, I'm going to deliver a message gathered with the force of a terrible blow. I'm going to be nothing less than savage when I run down that track. I'll run for America, and I'll run for you. We're Americans, Rachel, and we run free."

"Gallant Joshua, you cannot win here. It is a fixed race. They may let you have some tin, or even gold for your scrapbook, as my father has so much tin in his war chest. The Jew, however, is to be sacrificed on the scrapheap by which they make their medals shine. We are ants to be crushed, no more.

"You are a great runner, Joshua, and may win your gold em... medal, but they bury many men with medals here, and the streetwalkers rob their graves. You are at a crooked crossing, dear Joshua, in a city of losers, in a country that wants us to leave. We have no claim to feed the squirrels of the *Tiergarten*, or bask beneath the beauty of the lindens. This land is unholy; our God wants us to come home.

"Yes, run Joshua, on the beaches, on the old stones of the ancient city, near the wall where our temple once stood strong and mighty, or across the desert, and into the mountains of God. Come home with *me,* Joshua, to our sacred homeland, to Palestine."

She spoke in barely a whisper, taking his hand, and said the word again as if in prayer: "Palestine."

Joshua heard enough and walked to the door. As good as her word, he saw Hans the chauffer, standing stiffly by the side of the black, enameled automobile. Opening the door, he thought he'd create a disturbance that would shake the foundation of her intoxicating presence.

"Palestine means little to me. The race, only the race matters, and I'm an American athlete who will destroy their superman myth. Only America is my home, Fraulein Rachel."

"And Germany, mine, and sometimes, it is so hard to tell the difference, *n'est pas*?"

They didn't hear Hans enter the room. "You must return to the village now, sir. The authorities do not want athletes wandering about in night-time Berlin."

For Joshua, the intrusion was a godsend. He quickly opened the door feeling, however, at a point midway across his back where the 'S' was embroidered on his warm-up jacket, that her eyes were following him.

"Please, call me." Her last words stayed with him during the slow, rolling ride home.

***

In *Unter den Linden* scarlet banners, extending to within ten feet of the pavement and draping green flagpoles on either side of the avenue, curled in the breeze. Flapping in rows fifty feet apart along the central promenade, the swastikas seemed to dance in the wind.

There were streamers along the double-lane motor roads that led to the outskirts of the city. Wreathed in evergreen, beautified by the scarlet banners, unfurled in a dazzling array of illumination, bathed by the shadows that gave them shelter, a Berlin night was beginning to fall. He was witness to arc lights rising over the avenue, among the flags and the cherry blossoms, and the peaceful Nazi nation that was so unanimously adored.

She saw no difference between nations, he thought, but what of Palestine, to be carved from Arab nations. He should've held his ground.

"Please," she had said, imploring him for what purpose? But he wouldn't think about her, at least, not until the race was won.

There were dark clouds settling over the horizon above the impressive assembling of the swastikas. He counted the evergreens until he grew tired. Turning the wheel slightly, the chauffeur coughed.

Closing his eyes, he had visions of the race. Bobby Gillman would pass the baton, and he would take off down the cinders. He saw Bobby clearly in his vision. His hands would be sure. Even in the dark, they knew each other until each could feel the other's hand, touch hearts.

Joshua imagined the red clay infield, surrounded by the hundred thousand, hating him. Their hate only helped him run faster. Hate around the oval. Hate in their eyes: hate, now his fuel to hate them with Jewish pride, Jewish hate, smelled from the nostrils, seen in flesh, torn from the heart. Hate, the concept Nazis didn't seem to shrink from, didn't seem to care about the hate that would come back to destroy them.

He wanted to imagine what it would be like to be a Jew and to run for his people, not for glory, not for love. But in the imaginings of the sweetness of that savage run, he was abounding along the runway and racing skyward, the cinders alive, glowing with a brilliant hue, beguiling him now, not with hate, but something else, bewitching him now, her green eyes that would lay him down in the cool shade of surrender.

24

Arian Bandage was traveling by motorcade to a site just outside Olympic Village. A construction man, he liked the way buildings were made. Though the Depression had bankrupted the Arian Bandage Construction Company, he simply had a knack to change disaster into luck. Even when penniless, he refused to be broken, or beaten.

In 1932, he picked himself up and bought shares in companies in the real estate business in Chicago. He knew what properties were good to hold, and with good credit was able to gain controlling shares in many companies in hotel and real estate.

"I was a little lucky," he said.

Bandage was joined by a few American businessmen, consultants, and Wall Street financiers. They had taken some time away from the Olympic Games to see up close the new Germany for themselves. They rode in a Mercedes along *Stralsunder Strasse*, turned on *Bernauer* and stopped in front of the gate at *Strasse der Nationnen*. A quiet man in a black S.S. initialed shirt greeted them. He wore glasses, and had an odd, pasty white face.

Arriving in the tranquil village of *Oranienburg*, they saw quaint houses and white porches displaying streamers and pennants of the Olympic Games. Though the residents *of Oranienburg* kept a cheerful countenance, they often held their ears, or closed their eyes because of the tapping of hammers, the rumbling of heavy machinery, the dumping of concrete, and the shuffling of sad-eyed gypsies and bent workmen.

Had they another hand, they'd squeeze their own nostrils to hide the stench of progress. The workmen toiled in soiled, ragged clothes. Gypsies carried beams and large rocks on their shoulders. Why were they not smiling, them who must? "Happy are those to be working for the glory of rebuilding German industry," the neighbors lamented. But the laborers were invisible, blurred to them by the dust of construction, and the veil of forgetfulness that had settled on the town.

Bandage walked with his friends, a group of Americans, and a small circle of German friends. They passed a camp. He thought it was a camp, or a training facility of some kind. The pasty-faced man with gold-rimmed glasses said he built a three meter high stone wall inside, and trained his men there.

That German, another in a line of unimpressive looking faces, talked quietly about the German economic expansion, and the importance of mutual cooperation. His banking system reached from Cologne to New York. He identified himself as the *Reichsfuehrer* of the *SchutzStaffel*.

Standing by a lethal electric fence, one of the Americans laughed. "Could you say that in English, bud?"

A few of the Germans huddled. From inside the circle, the *Reichsfuehrer* gave the American a wicked look. Slowly, he composed himself.

"S.S.," he said, coming out of the circle with steely eyes, to face the American.

"O.K., bud, just asking," said the American, with a sudden sense of dread.

Standing beside him were the German and American businessmen who designed that place. Representatives of A.E.G., T.N.G, and parent company, AT&T, and C.I.E., I.G. Farben and Standard Oil of New Jersey, the Metalwork's Group, and Alcoa, the aluminum monopoly that had created a world cartel. Those were the initialed men of American might.

They had come together to share their vast empires. Petroleum, rubber, tungsten, steel, chemicals, aluminum, communications, finance, fuel, and electricity were the lifeblood of the nation. To have a modern nation, domestic production would have to be increased, or the regime might fold. Allies, and a new plan, were needed to support the aims of the Reich.

Bandage looked about and saw that Amescott Rhodes and Wendell Radcliffe, and the men of the newly formed Alfred P. Sloan Foundation. They had arrived in a second auto, and Henry Ford, of Ford Motor, and Charles Lindbergh, with Heinkel, the aircraft manufacturer, in a KdF Wagen V3, prototype of the little car Hitler adored, pulled up the rear.

From an adjacent road, in a wide arc on the gravel path, other autos with unfamiliar men converged. They were part of Himmler's Circle. Heinrich Himmler was the name of the *Reichsfurher* of the S.S. He was as close to Hitler as breath, in charge of that phase of the German recovery: the confiscation of a percentage of Jewish property as a price of forced emigration. What fueled the German recovery was an emulsion of cheap labor and American capital to reduce German war debt.

In their white suits and straw hats, the group didn't hear the grunt and groans of workers falling in the dust. Bandage could smell only concrete that he knew Germany paid handsomely for.

One needn't see the workers at all. They worked cheaply. Indeed, they worked for nothing at all. For accounting purposes, it was very tidy, very neat. One needn't mind the tangle of metal strung out in a looping chain. The idea was not so foreign to those bankers and brokers who had offices in Zurich and New York.

Thomas Watson, a one man conglomerate, talked quietly to his pal, Adolf Eichmann, the petty official who took the names from the punch cards off Watson's bulbous machines. Watson wore the most gilded initials of them all. He was founder and president of I.B.M. His international division leased those items to Germany, no longer for the census, but for one purpose only: the identification of Jews. Arian Bandage couldn't help admiring the efficiency of construction, the utility of design, and the dedication of a nation to a common cause.

Someone liked the perimeter.

"It's a perfect equilateral triangle. Barrack huts are there away from the entrance and the gate beyond."

"Why is that?" asked Bandage.

Again, the Germans huddled, needing to translate Himmler's words, but Bandage pretended not to hear. "We hope to put machine gun nests in the entrance gate," Himmler said.

Bandage turned with a wry smile, eagle-eyed toward the long perimeter of brick walls and cement, and the barbed wire fence coiling above. With pride, G.E., the American Company, and A.E.G., the German conglomerate, marveled at their lethal work. Above the fence, outside the perimeter, sparse trees and the hint of a vegetated life rose above the barbed wires in the industry of death to hail a more healthy capitalist enterprise.

Others by automobile came. They nodded to Himmler, not to each other. They came in business suits. Some had sent their doppelgangers, carbon copies of a philosophy that didn't have a name. What had brought them together were common interests and sound business ideas. Doing business with Nazis helped preserve American ideals.

Bandage marveled at the construction site, but held his ears not to hear, and finally removed his glasses, not to see. Deaf, dumb, and blind, he had no recollection later of that curious gathering at *Oranienburg*.

Damn, what kind of camp is this? Arian Bandage wondered, but he was reassured by another industrialist.

"In keeping with the idea, this camp would set the standard. Solely engaged for work and the training of …"

Here, the little man paused and raised his head sheepishly toward Himmler. Albert Speer, the man speaking, would use the workers for the nearby brickworks that would service Germany. It was to be pure German genius, the manufacturing of bricks from clay, toiled out of bedrock with a quarry on site, worked by virtual slave labor, serving the needs of the nation.

"Hence," he said, smugly to Bandage, "the motto and the idea of the camp." Bandage then turned to where the little man was pointing. The men of business rose as one. The idea had been planted above the gate in straight black letters. The souls of many would serve the state. The S.S. would enforce the peace thirty-five kilometers from the city of Berlin.

"*Arbeit Macht Frei.*"

Bandage certainly couldn't object. A motto like that was a shared philosophy. It was also purely an American creed. If only the communists and Jews agreed. Yet, he was blameless for the politics, for he was going to run the blacks and Jews in the same race. He sneered inside the perimeter at a black cat that crept along the tangled wires.

The climax of track and field would be in a few days, a pure sporting event that tested a man's strength with his lungs and legs. The blacks were doing well, but the Jews were another matter. Bobby Gillman and Joshua Sellers were scheduled for the four-man relay race. Blacks and Jews would be running around the track, with Hitler watching. What more could he do for the Jewish lobby back home?

Bandage's thoughts became abstracted. Still.., he remembered the cascade of black runners parading and strutting past the fuehrer's loge. It's a time to run the races, yet …

Bandage snarled, his sparse German rolling from his lips into the tangle of wires where the black cat scowled and seemed to imitate him. *"Arbeit Macht Frei."*

Then the Germans began laughing, hearing the cat bastardize the pure Aryan tongue – the language of Joann Wolfgang von Goethe and Beethoven. Even Himmler smiled slyly; then he opened his mouth, wildly contorting his face, and laughed out loud. Outside the gate, the group laughed wildly, too, as dawn in the guise of a rare German sun peeked through the morning clouds. *"Arbeit Macht Frei,"* Himmler said, and I.B.M., and A.E.G., and I.T. &T., and all the initialed men goose-stepped and laughed along.

By the time they stopped laughing, Bandage had already forgotten how happy he was in Germany under the sign. *"Arbeit Macht Frei."*-*"Work Brings Freedom."*

Then they toasted the words above the Iron Gate, not far from Olympic Village in one of the first, newly constructed Concentration Camps, and called *Sachsenhausen*.

There would be others.

PART 3

25

It was the morning of the Running Broad Jump competition. "They talked to Hitler," said a foreign correspondent.

"Really, talked to Hitler?" Jesse asked, with a wry smile.

"Well, those that could."

For what seemed a long time, nobody spoke. Then the correspondent said sideways. "He might want to meet you. He won't shake your hand, though."

"Really?" Jesse asked.

"From the horse's mouth."

Jesse smiled. He liked horses, but never imagined them talking. Now, he knew he should let it go. He was becoming arrogant, having tasted victory already. Racism was their problem, not his. But inside he churned. Anger was the enemy of his limbs, but it then seeped through every pore.

He made his way to the start of the Running Broad Jump competition, but his fists were clenched, and his warmup jersey still on. Down the runway, he ran with rage, neglecting his training, lifting off from the gut, smack against the take-off board. "Uhh," the crowd roared, his right foot leaping, with 'hate' the guiding force. Scissors-kicking and nearing another world's record, he cursed the tyrant. Everywhere, red flags waved at the finish. He had started his run six inches past the take-off board.

"Venz," "Uhh Venz."

The second attempt was no better. The takeoff seemed so far away. He was furious Hitler refused his hand. Gingerly, jogging down the runway, he timed his steps as he'd always done. But he'd have to shake the trembling. He fizzled in mid-air. A jump under twenty-three feet, a dismal leap, he'd have only one more chance.

The crowd still roared his name, but with an unmistakable buzz. The dread that plagued his cursed dreams had come again with fury. Even when sickly, he had run with his father. With every step, a dark voice had whispered, "Bet you can't." In dreams it was his father's voice. But his daddy never said, "You cannot," and his mom wide-eyed was in love with him. Yet, those memories made him shrink, his head burrowed into a turtle's shell. He was a fake; he had seen it in the eyes of Eulace Peacock, and that slight sneer of derision, when Jesse lost to him, and from those that stayed away from him, after a bad race. The track was often a cold and fickle place.

He tried breathing in a steady rhythm. His legs were heavy; he couldn't even walk the heat. Still, he carried the weight of his family, and the pride of his race. Worse yet, an Aryan was leading the long jump trials. He'd never heard of Lutz Long. The German cleared twenty-five feet in practice. "I'm just handing him the gold," Jesse said aloud.

Hello, Jesse Owens," said a friendly voice. Startled by a presence, Jesse turned, surprised to see the German nearby.

"My name is Lutz Long. That's 'L' like in 'Ludwig.' My English, not so good. I have wanted to meet you. You are a great athlete. Listen, those jumps mean nothing. But you must qualify." Jesse was shocked. His chief rival in the jump was offering to help him under the nose of Hitler. Long gave Jesse the key that could only defeat himself later.

"I am scared, also," he said, turning his eyes slowly toward the private box. The fawning faces surrounded Hitler. The initialed men were close by as well. It was in the air; a slight wind, and the tinkling of bells in which could be heard, with but little imagination, the sound of the letters: I.B.M., and A.E.C., and G.E. and A.T. &T.

Hitler peered suspiciously across the field. The two combatants seemed very close, indeed. A hundred thousand heads soon bobbed in the same direction while the rivals spoke amiably.

"I wish I were as certain as you I could make this jump," Jesse Owens said.

"Come with me," said Long. Owens followed along the cinders to the takeoff board.

"Jesse Owens, look," said Lutz Long, "Draw your mark a foot before the takeoff. In this way, you will make sure you do not foul. You will qualify easily."

"Why are you telling me this?"

"I have dreamed of this competition, Jesse Owens. You are the great champion. Winning in this event without you means nothing to me. Later, you and I will have a friendly go. We will only see each other. One of us will be champion. There will be glory, perhaps for both of us."

Owens drew the line he knew, but this time a foot before the take-off board. He would always be grateful to the blonde Aryan for what he gave him that day- timely advice in the most important moment of his life. Today, Jesse had to compete in dual events: the long jump, and the two hundred meter trials. He had to win the running broad jump. He knew he had to win them both. When dusk finally had settled over the great torch-lit arena, his name would be carved in stone, or not at all. If he didn't bag the triple gold, his dreams would be over.

If the Aryan, standing within an earshot, beat him in the broad jump, the Germans would rise as one, in a pandemonium of national ecstasy. The blacks would be blamed; he'd be remembered as an 'N," and a choker.'

The officials called the magical name for the third and last jump. The great throng broke into handclaps. Jesse heard them for the first time. He heard the name, "Uhh Venz," as if it were for someone else, as if in that hellish dream. The thunderclaps that time seemed to be mocking him. That same crowd now gave the adulation to the German.

Who was that blonde-haired German, it wanted to know? Unlike Blaske or Hein, or Woellke, Long didn't belong to any party. The unknown, with his classic build and Aryan features, excited the crowd. "Lutz," the crowd roared, sensing a great, upset victory. Long's name, and not Jesse's, echoed around the arena. Long was the Wotan arisen, Owens the pretender.

Jesse raced down the track into the roar that mocked his name, and soared gracefully and serenely, leaping to qualify, his legs clearing the fault line with ease.

Into the finals, first runner on the track, Owens bested the Olympic mark. Lutz Long rolled down the runway next, and landed with a great leap of his own, to tie him. The stands rocked with new frenzy.

Hardly before had Owens had any competition, and never from hated Aryan blood. But Long didn't fit the mold of an enemy. Owens didn't know what to make of him. He smiled warmly at Owens, as Jesse prepared for his last jump.

Hitler appeared nervous and exhausted. With Jesse ready for his last qualifying attempt, Riefenstahl's camera captured the moment. Hitler twiddled his mustache, crossed and re-crossed his legs. He tapped his knees with his fingers, seeming to ignore the pokes of his Italian guest.

Hermann Goering, Minister and *Oberbefehlshaber,* Supreme Commander of the Luftwaffe, sat in an eggshell and gray uniform, and cheered with childish glee. He was the collector of different titles and duties among which was the director of spy activities for the *Gestapo*, the Secret Police. He also took Jewish property for gain or confiscation. He enjoyed that job the most, amassing a personal fortune, while serving Der Fatherland and business interests abroad. Goering raised his hands overhead, cupped them together whenever a German even coughed. He understood nothing, and was roaring drunk.

On the next seat over, causing anxiety even among an avid Nazi audience, the Jew-baiter Streicher looked on with a whip at his side. His paper, *Der Strumer*, had been removed from the stands along the main thoroughfares, but the appearance of the Jew-baiter didn't hide the national disguise.

Long had given him another chance. Infused with the courage of the German champion, he felt he was in a real sporting match. That was what sport was about, friendly combat. Admiring him, he also applauded as Long's name was put on the message board that would soon crown the new champion- the results, not certain. Pausing for a moment on the runway, Jesse faced the monsters squarely. They were waiting for him to slip, the headlines already written that would exalt the new German champion. Near the Fuehrer, Joseph Goebbels strained his neck to see. He was already revising history. All eyes turned toward the infield. Jesse Owens would rise, or fall in that moment. But his hate, and the fear, were gone. There was only certainty, and he imagined the faces of his parents, and his dad calling him to run.

"Run, Jesse, run." And the track was the way to prove his worth as a man. America awaited the champion, and his race needed another hero, so that his people could dream the American dream. Years of dedication, and the solitary quest for a good name, stood with him at the top of the runway. The hardest race for a sprinter. The leap into the great unknown.

The Running Broad Jump Finals, Tuesday, August 4, 1936.

The place was set for pandemonium. Two warriors were rising through the air, in a spectacle of levitation, beyond human imaginings. How high would greatness soar, on a runway toward the twilight gods, or the flames that would rise for failure? Down the track, he ran away from flesh to touch the clouds. As he lifted himself higher, a spontaneous roar burst from the tiers. He thought he had gone deaf in flight, and had died somewhere above his heart, or that his eyes had been unhinged, and was carrying him into eternity, or the asthmatic night. He couldn't breathe, and he thought, if this were victory, death was the prize. He went farther than any mortal had ever been, past the magical twenty-six foot barrier, and into immortality that may have shattered, the very conception of white supremacy.

With one giant leap, he changed modern thinking about just what could be achieved by straining every limb, no matter the circumstance, or the hostile winds.

Lutz Long rushed over, the first to congratulate him. Owens went to his knees, breathless, he kissed the earth...

The stadium fell silent. Jesse dared to unrestrainedly laugh toward the reviewing stands. How they held his whole race in such contemptible regard. Didn't they know that mother earth loved all who rose above her garments?

In the silence of the stadium, there was only the whirring of Riefenstahl's projectors, and a human groan. The sound was almost imperceptible, the gasp before a shriek, or a tear coming from deep down an old, southern road.

"Very good, Jesse Owens. This is something for the memories, no?" asked Long.

Jesse gasped, heaving for the dank air that the crowd of Nazis expelled.

"So this was the fun you talked about, huh?" he gasped.

"For me, Jesse, the fun is over. There is pain in my leg now. I don't think my last jump will beat yours."

"Let me see," said Owens.

With Hitler leering, Jesse put lineament on the calves of his chief rival. Long approached the take-off board for one last chance. He hobbled down the runway, and leapt as far as he could. It was a game attempt that fell short of the new world's record, Jesse had set. The heroic Lutz Long had finally lost. But the two walked together, arm and arm, around the oval. Hitler was aghast, and Goebbels spewed hate in his diaries for those "Jew- Niggers" whom were beating the Germans.

Owens, again, was on the platform for the second time, holding securely in his hands another English oak and crown of laurels, and his second gold medal. But the crowd wouldn't let either champion leave.

The German unknown was hoisted on the shoulders of a mob that honored his heroics against the champion. Condescending to wait for the well-wishers and sycophants to depart, Hitler stood in a ramp way behind the honor loge until he was able to privately greet Lutz Long.

Standing proudly on the winner's platform, Jesse looked at the empty Caesar's box without anger. Once again, the Stars and Stripes were hung over the rafters of the arena. It stirred him to be the cause of the playing of the anthem of his nation. The majesty of the Star Spangled Banner kneaded his patriotic heartstrings once more.

Jesse Owens was more certain of his future, though he was hungry and exhausted. One more race, he thought, and his tired feet could race towards home.

26

After Jesse Owen's victory, Bobby Gillman was ready kick the Nazis out of the Fuhrer's Loge. Goering would be the easiest with his blubber belly. To get him over the top, and onto the infield, would be the problem. He might have to be hoisted. With a truncheon, he'd smack Julius Streicher in his ugly face. The Jew- baiter would feel some discomfort. Pity.

Hitler, though, would be more difficult. A wiry cunning man with a natural streak for survival, that weasel could worm his way out of most tight jams.

So, Bobby thought he'd have to come up behind him, grab him and trip him to his knees. On top of him, Bobby would slap his face, silly.

"What's a Jew, weasel," he'd say, kicking his butt like that.

"That's the way to deal with them," he thought, cheering Jesse on the sidelines as The Star Spangled Banner played again in fascist Germany. With Joshua and many black athletes at attention, tears streamed from his young face. He lit up the afternoon sky with a broad smile. He thought about his dad who had struggled to bring him to that place, and he wrote to him that night about the way he felt.

"I am so excited, dad. A brown thunderbolt has changed the world. Even the 'supermen' here cheer my friend, Jesse Owens. Something is happening dad. When Josh and I run, the world is going to be different, I swear. The Jew, this Jew, your son, is going places nobody else over here can imagine. I can beat whomever they throw at me, dad. I feel that strength.

We're going to kick butt and bust heads like in the old days. Pray for me. Your son, Bobby Gillman (I guess you already know my last name.")

Bobby also thought something else was happening there, but it would take another fifty years before it was said. In a manner suddenly unbecoming, akin to Hitler's arrival, pagan chants were unleashed by screaming Germans, in a hysterical aural orgy. That was not adoration for Owens. That was mob induced racism at its highest pitch. Those were the sounds when gladiators were introduced in the Roman pits, or the cheering for the lions when they tore the flesh. Those sounds held the fury of a frenzied expletive, a communal disregard of humanity and a sardonic display, the nations under the thumbs of the Nazi insurrection.

Yet, there was also so much beauty to behold, Bobby thought: the aesthetics of the beautiful Leni Riefenstahl, focusing her cameras on the American Brown Thunderbolt, the dizzying depths of the great arena, the handsome warriors meeting in sport, when Jesse Owens and the blacks ran to glory in the city of dreams.

"It was an alliance," said Gillman, his voice echoing in the vast, eerie halls of the Holocaust Memorial Museum in Washington, fifty years later, "between beauty and the beast. The crowd was having a feeding frenzy. They were trying to cannibalize Owens's flesh.

"Some say his victories were theirs, not *his* triumph. He had merely enlarged their appetites. But the Olympics of 1936 are not remembered as the Nazi Olympics, but for Jesse Owens and his triumph."

And Jesse was relieved. A great weight was lifting. He had twice won the coveted prize. Already two gold medals had fallen into the Ohio Bullet's lap. Later that day, he would begin his charge for yet, a third. The two hundred meters would be a shoe-in for the captain of the American squad.

The name Jesse Owens would be held aloft in the pantheon of great heroes. He would win his third gold medal in the two hundred meters the next day, and Bobby would still be on the sidelines, waiting for his one chance to run for Olympic gold.

Joshua was also on the sidelines, the collar of his warm-up jacket, hiding the side of his face. Bobby was ecstatic, thought he'd see the same expression on his friend's face. But Joshua wasn't watching the platform. He'd already turned to see the quick exit of the fuehrer and his entourage. For a moment in time, it seemed that their eyes met –those piercing eyes of Hitler, by instinct, had found an enemy worthy of his name-for Joshua had that sickly grin, and his eyes had caused Hitler's to blink.

Bobby wanted to know, "Who would win, George Raft or Hitler?"

Joshua put his hand gently on Bobby's shoulder, "Raft isn't a real mug, Bobby."

"I know, I know, but how 'bout Little Caesar or Jimmy C.?"

"Well, I'd say Hitler loses to all three because he's so jumpy. A quick jab to the face would do it, I think. Cagney would throw a pie in his face. Raft could kick him in the shins. Eddie G. as Little Caesar could pump lead into his gut. What's your angle?"

"My angle is about those Nazis," said Bobby, turning serious. 'We wouldn't even need the Hollywood mugs, Josh. Just let them come to Brooklyn. You know my father now talks peace all the time. He's worried about Hitler, and what he calls a Nazi menace. But in 1934, maybe, early '35, he took me to the Pitkin to see some MGM double feature. Next time you're in Brooklyn, Josh, I'll take you there.

"The Loew's Pitkin is the best movie theater in the entire world, I'd guess. It costs more than the locals, and we pay for the oval pool, the chandeliers, the castle, and even the goldfish kept in the pool in the lobby. What a place. Well, after the show, Dad wants to go to the city, and asks me if I want to come.

"Sure, dad, why not, you know?" I say, and we go. But we are not alone. Upstairs, from down the block, in Katzie's pool room above Abe Stark's clothing store, come a bunch of guys. I swear Joshua, they looked tougher than the Hollywood gangsters put together. They were part of Meyer Suchomlanski's mob.

"I don't know what he does, but he knows all the big boys. Yeah, he goes by Meyer Lansky now. You heard of Luciano, Costello, and the Italian mob. Well, Lansky goes with them. It's his business, but there's one thing he doesn't do. He doesn't do business with Nazis.

"So, we get into a DeSoto auto and head for the east side of the city, and go to a place in Yorkville, real quiet cause the mugs we are riding with are carrying police truncheons, baseball bats, clubs, and all kinds of hurting things.

"I have no idea how my father knows them. He never told me, and it's not my business to know. Everyone sitting in the car with those weapons, and dad reaches into his vest pocket, and all of a sudden, a bunch of tire chains and more weapons – knives and one gun, and then one Tommy gun, comes out of a mug's coat.

"They're worried what heat dad is carrying, and are ready to pump us full of lead. But dad was reaching for his white hanky, and makes a show of wiping his brow. Those are the mugs that we're riding with to Yorkville to visit a Nazi hang-out.

"The Third Avenue movie theater on the eastside played foreign, mostly German films. There was a lot of picketing over there, so they changed the name to the National Theater. As far as I know, a few people who sold tickets there, had some broken heads.

"When we get to the neighborhood, up one of the streets off Third, Lansky tells us to split into groups. Three guys take the stairs, two more, the roof. There are about eight of us, and dad and I are told to wait downstairs. We are to be the look-outs, though Dad doesn't know what we're looking for. But dad does what he's told.

"I am the more curious, so I climb the stairs. I get to the third floor landing, and see two guys making nice at the door, and hear a great commotion coming from inside. The door is open, some password must have been given, and a mug in brown shirt gives the old *'sieg heil.'* One of Lansky's boys grabs the arm and cracks his hand. When the Nazi screams, he takes him and throws him down the stairs.

"Lansky breaks up the Nazi meeting, and stuffs Hitler's photographs inside the goons' mouths. It was really hilarious, but frightening also, to see Nazis with their pants down, screaming and squealing like pigs.

"I watched Lansky, and one of his boys, hold the Nazi leader down, beat him with a stick and the barrel of a gun, and smear his blood on his spanking brown shirt. Then they cursed him and wiped his face with the swastika flag they pulled down from the walls.

"The place smelled of beer and smoke, and they took a few of the more scared blokes, and threw them out the window too. Lansky's brutes broke fingers, and all the while, he is beating them black and blue, and saying,

'Don't mess with the Jews.'

"And then he throws them out the window too. There's one more Nazi in the house, a boy about my age. Lansky calls me over and gives me a stick. He lays the kid out over a table, and whacks him on the knees. With him screaming, Lansky tells me to finish the job. But I can't hit the kid. I don't run like that.

"And then Lansky looks me square in the eyes, and he says something I never forget, but I don't know why. He says, 'If we can stop them for a day, just one more day, our people, and, he said, 'our people,' may stay alive, even for one more day.'

"So I punched the Nazi and broke his nose."

***

Hitler's box had emptied. Hitler, Goering, Goebbels and the rest, barreled down the tunnel. Nearby, Coubertin and Bandage followed suit. Bandage was a beam of light, a halo, self-contented. The sun reflected off his gold rimmed glasses as he paused a moment in the crush of dignitaries to savor the homage given to that *New Yorker Magazine*, Man of the Year, Adolf Hitler.

Lindbergh arrived, waving to the crowd that shuffled him along with heartfelt applause. Into the tunnel walked the nameless, initialed men with Avery Rockefeller and Rockefeller's accountants, Schroeder and Chase Bank. There were others hiding in the shadows of the alphabet soup.

American businessmen and Nazis, arm in arm, with Count Von Ribbentrop, Frau Goering, Albert Speer, and Count Umberto, talking sadly to himself. Julius Streicher strolled with Henry Ford, deep in thought. Other nameless faces pulled up the rear. Joshua sensed them before they came forward in sunglasses, and disappeared.

"I should, but I don't hate them." said Bobby, "because their swastikas can't stop me from running."

"Maybe it's not just the Nazis," said Joshua, looking at the unfamiliar faces.

Bobby looked up to see a shadow of an S.S. uniform, marching in his direction. Because of dark, threatening clouds, it was impossible to make out his features. His manner was quiet; his mouth closed. But his eyes gave Joshua extra attention. Then hiding beneath an umbrella, in a sudden down-pouring, he walked like a beetle into horizontal rain. Above in the tiers, Eichmann spooned with his lovely bride, abstracting information in his hard shell.

"Maybe, it's something else happening here," Joshua said.

And then a woman appeared and stared into his blue with her green eyes. Cautiously, Joshua walked up to her. He was confounded by purpose and desire, letting her steady him, as he fell backward into an embrace. He recognized the stiff bearing of the officer, Himmler, walking with a handsome man. His was the zenith of the alphabet power: Thomas Watson, chairman of the American Chamber of Commerce, president of the gilded men of I.B.M.

Bobby Gillman saw the transformation in his friend. Joshua held Rachel tightly, not caring where he was. The two walked down the same runway Owens had leapt to make history. At the farthest side of the stadium, they climbed the concrete to the highest tiers, disappearing from view behind Marathon Gate.

27

The honored guests that swept into the tunnel had reason to be happy. Hitler had decided to attend one of the lavish parties that were to be given that night. Joseph Goebbels had prepared a fireworks display, and a party for a thousand guests at the *Pfaueninsel*, the Peacock Garden in the Havel, decked out in Italian pastiche, on the wide expanse of water surrounding Berlin. Gaily lit pontoon bridges were made especially for that purpose.

Joachim von Ribbentrop, the Nazi ambassador to England, invited foreign guests to his villa, but the most lavish display of hospitality since the Roman Circus would take place near the new Air Ministry complex, in the 'wings' appropriated by Hermann and Frau Goering.

A woman who was an accomplished actress, Emmy Sonnemann, played the role of her life. She weaved in white, flowing gowns through the gathering crowd, touching her subjects with a white wand, and strode past adoring men like a bacchante.

The ministry was requisitioned by the new air minister, the minister of fuel and the minister of Prussia, one and the same. Goering had been pilfering more fiefdoms that week. A former commander of the Red Baron brigade, with twenty two kills in the Great War, he was wounded in the groin during a dogfight.

Afterwards, Goering cried out from pain, and for more morphine, becoming a drug addict, often seen disheveled and dazed. Unfortunately for 'Emmy', that was the state in which the host came down the palatial steps to greet his guests.

At the time of its construction, the Air Ministry building was the largest one of its kind. In the crisp, no frills style of National

Socialist architecture, it ran for over two hundred and fifty meters among *Wilhemstrasse*. It had a fearsome reinforced concrete skeleton with an exterior facade of limestone and travertine, a form of marble. Seven stories high, the edifice had over four thousand windows and seventeen stairways, its stone coming from no fewer than fifty quarries which took eighteen months for an army of unpaid laborers to build. Working double shifts and Sundays, the workers built a structure that could house four thousand workers, bureaucrats, and secretaries.

Inside the edifice protected by a large eagle, above the grand iron swastikas, outside the Hall of Honor, the *Ehrinsaal*, the Air Minister swished down the steps, tripping over a trail of little roaring lion cubs, which scampered for their young lives. He wore a cream colored vest.

"Emmy," said Goering. The ingénue turned wife-nursemaid moved the whining Reich Fuel Dictator down the staircase toward the entrance of the gardens, in the rear of the hall. Followed by an entourage of American and German businessmen, the gaily lit gardens overwhelmed their guests who walked into a shrine reminiscent of the great man's country residence of *Carinhall* in *Schorfheide*, in the forested suburbs of northern Berlin.

Sitting down to a lavish feast of pheasant and assorted culinary delicacies, the thousand guests 'ohhed' and 'ahhed.' Summer had brought a sudden surprise of Dionysian treats, including a piano recital and full ballet ensemble, performing in moonlight, the heady joys of a fascist, aesthetic delight.

Especially Bandage –his face already flushed, and his tears hurtling like a rush of glass, bursting through his gold-rimmed glasses in shards-was aroused by the performance of his fantasies of Bavaria, the snows of Berlin winters, and his secret desire for Aryan nymphs. He was the errant knight in ancient castled domes, his fancy to wallow among his lady squires. Wanting to lift the skirts of the dancers, and the veil of the Reich Minister's intoxicating wife-mistress, Bandage, as well as nattily dressed Alfred P. Sloan, like their host, could not raise themselves for the toast. But nothing prepared them for the dimming of the lights, and the festivities to come.

There was the hallucinatory scent of the garden metropolis, in what could have been mistaken for paradise. Indeed, Chip Finley, conservative member of the English House of Commons, left Germany with a dreamscape vision of a fascist, pure state in which he envisioned, like Bandage and the rest, a new world order.

It was becoming clear to Bandage, though he couldn't raise his head above the stein of warm, but freshly brewed German beer. He had seen it in the smiling cherubic faces, the frolicsome innocence of young girls, and the strength of purpose of the National Socialists. That was a nation serving a collective ideal. The ideal was exactly the same as the motto of his own nation: out of many…one: *E Pluribus Unum.*

Yes, in the dictatorship, only one voice could speak for all, he thought, rising above the Reich Minister who was snoring. He made his way to where the dinner crowd had gone. A buzz of fireflies were awash in the pale light of an enveloping moon.

Suddenly from below, great floor beams lit the night sky and highlighted a garden carousel. Children sat on painted horses and waved to storybook characters from Grimm and Anderson, and Bechstein. Pronounced Steen, or Styne, Eichmann, seated alone in a corner, wondered? There were wolves and monsters, herdsmen and hunters, and young women dressed as servants, alighting from the carousel, with pasted smiles and perfect grace, carrying trays of wines and liquors, and steins of beer, to their ever-thirsty guests.

A Jew in thorns, a Grimm's creation, hunkered down in front of Arian Bandage. Dressed in black rags that had been tattered by the play of a servant fiddler, the grotesque invader stole a piece of pheasant and ate it mouth open with an avaricious sneer.

"Tell it to go away," said Chip Finley, laughing in his beer.

But Bandage didn't find any of that amusing. With the 'Jew' seated above him, he rose with a rush and fisted the intruder from the table. "Dammit," he cried, visibly shaken. G-d forgive him, he pleaded. He didn't like taking the name of the Lord in vain.

There were squeals of laughter from the Nazi hosts, and from beautiful maidens who circled him with lightness and the allure of feminine grace. One sat down beside him, her hair braided and tied. Of peasant stock she had been raised in the collective and learned their desires, with steadfast sacrifice as her guide.

The pure fascist could not be made whole with the Jew within their midst; they strangled the Aryans' breath with that miserly stain that was the sole cause of war, inflation, and misery. Having consumed more liquor than the entire women's swimming team, he staggered to kiss a lovely, painted German miss. It was suddenly so clear, as much as drink could help make him see. A higher purpose awaited him there as president of the American Olympic Committee. America was much different from Nazi Germany, he thought, at least in terms of purpose and theater. But the similarities were clear, as clear could be.

To Bandage, the message was increasingly clear, although it had become so much warmer then. Airless and unsupported, with a vague feeling of faraway laughter, he had the sensation of having his clothes taken by deft, invisible fingers.

He knew the case could be made that he hated Jews, but he wasn't a rabid anti-Semite like his friend, Henry Ford. He would argue that few of his business friends disliked Jews. It was just a question of world view, and which vision would take the world of nations out of the Depression, and keep America out of war.

Only dictatorship was the aim, not of the proletariat, not of Russia and communists, trade unionists, workers and Jews, but of the builders, the contractors, the heads of the resources of industry, in service of the nation for the benefit of a grateful collective.

For Bandage, the purity of sports and National Socialist economic expansion were wholly consistent with the American capitalist system. He knew the Germans were trying to balance a tightrope between their need for rearmament versus domestic consumption. Looking across from him, where a yawning and a great stirring seemed to lift Herr Goering from his slumber, Bandage understood the dilemma. The new Fuel Dictator hadn't any idea about economics. But he knew how to rouse passions. He wanted, and got results, without having to bother understanding the fundamentals.

Just then he liked the Four Year Plan. Goering mulled over the idea of German autarky which his predecessor, Hjalmar Schacht, proposed just before he was ousted. Goering knew that the dual needs for foreign currency by the domestic and military couldn't both be met, except when he drank, or was under the influence of opiates.

The solution then was simple; the way clear. Bust the heads of Jews to grease the economy by confiscations, and appeal to the interests of U.S. collaborators at Chase Bank and the New York Stock Exchange.

Those problems, thought Bandage, couldn't be solved without the great facilitator, Adolph Hitler. Imagine the cursed Roosevelt dealing with that? He'd put everyone back to work despite the consequences, bankrupt the nation, give Social Security hand-outs and put millions on the welfare dole. He'd permit the communists and Jews to run wild, screaming and crying about this or that, cause chaos, like worker's strikes –who else but Jew- union inspired, - the very pulse of productive American industry ruined by them.

He began to hear rhythmic clapping from the carousel. The illuminated spectacle in the garden made him dizzy. The members of the corps de ballet and the thirteen beer serving Bavarian princesses had removed their dresses for discerning guests, and the thousand wandering spirits in the *Ehrinsaal,* came to a hushed interlude, as a dim light was cast on a lone speaker that roamed a make-shift stage like an animal in a gilded cage.

Or, so it seemed. The magical night had lasted until the pre-dawn drunken orgy was finally laid to rest. That was the epitome of National Socialism, alcohol mixed with cocaine derivatives and heroin, with lion cubs lurking in the hall.

The lads of I.G. Farben were users as well as inventors. They'd turned to the problem of synthetic opioid analgesics, using a drug called dolophine to help soldiers cope with pain during a war, irrespective of the fact that there wasn't yet an army of soldiers, a shortage, or a war.

On the stage, if it were a stage, was Hitler, if it were Hitler? The guests that had turned from the gaiety of Luna Park had come to watch the great man do Nazi theater. The power Nazi, the pure Nazi, the Nazi driven by religious symbol, Hitler thought he was higher than a deity, and he'd assembled his guests for his own perverted cause. It wasn't the speech but conviction that caused general weeping and lamentations, and the re-evaluation of religious faith. That Hitler, on stage, was myth in garters, a transvestite performer, holding an audience by the crack between its legs. That Hitler was the realism, no longer an abstraction, about the man, striven on horseback to ride off into the sunset of a messianic dream.

When that Hitler began to speak, its eyes rolled, and its powerful right arm commanded. Dressed, no longer exposed in Nazi paraphernalia, Hitler roused the guests to sign- up for the aesthetics of pure fascist political might.

"I ask myself, who are these elements who wish to have no rest, no peace, and no understanding, who must continuously agitate and sow mistrust? Who are they actually?" he asked, rhetorically, and the Germans among the guests answered.

The word rolled like venom from the tongue. It was fuel and loathing, and reason given for the simple peasant purity of power fascism. Bandage, not an intellectual by any sort, still thought that Hitler on stage hadn't ideas about his own performance, of how he might deliver his remarks with more clarity, or even to whom he talked. That Hitler could've been alone in a private psychiatric institution, run by maniacal idol worshippers that concocted his hallucinations to those of a convoluted idol.

"I know," he answered the frenzied collective.

"Jews," they had answered, "Jews," they repeated, "Jews," they were driven into hysterical applause.

Except for the men of Ford and DuPont, the others didn't come over easy to a full frontal assault. Anti-Semitism, for Bandage and many in the Himmler Circle, wasn't racially motivated, but born of experience and shrewd business sense.

Like Krupp and General Electric, the list was endless. They said, 'yes,' to the bubbly poisons they drank from Coca-Cola.

In the crowd, Lindbergh, said, "Yes," but couldn't bring himself to say, "Jew." He viewed politics in racial hues, but his thoughts were more complex, and too abstracted for a simple Nazi perspective.

Herman Goering knew the answer, had heard the same speech last May during the Labor Day performance. Roused from slumber and blissful opiate dreams, he watched his wife's lips as they curled in hate.

"You are disgusting," he said aloud, as she bathed him with that special look of familial devotion, the pitying look of the dutiful wife, her greatest offstage performance.

Hitler delivered his final words in a frenzy. "I know…it is not the millions who would have to take up weapons if the intentions of these agitators were to succeed," he said, and the crowd was brought to its feet.

"The Jew must get out of Germany, yes, out of the whole of Europe," he said, as he would have those words said, again and again.

But then the crowd of guests, already standing, thrust their right arms out in ecstatic salute.

"*Heil Hitler*," was the only ticket for that party, and Bandage and his American friends gladly paid the price. Though it would never be known for certain if that Hitler were Hitler, the results were the same.

I.B.M. and Eichmann, that silent mist, now in black *S.D.* garments, worked together like brothers, and shared greedy palms and outstretched hands. Bandage wanted so much to join them, but he stayed true to a greater command:

"The purity of sports," he whispered, as the frenzy of the audience bore holes in Jewish hearts.

"*Heil Hitler,*" they said, and Bandage raised both arms simultaneously. He was powerless against them, and his resolve to keep politics out of sports becoming, even for him, an empty, drunken promise. May the furies forgive him, he found himself shouting, above the hysterical voices. "*Heil Hitler,*" he cried. How he loved the power, and the menace of German might.

28

"Last man free," said Rachel, a broad smile on her face. Joshua was surprised that she was so carefree under the circumstances.

"It's good to see you, Rachel," he said. Somehow, he wanted to say more. "My father warned me about the games," she said. Imitating him, she laughed, 'Never forget you are a Jewess in a hostile land.'

'Then why are we not in Palestine, dear father, why?'" I asked.

It was only fifteen minutes after the last event, yet all of the one hundred and ten thousand had filed out of Olympic Stadium except them. Rachel had much to say. Walking slowly toward Marathon Gate, she used her hands in sweeping gestures. Joshua walked quickly, and even she was hard-pressed to keep up with him.

The collar of his U.S.A. field uniform had been tucked high about the neck. The blue jacket, zippered to the breastbone, was a tight, uncomfortable fit. When he had walked too far ahead, he turned to let her catch him, the uniform creased at the elbows, and his muscles strained.

The empty oval coiled around them, the seats, listening to their words like so many ears, the flags of the nations flapped every which way when the wind changed direction again. Rachel wondered if Joshua had been listening. Did he even like her? She couldn't be certain. Something in his bearing, the tense way he carried himself, was more likely hate than… love. She said that word again. Had she really been saying she loved him? Had she come to Olympic Stadium to offer herself to him?

"I don't have time for love," he said, his hand surveying the vastness of the largest arena in the world.

"Don't you now?" Her face turned as taut and stubborn as his. Her eyes made his blink.

She'd finally gained the advantage, she thought. He was altered by her passion. At the top of Marathon Gate, Joshua was trembling. Love wasn't possible, not here, not for him. "Then, when," she said, guessing his thoughts.

"Rachel, I just need to win the … emblem. I'm here to steal gold, not hearts. I don't care about love. I'm strictly alone, a song and dance man."

Her need was greater, her gaze persistent. "I have seen children wailing in front of headlights. I have seen gentle, old men being led around like dogs."

"Oh, please, I don't want to hear this, not now," he said, turning from the glow and the glare of her green eyes.

A gust of wind beating on top of Marathon Gate, the space between them grew greater. In a stadium of empty seats and invisible eyes, the red-green turf on the colorblind carpet, on the cinder paths under the darkening, charcoaled skies, saw her white dress suddenly lifted. Her petticoats underneath lay bare dark, smooth skin, lingering long enough for Joshua to tremble again.

She had bewitched the wind, the rain, and the lackadaisical heavens for a purpose as old as time. When she called him through the rustled grasslands, he followed, and wouldn't let go.

Afterwards, he knew he'd never be the same. The others had been sport; athletics carried on, in different ways. With Rachel, it had mattered greatly. Through her eyes, he had seen that paradise was possible, and that his rage could be stilled by a woman's charm.

Rachel gave him gifts beyond the stadium. She'd carried him on the wind beyond his dreams. She'd given him a greater song than vainglory. She'd taken him to the musical throne. After she left, the rains came warm and wild. He wanted to get away, yet that was the only place to be for...

"Love," he said, finding her down the steps that led from Marathon Gate.

A black-shirted S.S. blocked his way. "May I help you?" he said, cheerily. Then he saw Rachel. "Ah, a girl in white. I understand. It's a matter of love. After the rain, there'll be a fine mist, maybe even a rainbow. The Fatherland helps true lovers find their way."

Joshua left the amiable officer to find Rachel shivering on the grass. And there was a rainbow that arched skyward from one end of the stadium to Marathon Gate. The sky held intermittent sounds of thunder, and the illuminations of lightning lit up the track. The rain had ceased, and he used his shirt to dry her off. "Just once," said Rachel, "run with me."

"Here?" he whispered.

"This is our time, my darling, Joshua," she said, pulling her dress above her head.

If that had been Prospect Park, in Brooklyn, or on the track at the University of Michigan, spectators would've seen two people running with the speed of light demons. But they were just jogging and laughing, and kicking up remnants of a passing summer storm.

"Give me your fastest sixty meters," she said, now challenging him, and he took the bait.

He thought he'd leave her in the dust. He was exhilarated and loose, and strong. On the ninth of August, he'd be an Olympic champion. But a quick glance to the right saw Rachel gaining, then catching him and getting a resounding lead. Before he could open his mouth in amazement, she was gone around the turn. She kept up that pace for another hundred until Joshua accelerated. She was gasping, then, her head down. When he put his arm around her, she pushed him away. "Not now, my darling." She was tearful, her words gay. "Let us celebrate this day."

He laughed, "You'll need to wear something."

"In Berlin, at night? Don't you know clothes are optional?"

"Still," he said.

She smiled and found her dress, and with folds and alterations became modest. "Kiss me."

And Joshua did, a hunger deep inside, though she was brought to him by demons that disturbed his sleep. He thought he should leave, but she laughed, and so did he.

"I want to show you something."

"Yes?"

"In Berlin, we will see Berlin, if you come with me, yes?"

"Yes."

They walked out of the stadium and down the *Unter den Linden*. At that time of day, there was still traffic and foreigners gazing at the swastika and Olympic flags. But her choice was to disappear underground.

***

The underground train station had been built in time for the Olympic Games. Under new arc lights, it wasn't unusual to see lovers 'sieg heiling' before leaving for a subterranean rendezvous. Not that their meeting needed to be kept secret.

The Nazi aesthetics encouraged, even demanded a new woman, subservient to the State, and not to man. Outside of marriage, relations were permitted. No longer would women be ashamed to have an out of wedlock child. So, it was not unusual to see young lovers, hand in hand. The American and the dark-haired woman cautiously lingered. One was never certain of menace in a darkened passageway.

Joshua and Rachel knew not to look at each other. She was standing serenely enough, but he paced the platform and strained over the railing to search down the tracks. Soon, the hissing of steam and the rolling of spanking, clean rolling black cars came into the station and rushed them along, in and around the city, with the haste of a nervous suitor. Becalmed by love, Rachel tried to quell the loneliness she usually felt when travelling alone. Joshua had scooped up a paper, and began reading about exotic Asian and European cities, especially Italy and Japan.

The train was nearly empty until a youth got on, wearing black shorts and a dark, blue blouse with a large collar. Under his outerwear, he wore a light brown shirt and black neckerchief, held snugly in place by a leather toggle. The single shoulder strap of his summer uniform indicated his rank and number in white cotton edgings. The boy was of the *Deutsche Jungvolk*, the Junior Hitler Youth.

He took a seat opposite Rachel. Thinking she was asleep, and not yet seeing Joshua, he fumbled with his gray knee socks and touched the metal sheath on his waist belt that held the *HJ-Fahrtenmesser*, the traveling knife.

The boy stiffened when he saw him. He was used to an instant show of respect. Evil was everywhere, he had been taught. Leaving his seat with the train rumbling into another station, he thrust his right arm out.

"*Heil Hitler*," he said, in the cracking voice of puberty. Joshua saw that Rachel shuddered. She was afraid of that snot-nosed kid. He moved menacingly toward the child. Rachel saw that Joshua was about to cause a scene in front of witnesses. Across from her, she saw dim, heavy eyes, peering out from under a monocle.

"An American," she said, hurriedly, "an athlete."

"Oh, Jesse Owens," said a portly woman. "And you, American, Scandinavian, no? Are you German?"

"Why don't you say 'even?' "Am I even German?" Joshua didn't understand. He kept his eye on the boy who'd unsheathed his little knife.

"You're the guy they put on wedding cakes, right?"

What would James Cagney do tonight? He wondered.

The man with the monocle saw, but said nothing. The woman stirred. Suddenly, she was speechless.

"*Heil Hitler*," the boy said, again, but this time less certain, as the train slowed down.

"It's our stop, Joshua," said Rachel. She saw that he had developed a red streak along his neck. She knew he was going to do something before alighting from the train, and when he paused, Rachel stepped in between and mussed the boy with an open palm. She couldn't be stopped, even when the boy squealed and the passengers gasped. "I am a Jew," she said to the boy, and punched him in his little mouth.

"A Jew," she said, adding one lone finger, and finding Joshua, quietly walked through the closing door.

Joshua began laughing as the train left the platform. "I was only going to riddle him with some bullets. Why'd you do that?"

"I do not know," she said, "Can you tell me?"

Many years later, he would begin to answer Rachel's question. But Rachel's defiance would never leave him. Her laughter in the subways of Berlin always defined her. Now, they held hands, and laughed some more.

29

   Joshua escorted Rachel to the rich areas of the *Friedrichstrasse* as they floated with joy in a world apart. She didn't want to feel, or to see anyone but him, though a thousand Nazis walked by. He breathed her fragrance and embraced her charm. That night, and again, the next, they met, and on the third evening, he joined her in Berlin. The smoky haze of a cabaret seemed to be just the right place for celebration on the eve of his medal run. They would mingle, in tandem, with Nazis and their guests, and be the unseen stain that moved among them.

   It was the eve of the qualifying heats for the four man one hundred meter relay race. Joshua was ahead in the time trials against Davie Warren. He was also far ahead of Tom Grace, so that he didn't mind leaving the village once more. He was told by Robertson that he would race for the American team. He compared notes with Bobby, who said he was told the same. Tomorrow, then, it would begin with the preliminaries. Then on his twenty-first birthday, the day after, he would be an avenging angel. He would take on Deutschland, and give it a staggering blow. He thought about that crippled kid in Prospect Park. He had a promise to keep.

   Cigar smoke hung in the tepid air among the dense crowd in uniform, or not. Whiskey fell from low tables, and eager hands reached underneath to touch the night's giving's. After a few drinks, it seemed everyone was in love: the Nazis, the Americans, and the bizarrely painted clown who called the audience to attention.

   Quietly, Joshua and Rachel sat down. Joshua's eyes scanned the thickly set crowd, hunched together like a lone predator. He thought he saw the dark outline of Joseph Goebbels, but in the dim lights, he couldn't be certain. He had trained for four weeks with the squad and had practiced the difficult art of passing the baton in those vital twenty yards when the speed of the one finishing his hundred meters, had to synchronize exactly with the athlete who took the hand-off. He knew he could do that with his eyes closed, and take home the gold.

"The government has said if it continues to rain in Berlin, it will round-up and shoot fifty Jews," the clown said.

They were at The Scala, one of the three cabarets operating under the Nazi regime. The joke was well received. Even Joshua laughed, but the teller, Werner Finck, an icon of German night club entertainment, and founder of the Catacombs, in the decadent Weimar Republic days, was already marked by the S.S. to be the first artiste to be taken into 'protective custody' to join the gypsies and thieves at the concentration camp at *Sachsenhausen.*

Goebbels had decided that politics and theater never mixed well, except as it served the state. Only the revues were kept because times were hard, and the people needed the escape of entertainment, and the love of anything German, marching in precision.

He saw men whom he had seen in newsreels; a diplomat, an aviator, a dour car manufacturer, an ambassador, a gun smuggler with a wide smile, and those who sat tight-lipped, although their intestines were cracking with suppressed laughter. He whispered to Rachel, his stein raised with hers for a toast.

"Tomorrow, then, for America, for your people and mine."

"My people, Joshua, are yours as well," she answered, as their eyes touched even before their glasses.

Before he could respond, he was surprised by the sudden commotion from the stage. The emcee, in clown costume, was being whisked away by two plainclothes men in raincoats and black hats. An *S.S.* officer in the first row rose, and said,

"No longer can Germany tolerate the Jew decadence of the past."

The emcee was screaming, his feet fluttering behind the rest of him. The crowd, sensing that was part of the act, applauded and laughed loudly. Indeed, a chorus of laughter shook the cabaret, matching the emcee's muffled shrieks behind the raised, red curtain.

"What a funny man," said an ordinary face, the last accolade for Warner Finck who would be away from home a long time.

"Not so funny," said a lame man with the black eyes, "he ridicules, not the Jew, but our own racial policy."

"And what will happen to him?" the same man asked. He wore gold rimmed glasses, and was much taller than the rest.

It was Joseph Goebbels who answered Arian Bandage. "He will have the sense kicked into him."

His companion had slumped down in his seat, his eyes darting over his glasses in a troubled pose. Bandage recognized the pair of Olympians who had just come through the door to watch the stage revue.

Goebbels' trained eye followed his path into the more softened light at the rear of the café. He noticed with a bemused expression, the deposed champion, Rachel Brach, and gave an indifferent stare towards her American companion. "They are no longer of interest to the Reich."

"Who?" asked Arian Bandage from a crouching stance.

"The Jews, or the auxiliary, jungle tribesmen. We have grown indifferent to the games. The purpose has already been met. The world has proven, - America has proven, - it will help us with our new Four Year Plan."

"Four years," said Bandage, distracted by a sudden call to attention, and a blast of music, piped into the make-shift theater.

"Yes, by September, 1940, Germany will be ready. Meanwhile, the world, *your* misguided America, can coddle its Jews, and we may have to search farther for a solution to the Jewish problem."

It was impossible to hear the Minister of Enlightenment and Propaganda. A bevy of beauties showed their long-legs and tapped synchronously across the barren stage, in sequined Prussian military costumes. Like deft swordsmen, the women raised their gleaming weapons so that the male audience could admire their form, their supple attractions and ample allure.

Twenty-eight pair of bare legs marched in perfect precision. Hips thrust, calves exposed, and with a slight turn, derrieres performed military maneuvers.

That was the one accepted form of entertainment that could not be taken from the masses, no matter the circumstances, Goebbels knew. It was also his favorite pastime as well.

From the rear of the cabaret, Joshua found Rachel's lips, focused on him. That was not the place to talk of Palestine, she thought.

And Joshua would've been content with his petting party in the corner of The Scala, except for the presence of those eyes that seemed to triangulate on his table; the one, blazing, studying, and cataloguing alongside his companion of the leased machines. The other was barely focused, even shame-faced under his gold-rimmed glasses. Arian Bandage, desired the ladies from head to toe, but was disturbed by Rachel and Joshua's presence in a way he had never known.

Bandage rose bravely from his slouching positon, and caught Joshua's full stare. Gratitude, even admiration, flowed from the

Olympian's eyes. It took a great man, Joshua thought, to fight all obstacles and field a multi-racial team in the heart of a racist nation.

Joshua hoped the message was as clear as an embrace between a father and son, departing for war. He would represent America proudly, and when the dawn broke and the preliminaries began, he would honor his nation with victory. He was going to honor, not only to his own kind, but Bandage's name as well.

But Bandage had a different thought, watching Joshua with a taut, cryptic gaze. What if Rachel Brach joined the chorus line? Her dark hair would then be noticed, a discordant note in the symmetry of the ideal. At first the German girls would welcome her. They would shower her with affection. Her sword would be gleaming; her hips, proud, and her posture perfect. Each nuance would capture the moment for a while.

Then, unnaturally, she would exhibit the foul breath of separation, perhaps her diet was tainted, and then would the Aryan fear her presence; their blood would be made unclean, even by her fragrance. The girls on the line marching, muscular arms waving swords, and the cracked sequins between their legs glittering – those were the girls with strength and allure.

Goebbels and Goering wanted four more years to bring the new Germany back among the powers of the earth. America was the engine of that process infusing capital and know-how, reducing the reparations debt. Wall Street, as well as the greater nation, would profit handsomely from mutual respect. Goebbels said the Germans didn't care about the games, but Bandage saw the greater implications of the Jewish victory that would begin tomorrow, for he had read Joshua's mind.

On the stage, the girls paraded, revealing much exposure for the screaming crowd. Their high Prussian headdresses discarded; flowing auburn, brown, blonde, even orange hairs brushed around the stage. Who could deny that delectable world that was also good for American business?

It was only the Jew-communist who saw another world. Joshua could revitalize Jewish interests, help create a frenzy of Jewish sports enthusiasts, help destroy an Aryan myth, and more. A Jewish victory, more than embarrassing the fuehrer, could threaten the Master Plan.

Why would Jews immigrate to Palestine if they were sustained, and not marginalized by America? Germany needed world-wide domination of the Jew, and then Jewish blood as fuel to satisfy their quest, their ideals of one world, under the dictator of the people. Service of an entire world to one world purpose, Bandage thought, wasn't a bad idea.

What did Joseph Goebbels say about a four year plan? *America could do that plan in three.* Working together with the Nazi Reich, America would help ready them by September, 1939, not 1940. Germany could have another year of golden prosperity.

It was not race prejudice, but since their massive protests, Bandage had no love for Jews or dark- haired beauties. He would permanently ban the brunette, Holm-Jarrett, from ever competing in an amateur event again. And the Jews, Joshua and Bobby Gillman, the word 'Jew' now rolling from his lips, were like a disease.

No, that would not do. Leaning on the crooked shoulder of Goebbels, Arian Bandage rose. He was a little wobbly. "The phone, *damnination*, I need the phone while it's all so damn clear." And he was helped by many arms. It was only business, after all.

The clock had just struck twelve, and the beautiful chorus twittered like birds, bending over, to and fro, "Cuckoo." And Rachel kissed Joshua who felt suddenly alive. The strength in his limbs was ready to take her again, but there was little time for play. In just two days, on his birthday, he would know what Jesse knew three times over-how it felt to stand with the oak tree and the laurels of victory.

"Until then," he whispered, as he held Rachel, "when we'll have the last laugh."

"Yes, we have tomorrow," she said, holding him with all her might, but her eyes watched the drunken display near center stage. A man with horn rimmed glasses was being restrained from kissing the feet that were still tapping on stage. Rachel laughed at the greater spectacle. She was content to believe that fate would be kind to her Olympian in his race for glory around the unforgiving graveyard for would- be hopefuls.

"Until tomorrow," she said, drawing closer for one more kiss, one more time, in the city that was about to run out of time for the likes of them.

30

Saturday, August 8, 1936

Coach Robertson limped inside the athlete's quarters, tapping his cane and talking quietly to a few of the runners. He spoke to Jesse Owens and then to a newshound, when Jesse cringed. His eyes seemed to find Joshua's, seated nearby, but his eyes were closed, and Jesse had no grin. A rumor had circulated that there was going to be a change for the 4x100 meter race.

The naming of the runners was all but certain. Dave, Tom, Joshua, and Bobby were already in place. If there were a change, Bobby thought, then it would be in Warren's position. In the competitions, it was Davie Warren who consistently came in last. He thought, as rumors had circulated, that Ralph Metcaffe would take Davie Warren's place.

But Ralph with two, silver, and Jesse's three, gold were tired athletes. Jesse slumped forward. His eyes were heavy, he had had little sleep. The committee had told him he had to pack for yet another European meet after the Games. Jesse won the two hundred meter gold medal as expected, two days before. During competition, he had lost ten pounds. He was gaunt, starry-eyed, seemed drugged with exhaustion. He and Ralph Metcaffe had never passed the stick to each other. What they added in speed was lost if a fatal error occurred: the wrong pass of the baton. So just what was that meeting about?

Tom and Davie had become closer to them. As time went by, the forced competition didn't matter. The four would race for gold unless something crazy happened. Tom played the guitar, and Joshua curled his hands and impersonated Tex Ritter in "Sing, Cowboy, Sing." He was hilarious, his body roaming the room as if he were riding a horse.

Joshua told Jesse he'd be willing to use him in the next Tarzan movie, after he made it big. He could play the "auxiliary, jungle tribesman!" Jesse doubled over with laughter. He stayed on the bed, laughing, as he imagined how American audiences, blacks, especially, would take to that. They would tear the seat covers apart.

Davie told stories of famous pilots of the Great War. He said he wanted to learn how a Trojan could fly. Mack Robinson spoke fondly of his younger brother whom, he said, did amazing things with a ball and bat. Matt told them to remember the name, Jackie Robinson.

***

The meeting got crazy soon. Davie was standing, but smaller than The Dean who formed a circle around him, surrounded him like a bear. Robertson was at the door, tapping the cane and trying to choose his words, his head down, his eyes unseen. When someone banged at the door to the rooms, The Dean scowled, "Get away!"

It was a gangster film. Robertson was the look-out. Nobody could go in or out. Suddenly, from the cane, lead pumped into Bobby Gillman's brain. Robertson let them have it straight between the eyes.

"The Germans saved their best for last. We have reports they are training in secret. They want to humiliate us. So are the Netherlanders and the Finns. We're going to make a change."

Dean came closer to Bobby's missed heartbeat. Around the circle, air grew suddenly scarce. Jesse blinked uncomfortably. He felt like glass. Robertson coughed and cleared his throat. His face showed the disfigurement of long ago. It grew uglier with his words.

"We have to send our fastest men. The four man team will consist of Jesse Owens, Ralph Metcaffe, Tom Grace, and Dave, Davie Warren."

Bobby rose. "That's not true. The Germans don't have any threat of any kind. There is nobody on their team who is a world class sprinter, and none have ever been in world competition. Nobody, Coach, and that's the truth."

The only sprinter the Nazi had was Erich Borchmeyer who was fifth in the hundred meter run. Bobby thought all seven Americans could beat him. Damn, anyone in Prospect Park could beat them.

"I have unassailable information," Coach Robertson said.

"Coach, "it was Jesse Owens, and he commanded the floor. He voice, hoarse, and body run down, it was hard to talk, hard to make a sound. But he looked toward Joshua and shared hearts. His head sank into the middle of his words.

"Let Joshua run this race. He's been at it for a month. He's beaten all competition. I'm tired. I already won three gold medals. Bobby and Josh deserve their race."

From the center of the room, a small hulk crouching with all the venom it could muster, pointed a finger and cast a shadow on the bare walls.

"Shut up, you'll do what you're told," said The Dean.

No matter the false legends, the tale of Jesse's ambitions, or other authoritative fictions, Bobby Gillman knew the truth in his heart. Owens was a true friend, and a man of courage and fair-play. Yeah, he may have said a few words. He was exuberant about his performance. But he'd never want to replace Joshua who shared a special place in Jesse Owens' heart.

Bobby would remember that moment until his dying day. He was red-faced by then. It was as if he had been punched in the gut. It still hadn't sunk in –the finality, and what the words of the Coach really meant. But he held back somewhat. He was eighteen years old. In four more years, he would be the fastest human on the American team. He thought about the land of the rising sun – Japan, in 1940. He would have to filter his tongue, not to say the thought that was on the lips of everyone. The foul word nobody dared to say was 'Anti-Semitism.'

"This won't sit well with the American Press. They're going to say it may not be coincidence that two Jewish boys were let go at the last minute," he said.

"Well, you just let me handle that, "said The Dean, clapping his hands, dismissively.

"Okay, so let's go, there's a race to be run."

Only much later, did Bobby know how wounded he'd been – he was a casualty, then, in a time known later to the world as the Holocaust. And Bobby saw that Joshua had lost more than a dream. He seemed to lose something, put his hand to his head. His face had whitened, the color drained. His body seemed unsupported. He slipped out of the chair.

The face of his betrayers was the hardest blow to take. It was blackface for real. It was as if Joshua never raced Warren or Grace to be faster than them, to beat his rivals. It was as if he were suddenly strangling, the entire weight of the Earth beating down on him.

Even though he had beaten them; beaten his nearest competition again and again, he was still the "also ran." But this time, Joshua stiffened, he wouldn't be racing again. The thought pounded him senseless, though he tried to make sense of that concept.

Just yesterday, during the last competition, Bobby and Joshua were one, two, and Davie, gasping, a poor third. Robertson wanted the fastest to run against an imaginary Hitler attack, and divined Warren to be one of those runners, though his own eyes saw Warren fade consistently to last, and his coach's own words had already named Sellers and Gillman to the four man team.

"Joshua," said Bobby, hoping to bond with the fallen athlete. "Joshua," he said, again, as the others filed out. Luckily, nobody saw that he was crying. He wanted to share his suffering with his companion. The others barreled past Robertson's cane, eager to leave the airless chamber where hurt had been given and taken. But Joshua was already gone.

31

Sunday, August 9, 1936, Berlin, Germany.

A hundred and ten thousand citizens of the Third Reich, packed the Nazi stadium as before. The popular relay event was about to begin the finals. The Netherlanders came on the field first, followed by the Italians, and the hometown German favorites.

On the sidelines, the Americans clustered about the assistant coaches. Bobby Gillman still hoped for a miracle. The coaches had changed their minds before. Newshounds knowing something unprecedented had happened –the first ever disqualification of able and fit Olympians from an American team- waited for the absentee coaches, and the official word.

Men in white butcher's frocks were busy cordoning off the track area into quarters. The twenty yard distance was carefully measured from which the runners were to hand over the precious baton. The race was to begin at the far turn, and end in front of the Honor Loge, where Herr Hitler and his cronies, eagerly bobbed for a better view.

Bobby Gillman, his eyes moist and heavy, didn't take part in the final pairings. He didn't want to play odd man out. Hands in his pockets, he walked away to the infield to watch the race.

Yesterday, Bobby also witnessed the trial heat along the infield and licked his wounds. When Owens handed off to Metcalfe, it was him that took the baton and raced for glory. Inside, he was hurt, confused, and angry. But a patriot all the way, he rooted for his country that won the race easily, and tied the world record of forty seconds.

Those "'secret" Nazis work-outs were worth a dead last finish. Bobby cursed softly, but he didn't know why. Again, he thought of Tokyo, four years hence. If he were angry, it was mostly at himself. Had he done better at Randall's Island, he'd have easily qualified. He might even have been a medal contender in the hundred meters.

He looked to the honor loge, saw Hitler grimace at the poor Nazi showing. Near him, wearing his patented framed glasses, Arian Bandage sat down without a care in the world.

"A boil in your throat," Bobby cursed, softly, in Yiddish. But he turned quickly around, afraid that his words would be heard.

Maybe the expulsion from the team was a bad dream, he mused later, inside a restless sleep that had him wake up to put on his running shoes, and go down into a crouch to wait for the handoff of the baton from speedy Joshua, but Joshua wasn't there, and the baton dropped into the fog that woke him. He no longer knew where he was, or what part of that dream was true. Joshua hadn't been on the infield, or in the Olympic Village. Poor Joshua, he thought, fully awakened. He knew that blow below the belt was hardest on the Michigan sprinter. Poor Joshua, he thought, awakening again, as if he were moving in triplicate. On that foggy Sunday morning, it was an imperfect day to have a birthday party celebration in Berlin.

"Owens, front and center," bellowed Dean.

"Yeah, here Coach," said Jesse Owens.

"Metcalffe. You ready, boy, to run for gold?"

"Yeah,' said Metcalfe, adding, "boss."

The Dean stiffened at Metcalfe's sarcasm, but soon beamed with pride. His own men would take the field for the blessed Trojans of U.S.C.

"Davie, and the Golden boy –Tom Grace, an American hero, you two let's go for gold."

"Right here, Coach," Tom Grace said, somewhat softly as he peered at Bobby Gillman, and shared his pain. Tom Grace, throughout his life, would maintain that Joshua Sellers and Bobby Gillman were replaced for one reason only, anti-Semitism.

***

The 4x100 Meter Relay Finals, Berlin, Sunday, August 9, 1936.

The starter raised his gun toward a pale, gray sky. The runners for the four man event got set, and took their marks, and when the shot rang out, were up and off around the cinders.

From the start, it was no contest. Jesse Owens opened a five yard lead over his nearest rival. At the first hand-off, Metcalfe cleanly embraced the baton and extended the American lead to eight over the hapless Netherlanders, and the Italians who were surprisingly making a bid for second place. Far back, the listless Germans ran well off the pace.

Then trouble happened so fast that only an experienced relay runner, or an adroit newsman, could tell. Metcalfe was running fast, much faster than Davie Warren, and too fast to pass the stick cleanly to him. That was the vision Bobby Gillman had already imagined. That was the horror awaiting the hapless change at the eleventh hour. The excuse for the change, the Germans, measured twenty lengths off the pace. But American teamwork, borne of practice and care, was gone.

Metcalfe was so fast he was at the edge of overstepping his bounds. One of the judges moved toward the sidelines, his body hunched, his hands about to lodge a protest. Bobby Gillman, believing the Americans had fouled, groaned from the sidelines.

In the momentary process of decision, the judge relaxed and made no further movement. No foul called, Warren responded to the challenge and improved the American lead to ten yards. The Italians nosed past the Netherlanders for second. Tom Grace came toward the finish, waving the baton in a final burst, screaming in victory; his face, heated with fury, as he thrust his fist with the stick, aimed high towards the face of the Nazi fuehrer.

The Netherlanders had dropped the baton, and Grace breezed home to a new world's record. The Italians were far behind, and the Nazis, whom were "saving their best for last," were, indeed, last to finish. The time was under forty seconds, a new world's record.

32

Sunday, August 9th, 1936.

Joshua was in a corner of the stadium split like an ax that had cut him in two. A world apart, he faced the track with heavy eyes and a howling inside his head. It was that little fist, like a child's, pounding, pounding inside his head. His lonesome gaze always returned to the Chancellor of the host nation. From where he would be handed the baton, and for his start in the one hundred meters around the oval, he'd be able to see the plush place where the monster sat. Hitler would have to watch a Jew beat a Nazi, beat all Germans of the master race.

That would be his moment of triumph, and a promise kept to a crippled kid in Prospect Park. By then, his resolve was translated into German past that thin line bordering on madness. The words of the coaches yesterday no longer mattered. It was now his twenty-first birthday, not a time to shatter dreams.

One last time, one chance, he knew his legs could outrace Jesse's that morning. He could tear down that track, and give the Americans a lead that they would never give back. His heart told him he was going to race today. G-d, he would never be that close to Hitler again. He wanted the Nazi to smell his rage. He didn't feel that way before the meeting yesterday, but he felt that way now. Rage his friend wanted an answer. The wolverine had bloodthirsty veins.

He had been altered by the meeting, but not in obvious ways. Even Rachel wouldn't understand. Her Palestine and lofty ideals were too distant. She was going there not to fight, but to flee. She'd never know that Jewish vengeance was brought on screaming, fleshless wings. If he ever saw her again, he'd tell her that. Tell her he was held back in the temple of doom.

   He had to whisper there for fear of disturbing the hell borders. He saw, where songs and poetry used to reside, a montage of human faces being sliced of flesh, of graven images that would send crippled kids into furnaces; of wild, unwavering dances to the gods that stole that race.

   Joshua thought about Schiller and his cranes. They flew from *Ibycus* in horrific flight to stop an injustice from triumphing again. He thought about the true meaning of what that race was really about. The tormentor had traded places with the scapegoat in the last battle of the apocalypse.

   Robertson said secret work-outs bothered him. Hadn't he known that Joshua could beat even Mercury today? What the real truth was, they'd never say. Yet, it may have been so simple. Who fit in and who did not? Who walked among men, and who was forced to kneel? Whose vision would come out on top, Hitler's, or his?

   Joshua was ready, cool and determined. When his teammates circled the coaches, he removed his warmup jersey. Joshua remembered sandlot games, and the rules that everyone knew by heart. In baseball, it often happened that a small group of friends didn't have enough kids to finish the game. If one was a runner on base, but he was also called to bat, an invisible runner could be imagined to be on the base pads. He was called a ghost runner, and had a job to do. That runner would be moved along by the movement of the batter. When the ball was hit by the live batter, the invisible one took off around the bases. When the batter reached third base, the ghost runner would score. Joshua walked over to his teammates. He was going to race invisibly. He was going to move everyone along. He was a ghost runner now.

When Metcalfe almost fouled, Joshua was brought to his knees. He inched his way along the infield, closer than anyone had ever been to the Honor Loge.

Miraculously, unnoticed due to the race, he rested under the hateful gaze of the monster whom he wanted to see. But Joshua was even madder than him. He was robbed and humiliated in front of strangers. His own American family had made him an outcast among men, and, suddenly, he was not an American, but an object of ridicule, condemned on his twenty-first birthday, by the one hundred and ten thousand Nazis who'd kept one of the fastest men on earth under its collective fascist heel.

Joshua couldn't find words to describe how he had been altered. A good word as any, Joshua felt violated. The pain was unendurable.

He was a hairsbreadth away from them, now, from Hitler and the rest. He was so close, he could smell them. The weather was dry and clear. The time, 3 P.M., on an August day, his birthday. Hitler should know his pain, but not only the Nazi leader. Who was he, anyways?

Joshua wanted to scream to the entire stadium, the entire Nazi nation; even to their unborn, and to the next generation. His hand grazed the balcony where in a startled way the leader of the Nazi nation sat. He was being pricked in the ribs by the tireless Italian Count Umberto again.

Joshua was also startled. His arm was already in a fighting pose, and his hand was poised to deliver a staggering blow. He saw that Hitler was scraping some inner skin off his agitated cheeks with his tongue. Joshua smelled some foul pomade. It may have been Hitler's, or Umberto's. The Count kept talking, and saw nothing but Hitler's ear. A fly came and buzzed about.

Then Hitler turned unperturbed at Joshua, and the fist that lied squarely there, ready to smash the bones beyond Hitler's cheek. And the nose. And the mouth. He'd tear the flesh from his mustache. Rachel said the Nazis did that to the gray beards of old Jewish men. He would not stop until there was nothing left of him but blood and bones.

He was close enough then to curse him. "Kike."

Hitler faced him bravely, but his eyes blinked. Somewhere inside him, the word must have had meaning. Joshua's presence was a memory in a twisted brain. Nazi projective fear had come of age. Those were the Jews, thought Hitler. Those were the ones who would make them afraid. Because they need to destroy us, we must root them out, never to return. But Joshua stopped his punch in mid-air.

He didn't want to hurt Hitler. He just wanted to give him a love-tap from the Jewish nation.

He closed in a circle of distraught. 'I stopped my punch in mid-air,' he thought, as much confused as anybody else.

It wasn't even Hitler's fault. The treachery had come from much closer. The betrayal wasn't planned by Nazis, but by his own people- by Americans who were nearer to his heart. Would anybody listen to him? Would anyone ever hear his voice again? Joshua felt dizzy, as many hands came to grab his fist that was flexed to deliver a staggering blow. 'I'll smash him,' he thought, his eyes deciding that, as the furies rose towards der fuehrer's filthy face.

Then, there was shouting at Hitler's Loge, and at the finish. Tom Grace rushed in with raised baton, and a terrified cry. His proud run had ended in shock when he saw what his teammate was about to do. Onto the track, the coaches came: Lawson Robertson, the old man with a cane, followed by the Methodist bear, hateful and proud, The Dean, a slob through and through.

But even they weren't to blame. Joshua scanned the seats directly above the Fuhrer's Loge. He found the man in the gold-rimmed glasses.

Into the general pandemonium, a dozen of Hitler's elite S.S. guard wielded their weapons. Yet, before one frame of film could be shot, Joshua was subdued, but not yet pounded into oblivion by the S.S., no longer smiling, but gurgling with hate; their white truncheons, suddenly transformed to black shakos and more weapons, a storehouse of Berlin's illegal S.S. instruments of torture. His would be a quick interrogation. But then, an event happened simultaneously.

Greg Morris had been declared the winner of the decathlon. The Americans had swept the Gold, Silver, and Bronze. Near the honor loge, the American champion groaned like a creature in a man-made jungle trap, and jumped into the lap of his mistress, Leni Riefenstahl. Morris used two hands in one motion to rip off her blouse. Goebbels got his ill-gotten gift. He knew he had dreamed it before- that scene frozen in time, but only remembered in Riefenstahl's warped memories when she had reached the ripe old age of one hundred and one, and died. Soon, with cocked guns, the entourage of Nazi police paused to watch the three ringed circus, in which everything wasn't as it seemed.

Into the arms of Joshua Sellers, came the four man Olympic team. Tom Grace, the last man on the run, hugged him first, and then came Jesse Owens who had just won his fourth gold medal of the Olympic Games. Jesse tried to hug Joshua in friendship, though neither could look at the other; the one, ashamed, the other, hurt beyond expression. Jesse had run in Joshua's place. Jesse felt he stole something precious from him that could never be replaced.

Coach Dean was there frantic and bellicose. If the Coach had just one moment alone with Joshua Sellers, he'd waste that 'damn' son of a gun. Coach Robertson's cane was raised ready to finally shoot the bullets Bobby Gillman had imagined.

But Joshua wasn't finished yet. While the coaches tried to downplay the events near the fuehrer's box, Joshua saw the face he was really looking for. Bandage's appeared from above, whitened into a mask, and he seemed scared to death. His massive arms came down in a bear hug to grab Joshua who looked inside the intruder's evil eyes without flinching, and that time paid him no respect. His hands were held securely behind him, but his heart and mind were enough to stare Bandage down with a greater rage. Joshua saw what he never wanted to see before when he was growing up in the streets of Cincinnati- the ashen face of race hatred. That was the reason for the face that had betrayed him then. At that moment, like lovers on a mission of mutual hate, Bandage pursed his lips, but Joshua spat first.

Bandage wasn't alone for Joshua to hate. Breaking through the hold of his teammates, who formed a wedge around him that shocked the S.S. into lowering their weapons, came another cordon, a gauntlet more powerful than Joshua Sellers could bear. He'd seen them before in the eyes of his betrayer. Bandage had served them, and catered to their interests. Those were the alphabet soup of the initialed men that cheered him on at the pier, who came aboard the Manhattan, adored the ladies and laughed at the Jewish jokes at the cabaret, or at Goebbels's parties, or at the lavish air ministry affairs. In attendance were the faces of the American financiers who held Joshua down in the strongest grip of all –the one hardest to break, the invisible grip of anti-Semitism. And Joshua began to understand the extent of his betrayal, when loving eyes came to save him.

Nobody stopped her at the gate. She was still the German champion, and her love was stronger than their hate. Bathing his face with the light of her kisses, Rachel heard the catcalls coming from the Honor Loge.

Even on a clear day, spit fell like rain. She thought she heard Hitler hissing, but she didn't dare look up. The world had turned upside down, she thought, shielding Joshua from the searchlights aimed at his swollen eyes. He walked bent over, bloodied, but thought his sorrow was no disgrace. He knew that was what it was about-to be humiliated- on his twenty-first birthday. Not by his enemies, but friends. As if Jewish blood was somehow contagious, the circle grew wider, and he was left to pass.

The heels of history were also passing him by. Hitler wanted to see the American swimmers. Goebbels wanted to adore a new female aesthetic. Leni Riefenstahl had passed already into history.

Rachel walked him through the gauntlet, his eyes closed, blinded by the knowledge they might never really open again. Rachel held him, and didn't let go. She saw past the top of Marathon Gate, toward the steps that led down the bustling streets of *Unter den Linden*, the train station, the ships of call, the European nations, the transit visas, the payments of transfer, and their final destination, delivered from Nazis and their ever-widening circle of friends, into a new world to fight for, to be built from ashes, when the fires no longer would rage so furiously against them.

"We are going home to Palestine. You will see, it is a home that will never be taken from us, ever."

And Joshua knew that he was no longer welcome in America, the land he loved, the home he knew.

"Palestine," he said, "a home I don't know, and the earth I can't touch."

"Imagine,' she said, imagine with me, paradise."

If it were paradise, then it would be a paradise of broken pieces, he thought, walking through the Nazi gauntlet toward that abstracted desert in the East.

33

The climax of the Eleventh Olympiad came with the victory of Son Kitei, born in the Japanese colony of Korea. The victor greeted well-wishers from behind swaths of wet sheets. He was surrounded by weeping fans that tiptoed over to him with rose petals. Putting their heads silently on his breast, even hard-nosed Jap journalists burst into tears.

"We have been preparing for this event for twenty-four years. Now that it is here, we can hardly believe we have won."

Son Kitei smiled. What else could he do? A student in Japan, but homesick for an oppressed people, Son Kitei, (which wasn't even his real Korean name) cried when the Japanese flag was raised at the medal ceremony. His own coaches, knowing his tears weren't for joy, wouldn't let him take the Grecian mask in honor of his victory.

That night, Dr. James A. Naismith, the founder of the game of basketball, searched feebly for the reception that was being given in his honor. In making out the invitations, his name had been omitted by the United States Olympic Committee.

The good will between nations was also lost as the Games wound down. Angered by a ruling in a soccer match with Austria, Peru packed and went home. Leading 4-2 against the favored 'hometown' team, it was alleged that some of the Peruvian fans attacked the Austrian team. When the referees decided to replay the entire game, Peru bolted for home.

Among the United States squad, the strain of the past two weeks began to show. Led by the female American swimmers who had still not forgiven Bandage for the dismissal of Eleanor Holm.

"The committee didn't mingle with us, and spent a good deal of time squabbling among themselves. There were so many times when small favors which meant nothing financially would have made us happy, but our officials could not, or would not see things that way."

Another was even more upset. Mrs. Dorothy Poynton Hill said: "I think there wasn't a happy athlete on this Olympic trip." After capturing her second high platform diving championship, Mrs. Hill joined her other teammates who made a quick exodus from German Stadium for home.

Only Margorie Gestring enjoyed her stay. She had become a star atop the Olympic world by her victory in the springboard competition. As the youngest athlete ever to win a gold medal, she faced the trans-Atlantic radio cables, and a sea of international reporters, to thank her parents. Meanwhile Mrs. Rawls, who placed second, and was her closest competitor, booked an early passage on the U.S.S. Roosevelt. Other Olympians followed suit.

Perhaps, the last ones to understand the true nature of the Berlin Games, the American Olympians were tired of the propaganda of the New Reich and the United States Olympic Committee. For as the Games approached an end, Nazi newspapers were more nationalistic. Editorials proclaimed the Nazis supermen. Counting all medals equally, in a rare display of Nazi democracy, the Nazi scoring system had them far out in front. They claimed sixty-five points in the equestrian competition, eighty-seven in gymnastics, twenty-seven in cycling, nineteen in fencing, forty-three in canoeing. Added to the fifteen medals in architecture, and other non- athletic events, the Nazi Press didn't mention the abysmal showing of their male athletes in track and field, or that, in a male-dominated society, it took a superior performance by their women to put them over the top.

In the past, Americans stayed on in European capitals when the games ended. The Eleventh Olympiad, however, broke that tradition with outward hostility toward the American Olympic Committee. The leader of the revolt was also the captain of the team, four time gold medal champion, Jesse Owens. By the time the embers had died away on the sporting pageant, he was suspended by the Amateur Athletic Union, and threatened with having his name erased from the records he had just broken. Jesse came into conflict with them when he refused to honor commitments in post-Olympic competitions.

With all the money he had spent, and with no provisions made for him for food and lodging in the capitals of the Scandinavian countries where the American athletes went after the British Empire Games, he knew he had reached the end.

Without considering the circumstances, the A.A.U. suspended the champion. In America, Owens' family reacted to the news. His wife was shocked. She told Jesse not to finish his last year at Ohio State, but go for the money instead. "'In my house, I'll make the final decision," Jesse said, "at least, until I get home."

Although his medals were not taken away, he was very upset. "I'm sick of running. The track business is a racket where the A.A.U. gets all the money collected in the United States, and then comes over to Europe and gets half the proceeds. I've lost sixteen pounds, and I was skinny when I started. I need to go home."

34

The sun set between the pillars around Marathon gate. The great fire on the altar of the gateway rose in a last thrust skyward as the victors of the final competition were crowned. Soon, the floodlights shone brightly over the oval as a gun boomed a distant reprise. By the bell tower, on the near horizon, a white-clad army of choir boys, marched in single file, while the trumpeters climbed the tower with their trumpets outstretched along the dying pastel sky.

Rockets fell over the stadium and burst into beams of white, swirling flames. Simultaneously, in regular intervals, searchlights from outside the arena converged in a dazzling array that bombarded the stadium with crossing white lights.

After the blast of trumpets, and a march from the majestic Berlin Philharmonic Orchestra, the flagbearers of the nations formed, as a line under the lights near the rostrum of the fuehrer, signaling the final moments of the Eleventh Olympiad.

In reverse order the athletes came. Germany, the host of nations, in Nazi snow white, appeared first on the green turf and red cinder path. They were followed by the athletes of the United States, Uruguay, and after a parade of other also ran's, Greece filled the great arena to capacity.

With the large scarlet swastikas of the host nation, waving on all sides of the hallowed rostrum, the white-haired father of the Games, Baron Henri de Baillet-Latour, said:

"In the name of the International Olympic Committee, after having offered to the Fuehrer and Chancellor, Adolf Hitler, and to the German people, to the authorities of the city of Berlin, and to the organizers of the Games our deepest gratitude, we proclaim the closing of the Eleventh Olympic Games, and accordance with tradition, we call upon the youth of every country, to assemble in four years in Tokyo, there to celebrate with us, the Twelfth Olympic Games.

With booms of cannons and bursts from the orchestra, and a chorus from Beethoven's hymn, 'The Flame Dies,' fifty-four white- uniformed girls walked to the rostrum, bearing laurel wreaths, and faced the flag bearers before placing the wreaths on the flags that were lowered for that solemn time.

As the farewell song ended, the Olympic flame on the altar above Marathon Gate, seemed to suddenly die down. With the dimming of the lights, the crowd stood in silence until white-uniformed sailors unfastened, and carried the Olympic flag to the rostrum where it was threaded and presented to Lee May Garland, representing the city of Los Angeles as the last host city of the Olympic Games. Walking between twelve German fencers who guarded the great flag with drawn swords, Garland gave the Burgomaster of Berlin the banner that was to be held until the Tokyo Games of 1940.

***

At about the time the Olympic flame died, and the first burst of cannon and flares were heard in the stadium, Joshua Sellers began walking aimlessly in the streets of Berlin.

A week of misery had passed since he was told he couldn't run on the red cinders. His was fire that had suddenly stopped raging; an animal struck by lightning, but still alive. When teammates offered support, or gave him money they thought he needed, he reacted strangely to the humiliation he felt inside.

Over three hundred athletes, some with a dollar, some with two, came shamefaced to his quarters, as if they had something to do with the treachery of the American coaches. After the first refusal, Joshua took the money. He counted dollar by dollar and paced the floors of the athletes' quarters. Left to himself, neither books nor music helped relieve him of the oppressive weight that hung over his head. Only the thoughts about that money could relieve him from more dangerous thoughts. Vengeance was a lead weight about to burst into the toxic air.

Joshua thought he was bleeding during his troubled dreams about the outrage –there was no other word, he thought – given the chance, he would climb the pedestals again toward the honor loge and meet the fuehrer with a stronger hand.

Over the years that followed, he would relive that moment, each time hate thrusting an iron fist into that flat jaw that held such contemptible regard for his race. But then, he didn't want to kill Hitler. He only wanted to get his attention.

Joshua felt he had left the home and hearth he knew, those guideposts anchored on solid earth that he no longer felt to be his own. There had not been a sudden shift of the seismic earth, but he felt no longer whole, or part of Michigan, or the cinders, or the American songs he loved. He was displaced, chewed up, and in choose-up, he was the odd man out.

"No Jews allowed."

Those signs displayed in every place of business were now directed toward him, not by individuals or by foreign government decree. That sign came from the country he loved – his country- only America had betrayed him. America's dark hand played for gain, in the time known as the Holocaust. America had paved an easier path for the Nazi serpent to swallow Jews and mankind.

He made that leap from self to all Jew as an entire race of outcasts. He had thought he was first an American, a son of the strongest nation on earth. Nation above race, above ideology – he'd competed against fascists to the steps of glory only to fall from grace. The race to avenge his race wasn't going to happen. He was used by Americans into helping Hitler make the world *Judenfree.*

He had stepped out into a crack in time. A rising sun and red summer moon were all the same. He cried beside the artificial lake, and in a lazy mist after the Berlin rains, he found a place to wallow in misery.

Out of the shadows of the lake, he began to feel surrounded by the presence of ghosts, similar in form, with eerie shapes. He welcomed their presence beside him.

His mother came first with sad, blue eyes. She welcomed him home, but had nothing more to say between the pot roast and boiled potatoes. With a wave of the hand, he tossed the food away.

His classmates from the early days held hands and danced, and prodded him with bones. Joshua could feel neither the anger, nor rage that had once engaged him with their taunting, and tossed them into the murky mist.

He saw Rachel, her green eyes hovering over the dark waters in glistening emerald glass, that soon gathered seaweed and leaves that were falling from the lindens, to cover her in natural cloth.

"Go away," he said, sadly, but startled, when out of the distant waters, rose the form he had been waiting for. His father sat down beside him, touching him with a weighty grip. Joshua sighed with childlike pleasure as together they watched the mist swirl above the waters, and rush toward them, at a feverish clip. He had so much to say to the man he had hardly known. What better place than there by the mist, and the muck, and the magical waters? Joshua said, "You look wonderful, papa."

"Must be the formaldehyde," said the ghost.

"Forever is a long time without you," Joshua cried.

"Ahhh, it is not me who creates paradise, or destroys dreams. I am always close to you in your mind and heart."

"So what am I to do now?"

"It is not in your hands."

"There is no free choice, not for me, and not for the Jew. There aren't any dreams, not honor, not glory."

The ghost laughed, "I have often thought the same way."

"They aim to sacrifice the Jew to feed the German war machine, not just in Germany, but everywhere, even in America. Nothing is accidental."

"I was given the gift of speed only to be persecuted for running."

"I know, I know- and breathe but do not snore."

"But which way must I go?"

"East," said the wind, said the fog, and said the lackadaisical heavens. "We seem to always head east," it said, and was gone.

***

But East wasn't beyond eternity. It was there in the *Kurfurstendam* that played that "Jew-N' sensibility," called Jazz. Goebbels said East was also the promise of the Nazi future.

His head ached by the time he reached the streets of Berlin. Feeling dizzy along the roads, he came within the pulsating sounds, and the gaiety of the outdoor cafes. His hand rose to his temples. Music makers played their accordions while dreaming of more steady work – perhaps the S.S. were hiring, they thought, while happy tourists talked and drank coffee, Nazi imported Coca Cola, or German beer. He walked into the garden past the low shrubs and bushes. No light came from the houses there, despite the darkness of the Nazi night. Even the porch light was extinguished but for the frantic flying of fireflies, and the earth was cracked into darkness that overwhelmed his senses.

He was moving backwards in time with an unsteady gait. Disoriented in space with no moorings, no compass to guide him –was it the earth or him shifting in the sands, he couldn't be certain.

Running, (if he were running) toward the side of the house, he saw a lone light that flashed from within. He was horrified to discover he had a knife that, suddenly, gleamed in the reflection of light. A candle had been lit in the guestroom, he guessed.

He crouched under an open window like the dash man on his mark. He thought about the starter's gun, and the ritual of running. The ghouls in the crowd always hypnotized by the speed on the cinders. Many believed they were really watching an execution. How many really wished to see that pistol that pointed skyward, suddenly turn on one of the dash men?

After the starter orders, 'Get Set,' the crowd would be joyful for the bullet to descend into brain matter, or the back of the neck. That was the way the 4 x 100 meters relay was really run. His blood was shed, and he'd faced the bullet squarely-a casualty on Nazi soil. Ironic was history, he thought, raising the knife and stepping in between the curtains.

The candle's flame shone in bright and dark shadows, and flickered in concert with the fireflies that paraded blindly on the porch way. Moving closer to the light of the flame, Joshua brushed a nightstand that came from the foot of a small, Louis X1V, French-styled bed. He didn't think to look past the small footboard to the brass head. Had he been more awake, his entrance would have caused greater commotion, had someone other than him had been hiding in the shadows.

Walking to the guestroom, he heard a gurgling noise from down the hall. A great German grandfather clock with clear toned bells struck the hour. Afterward, the house on *Gregorstrasse* was voiceless, except for a slight undertone that Joshua thought to be a kitten. From the room he walked past, he heard an unmistakable human cry. Bewilderment was transformed to horror, as soon as he rushed back through the door.

With only the lone flame as his guide, Joshua stood in the middle of the room, his hands grasping the weapon. His eyes scanned the walls and the closets, and rested on the bed and the drawn curtains that rustled from the soft night winds. From the head of the bed, he saw Rachel lying there, and beside her, was *him.*

Joshua didn't know who the apparition was, and who himself was- him in bed with his lover, or him standing there in the shadows with a knife? Rachel awoke to the horror of the moment. Joshua had already left her bed for a more uncertain union with a tenuous ghost.

"Good-bye, Rachel," he said, dropping the knife. "I hope you find Palestine."

"They took your medals away," she said, rising from the bed, "but there are other dreams."

"What dreams?"

"Dreams of life, and, hope and, yes, love."

"It's time to go. It's really time to go. Get dressed."

He helped her out the window. She or he was bleeding from somewhere. He picked up the knife as her legs brushed- up against the low shrubs and bushes.

"Please," she whispered. Their hands clasped tightly. He lowered her gently on the grass.

"I'll find you when this darkness turns to light," he said, and let her go. His head was throbbing violently.

"Then you will never see me again."

"Go now, if you value your children's souls, you'll go tonight. Here's some money to buy an exit visa. It's enough to get you to Palestine, and take this," he said, handing her the knife.

"Slit anyone's throat that tries to stop you."

"And you, where will you go? This is no place for you."

"Ever see an animal without its head? I'm already dead, only the time is unknown."

Leaving her, he touched the pounding in his head. That little fist again, pounding him into oblivion. He knew he would never see her again.

35

He reached the grasslands, and beyond a cluster of woods another path, clamoring with sounds of deconstruction. The Olympians were gathering for the close of the games, but he had tired legs held down by the weight of his misery. In the awakening of the early changes of autumn, he ached for her with the palpable grief. "Rachel," he said, staggering along. But an inner voice mocked him; he was nothing but song and dance.

His heart beat faster when the American flag was unfurled along the parade grounds. He knew he'd have to live with the decisions he made about her, but what else could he do? America was still his home. He was a wolverine struck dumb on the tracks to glory, and not allowed to run. Betrayal had come not like a lightning bolt, but only in spasms that shocked the senses and confounded the heart. Taking off his running shoes, he ran shoeless through the thickets that burned through his soles.

He heard shots bursting through the village from the periphery of the adjacent parade grounds. A Nazi honor guard fired twenty-one rounds, and cannon boomed, seven more.

Floodlights basked the area where the dignitaries said, 'good-bye.' Von Ribbentrop and Bandage embraced. Imagine, they'd never thought they could weep so much from joy. Adolph Eichmann in full S.S. dress uniform listened to the words of the chairman of I.B.M. Watson told Eichmann it was just a matter of a few punch cards. Soon, he'd know all the names of the Jews. Yes, it was possible not just in Germany. In a little more time, you can begin cataloguing all of Europe."

Not usually prone to emotional responses, Eichmann opened his eyes wide.

"Even, Tommy ..." he started, but needed help.

Turning around, Tom Watson provided the quick answer to a monster's dream. He didn't want to be quoted. "Yes, even in America. With our business machines, there's no more room for *them* to hide."

America was their true partner in the growing racial war. Even Goebbels was shocked by the turn of events. Imagine the Jews of America catalogued? No country would harbor them. "So," Himmler told him only yesterday, "the world joins us after all. The Jew is on the edge. The nations will not stop our march to push them off."

"Theodor Herzl wants a final solution," said Eichmann.

"Well, then, Adolph, take your young wife and go to Palestine. See what can be done to move the transfer along. Of course, I believe, as the fuehrer has stated, there is only one final solution."

And Eichmann really looked forward to that trip to Palestine. He was a true Zionist, he thought, the last friend the Jews had in the world. At night, with his young bride, he thought of a trip to Palestine. The possibilities for play were endless.

American athletes doffed their straw hats and formed a lone line for the last inspired playing of the Star Spangled Banner. As their hats were tossed into the air, one great boom from a brass drum ended the ceremonies. Then the Olympians, under a crossbeam of headlights, seemed to disappear. The parade grounds were illuminated in a pre-dawn light that saw the presence of the last three buses that had not left the grounds. The top of the drab grays were down. The glistening, blue dress uniforms, bobbed in unison. Well- wishers came to whisper one last *auf wiedesehen*.

A lone trumpeter played Taps, mournfully, as the American banner came down, and the first of the three buses rumbled along the grounds. The second started with a jerky motion, hurtling the athletes forward. But the shock only lasted a moment as they passed into the hopes and memories of a new day.

And then the trumpeter wailed a lonesome reprise, and a drum rolled among the sounds of skyrockets, darting across the horizon to light a dazzling sight for the last bus to glean. In the haze on the infield tucked away from view, a man dressed in the black cloth of a reverend, waved a solitary wand.

From down the road, the monolithic stadium glowed like a jack o lantern, as floodlights flashed and sirens resounded. The noise was deafening; the last of the buses rumbled along the spacious grounds toward the well-lit Olympiastaad.

Another round of rockets glared above Olympic Village for the last awesome spectacle of the resurrected Grecian games. Brown- shirted Wehrmacht troops began to fill the empty spaces where the Americans had stayed.

It was time for the last unaccounted athlete to survey the site. Joshua had known, even before his high school days that a moment of glory could pass in the wink of an eye. That eye was closed now tearless for him. The starter's gun would sound no more. His speed and strength had already disappeared. High above him, a lone winged bird, screeching from a slender throat, flew over the garden and joined a swooping squadron with heinous cries.

He walked across the field toward the bastion of lights until he saw the last American bus, sputtering on the pavement some one hundred meters away. Above him, the gray dancing squadrons kept the gathering of army dogs at bay and paved a dark and foreboding path for him to follow. 'Beware,' they seemed to say, but Joshua heard nothing. Someone was shouting his name from the bus.

"Run," but he couldn't run; nor could he leave, as the bus turned and raced back for him. A hand reached over the railing, and something glistened nearby. Joshua lunged for the glowing object, his feet beginning to move, as the bus turned to pull away again.

"Run," said Bobby Gillman, again. It was a plea.

But still he couldn't run, seeing only a gleaming object that helped him along the way. He felt many hands lifting him on the bus, hearing the sheltering voices of friends below the flapping and screeching that came from above.

Bobby was more startled from what happened in the sky than by the sudden appearance of his lost teammate. Gray squadrons flapped and whooped about the bus with ghoulish, gleeful, cries. Things vast and vengeful were swooping down.

"Look at that!" he said, flailing his arms.

Joshua turned toward his teammate. Gillman had the hope of youth still in his eyes, but for Joshua there was nothing now but the object Jesse Owens had passed to him.

He thought about Rachel. She was strong and would survive. She must understand how he couldn't abandon America, nor ever stop loving her. He saw the wings come whirring above, and felt cold and chilled. He thought, perhaps, it was warmer in Palestine.

"What are they?" asked Bobby, shouting in wonder as the birds rushed by.

But for Joshua, they had come too late. He answered coldly, his emotions confounded. Hope and despair reigned together in his heart. He thought one last time of glory, and the dash men who ran like gods down from Olympus.

"Cranes, they are only cranes," he said, his anguished face peering into Jesse's saddened eyes, before tossing the object, a baton, high off the sides of the bus.

But the cranes swooped down in a furies' might to take the stick in mid-air, and with vengeful beaks, thrust it over the heads of the dignitaries before flying away into another screaming, gleeful, Berlin night sky.

36
Havana, Cuba, December 26, 1936.

Julio MaCaw was at least three times the circumference of Jesse Owens, but the sprinter was desperate for a pay day after the glory of the Olympic Games. He had listened, graciously, to the offers from American businessmen that had proved to be nothing but hot air. And he had three mouths to feed, though Ruth would have starved rather than agree for him to go to Havana. But Jesse never had a problem rolling the dice and taking his chances. Besides, he was taken to racetracks by Coach Riley, and watched how the horses ran with ease.

Horses, of which Julio MaCaw was a pedigree, had always run the way Jesse wanted to. With strength in his legs and lungs, and eyes focused, never wasting a muscle to pride or vanity. Jesse had wanted to race the horses and pulled Coach Riley by the sleeves. "No, no, Jesse, that's not the lesson." Jesse just couldn't resist the track.

Well, America, still didn't like its heroes doing degrading work. Bandage wouldn't lift the ban against him. His reach became stronger, as time went by. Only Jesse knew he couldn't eat Olympic gold medals at the family table. The Cubans offered him two hundred dollars for the event. The National Sports Festival included the first post season football game played outside the United States. And Jesse arrived on a boat with players from Villanova and Auburn to play in The Rhumba Bowl.

In Cuba, there was laughter and dancing under the royal palms, known as the feather-dusters of the gods. Wide avenues of the Prada greeted him. At the casinos, a black tie studded event, Jesse watched the roulette wheel spin, and the young women turned up in flowered dresses to admire him. He thought of Ruth and his little girl, and resisted temptation.

Little care did the rich show when Fulgencio Battista staged a coup d'état to seize power. He almost cancelled the Rhumba Bowl unless his face would be on the greeting card of the event.

Fate had brought him to Havana. At least he had found a track. Men in sports coats, and woman in gaily colored dresses, flooded beneath the grandstand. They drank, or smoked at special tables, felt the tropical air, and listened to the rhumba piped in on saxophones and trombones. On the track, the dust was already whirling when Julio MaCaw came out to greet him.

Inside, he thought he was a freak in a freak show, but his typical charm won the sponsors over. "I don't need a forty yard handicap," he said.

But he did. Jesse went all out. Not an Olympic best, but enough to hear the rage of muscle and the breath of the horse, barreling in on him. Down the track, Jesse was frightened. He knew Julio was boring in, but he never looked back, and won by a horse's neck to the delight of the merry crowd. When his hands took the winnings, it was shaking.

He couldn't wait to lay down the money to his wife and child. He couldn't wait to get back home. It was a new year in track and field, and he knew he was going to miss it. But now the track was clear for Joshua Sellers. Joshua was going to get his turn.

37
Ferry Field, Ann Arbor, Michigan, May 7, 1937.

"Take me back to my boots and saddle,
" Oh, oh, oh, oh; oh, oh, oh, oh, oh we,"
Let me greet each blazing morn
In the place that I was born,
With my buddies Slim and Tex,
And old J.C."

Joshua awakened to a new dawn. It was 1937, and no dust in his eyes, or lungs. The past was the past, and he ambled along the grass of Ferry Field, and never looked back to see what was following him.

Jesse had turned professional, and Bobby Gillman played on the gridirons of Syracuse. The track was Joshua's alone. At first, it had been an odd feeling, more like paralysis, than running. He got stronger, better, faster than he was back then.

But he stopped himself before he thought about what happened. He wouldn't wallow in the past, and now he was the Midwestern champion, and the NCAA champion of 1937. And afterwards, he knew, the starlets wanted a piece of him. He knew he was on a fast track to stardom. He would be on the Johnny Mack Brown, Gene Autry, John Wayne, and Tex Ritter team. The lonesome, singing cowboy from Cincinnati.

"So, ride cowboy ride,
Though the dust is blowing for miles round
There'll come a day,
When the cowboy life will pay,
So ride cowboy ride."

It was "fleet," Joshua Sellers, dominating the competition. No longer "second fiddle," he had raced to the front. Last month in Los Angeles, he tied the world's record, timed in 9.4 seconds for the 100 yard dash to become N.C.A.A. champion. He used his speed to make connections. Soon after graduation, he would have parts in ten movies. He had a new gal who would soon become his wife, singing on the radio, and photographed with Bette Davis, and the stars of Hollywood. He was getting such a name that someone wrote him to borrow a thousand dollars, though Joshua had made only ten dollars that day.

He stared down the track at Ferry Field for one last meet. Already the champion, he wanted to go out in a flurry. In the stands, a few had come to watch him. Some took photos, others just blended in. The champion of the Midwest, N.C.A.A. fastest sprinter of the year, it was all now just a screen test. He thought how smart it would be to ride onto the track on a white horse, singing. He looked up into the sky, but couldn't see, though he'd swear he heard a whooping, gleeful cry. He saw the crowd as a blur in the swirling dust. A man, taller than most was wearing a brown hat. But Joshua didn't focus on him, though the hat came off and waved towards him.

Getting serious, as he did that year, he dug deep into the cinders to get his traction. That stance that could burst fastest out of the cinders. But he began to cough as the dust blew down the track. He spied the crowd again, but nobody waved back.

The race began, and he had a sluggish start. He didn't even know his rivals' names. There was always someone creeping up the rear. But the dust in his face and lungs brought home what he never wanted to know again. It was the dust of defeat; the dust in front of him.

Joshua saw that smile, again. The urging hand, the grin of the champion. He was calling him.

"Come on, come on," the voice said. And Joshua ran with vengeance and sorrow. He raced until there was no past, no tomorrow, bursting past the "also rans." That was his track, his season, his glory, at Ferry Field in Ann Arbor.

***

A plaid sports coat and brown hat, held in one hand to his heart; the right came forth, strong, and firm of grip. But Joshua had the swagger. Jesse, though much taller, seemed to fade. His smile, though, was softer. His words, clear. "Heard you had a good year."

Both found it hard to talk.

Joshua had heard Jesse's name defamed. When word came he was racing horses, Joshua, like the others, was ashamed. That was his captain, Jesse Owens, the champion, everyone's hero who beat Hitler. Jesse held his hand, as he did once in Chicago, and as he did on many tracks, and wouldn't let go. But Joshua's head was turned. He couldn't face him squarely. He wanted only to look forward, not back, and Jesse seemed to know.

"How's Ruth? And the baby?"

"Just fine. Little one's growing all the time."

"So, what brings you this way?"

Jesse took out a Camel's cigarette for emphasis. He kneeled down and drew a circle in the settling dust. That was the same place Owens made his very own, the place he shattered world's records. How long ago, he wondered.

"A little more than a year," said Joshua. He still had that ability to connect to him in strange ways.

"Then, tell me what I need to know? Jesse asked.

"That I just can't pull out of a hat, J.C."

Jesse pointed toward the circles he drew. He had searched for, and found a stick to use. He passed it back to Joshua who winced. Was Jesse toying with him? "You know I don't take sticks from the back hand anymore?"

He became flushed.

Jesse understood. "Hey, Joshua, it's me. We both run first now. It's agreed. Come on, squat down, I need to show you this."

And Joshua did, smoke from the Camels, settling in. Jesse pointed to what seemed to be a globe.

"In this whole world, Josh, is there no room for me?"

Joshua couldn't field that question. He was afraid to look into Jesse Owens' eyes. To see the heartbreak that he thought was his alone, now in the heart of the captain. At the soul of his undoing, in a place that would be remembered as housing the greatest one day spectacle in modern sports history. When Jesse Owens broke three world records in forty- five minutes on the University of Michigan track.

"And you were hurt," said Joshua, reading Jesse's mind again. "And it was my fault."

The night before, there had been some drinking and carousing with the Dekes that had let Jesse in. They weren't going to let him stay off-campus as they made him do at Ohio State. But Joshua was caught between a rock and a hard place. Tomorrow, they would be rivals, so tonight he might gain advantage. Later, Jesse only remembered being jostled when he tripped down the stairs, bruising his back so bad, he almost didn't race. But he forgot what had happened before.

"I tied one on, got drunk, and smashed the bottle on the concrete outside the door. I remember I said I thought I could walk on glass. I knew you'd come save me. You always did because you took care of all of us, the way you did, captain.

"You were closer to the instincts than me. You wanted to watch out for me. I remember you racing out the fraternity door and leaping towards me like Tarzan through the trees. You grabbed me away. You twisted your back. You did that because of me. And I'm sure you knew what I was doing, and why, but you still came. Why?"

"I needed you, Josh. We were both on the same side. My place could only be first, if you were there beside me."

"Beside you? I wanted to run through you. I wanted to beat you in a foot race. I wished I never heard your name. And you were just pawing with me."

"Oh, look at you, now. Look at me. I can't support my family without becoming a freak. Which way do I go, now?"

Joshua remembered the ghost of his father.

"I don't know where the heroes go to find peace. I don't know now that the world seems to want war, not peace. I'm sorry, J.C., I just don't know."

Joshua rose first, and Jesse faltered. Joshua gave him a Jerry Ford bear hug, and this one time, washed away J.C's tears, as Jesse had done so many times before, for him.

That was not the way it's supposed to end, Joshua thought.

Now, Jesse was clairvoyant, his heart exposed.

"You want another race?"

And Joshua smiled, wickedly, as Jesse pawed at him with the backhand, lighting up another cigarette, and holding it in the other palm. Like a drunk, Jesse Owens let his sports coat flutter in the dust, his tie getting caught around his neck. His expression, tight and unsupported.

"Yawl think I'm shamed because I raced Julio McCaw. But when I ran down that track, there was no greater glory. How could a man measure up to the natural gait of an animal that has no shame, no pride, just G-d given speed that could have eaten me alive?

"Come on, competitor, race me."

Joshua was red- faced. He was furious with him. What was the point racing him?

"That don't make any damned sense, anymore."

"But you still want to win."

And Joshua knew that was true.

Joshua ripped and clawed. The earth was cold. A prairie dog came out of its burrow. It saw Jesse follow Joshua's lead. Billows of smoke and dust surrounded them. Night began to crawl from the tiers, from the track, and from the surrounding forest, and down by the lake. A peaceful night descended in Ann Arbor. The races done, the woods and the thickets came alive. But Joshua was ferocious; he would dig a tunnel under the earth to hide. Jesse watched him, a twinkle in his eye.

The ritual done, one in shorts, the other dressed in street clothes, prepared to best each other.

"Where's the finish line?" asked Joshua.

But Jesse took off, without answering, and ran towards the night sky. Joshua caught him, the dust rose high. It seeped into his nostrils, his lungs. Soon stride for stride, Joshua bore down, a question, in his eyes. But Jesse was laughing. He had stopped in midstride.

"Can you feel it?"

"What?" asked Joshua, the hunger to outrace him, gnawing at him once again.

Jesse put his arms around him, but Joshua recoiled.

"What?"

"Oh, I can't say. Maybe, ghosts who are unnaturally paired. We can't change history, or the future, even if we dared. This is our turf, Joshua. Yours and mine. You are the competitor, but the earth is not yours, or mine."

Jesse moved forward, tried to touch, to poke, yes, and to paw at his friend. But Joshua stayed grim and unavailable.

"Got a song for me?"

And Joshua began to thaw. There was always a song for the singing cowboy.

A new one was making the rounds, but not yet released. Joshua had offered to do that song in Hollywood, but there were no takers. Jesse had heard it too, when he was in Havana. If only they knew the future.

"*Oh give me land, lots of land, under starry skies above, don't fence me in.*"

"Let me ride through the wide open country that I love, don't fence me in."

"And let me be myself in the evening breeze,"

"And listen to the murmur of the cotton wood trees,"

"Don't fence me in."

And then, evening fell in a hush in Ann Arbor. Jesse seemed to get what he came for, and embraced his friend. But Joshua was ashamed and too angry to look him in the eye. Walking the last gauntlet through a grateful crowd that gravitated their way, they heard the cheers together for the very last time.

PART 4

38

Gerald Ford was portrayed as a bumbling clown, unfit to hold office, who couldn't be trusted to walk down a few steps without falling. He'd done that a few times, and the nation, still simmering with fury, held him accountable for pardoning Nixon and Tokyo Rose.

Years had passed since his days on the Michigan gridiron, but he was still strong and athletic, and could break a man's hand in his grip, if he wanted.

He'd healed the nation after Watergate, but still was reviled. Without mandate to rule, he wouldn't defeat the Democrats in the November elections. He was the President who, by his will, alone, held the country in his great big paws, and wouldn't let go until it had become more civil.

"Gerald R. Ford is a gentleman in every way," said Bobby Gillman.

"Stand still, Bobby," ordered Martha, his wife of almost forty years. She was trying to straighten his black tie. "Look, it's not every day we get an invitation to the White House."

"Well," she said, "they're finally going to get it right."

One look from her husband and she knew to add, "at least for Jesse."

"He became so large through the years. We became little. Nobody even knows the story or cares anymore."

Changing the subject, Martha said, "I hear the entire U.S. Olympic team is going to be there."

"And well they should. Ike made him Ambassador to sports, but that didn't stop the IRS from bankrupting him. Jesse rose above sports. He was the one true Olympian. You know, Hitler was kinder to him than America ever was. He never even got a telegram of congratulation, not from Roosevelt, or Truman, not until now, forty years later, finally, an invitation to the East Room."

"Still," said Martha, swelling with pride. Jesse was a special friend for her as well as her husband. "Still," said Bobby, understanding the accomplishment and the road that was traveled by the Brown Thunderbolt, the champion of champions.

"And him, will he be there today?" she said, about him who needed no introduction. "I don't know. He took that race harder than me. My whole life has been broadcasting sports, getting to interview great people. In a real way, I am always playing sports. But him, I can't contact. It's as if he has fallen off the earth."

"For him the earth was flat."

"Pity."

"There now you can look at yourself."

In the hall mirror, Bobby couldn't recognize himself. It wasn't the gray hair, or the balding, or the way he'd begun slouching. He'd already accepted the progression of age. Heck, he thought, he was fifty-eight years old. He'd earned his stripes. It was the eyes that had changed. The smile would always be the same. With some cosmetic dentistry, the teeth lined up in a straight row like little white soldiers. But the eyes were not cock sure, the way they were when he was young and had dashed on the cinders.

He was going to take the handoff from Joshua and run along a ragged fold of Nazi skin. He'd clog their bones, rankle them to know there was Jewish blood that was going to transfuse them.

He did take them out, didn't he? He thought, but that was in the war, and that was much later.

He walked over to his display case, as he did every day to see the commendations from presidents, trophies from Syracuse, fistfuls of medals and ribbons, and photographs that were taken with him, down through the ages of twentieth century American sports. Those of American heroes: Dempsey, Louis, Ali, Ted Williams, Johnny Unitas; the list was endless-and he had known them all. He must have broadcast five thousand football and basketball games and been honored in every which way possible. He said he once announced a circus to a blind audience.

There were other medals and ribbons. But on his mantelpiece, inside his trophy case, the centerpiece was left bare. He liked to repeat the story as he got older. It became harder for him to leave it alone. Because of his age or disposition, he was allowed to say as he pleased. Martha, of course, had heard that lament many times before.

"That spot is for the medal they didn't let me earn just because I was a skinny Jewish kid. Imagine that, not letting an innocent kid run just because he was born Jewish?" he said, the words always hard to say. "It's about him today. It's about Jesse," said Martha, helping her man straighten his back until he could walk out the house again with the purpose and swagger of a champion.

"How much time do we have?" At those times, Martha knew what was coming.

"About an hour, but then we must get to Penn Station." They could, though, take the shuttle at LaGuardia to D.C.

"I need to run a ways," he said, limping somewhat, trying to fight the slouching that comes with age.

"So, run, Bobby," she said.

Martha would never fight him about that, though he often appeared unable to walk, let alone run -that same man who seemed to need oiling at the joints, who on days before a snowstorm couldn't stand straight, was suddenly transformed as soon as he got down into a crouching three point stance.

He shed that dreaded formal wear when he ran. He was born to wear sweats and shorts. But nobody now paid much attention to the old man.

Bicyclists whizzed by on the paths, and in the park, it got only worse. Bouncing with basketballs, black youth showed off the between the legs dribble. Those whites along the horseshoe were throwing discs or kicking soccer balls. Only once in a while, he had seen the flight of a football or heard the smack of a bat when it hit the ball.

Sitting in the spring grass, boys and girls of college age ate fast foods and tossed the wrappers on the ground though receptacles were but a slight walk away. And the kids were fat, he thought. They were almost obese. The girls and the boys- their bellies barricaded the walkways and paths where some lined up for the carousel and none were even wearing running pants.

Running, he thought, was a joke. Those didn't even like to walk. Once in a while, he saw a lean black kid, boy or girl run across the meadow. Running clubs in Queens and Far

Rockaway and committed high school coaches aired out some of their fastest sprinters.

In the ethnic melting pot, groups divided on racial lines or on strict neighborhood boundaries. Though he lived now in Westchester, Bobby Gillman worked the whole city. On Saturday mornings, he broadcast the high school football games. When he got to Brooklyn –for Boys High, or Tilden – especially for Madison, his alma mater, Bobby walked the neighborhoods and observed the passing of the generations.

When he ran in the park, he was always shocked to see games going on he didn't know. Cricket, an effeminate sport to the American sports fan, was being played in the lazy style. How could they not blast a ball with a stick, to hit it as far as the eye could see? Mickey Mantle wanted to murder a baseball. Those boys looked like they wouldn't get their hands dirty. Where was the America he knew and what had happened to its youth? They were fat and didn't move. Except for the blacks, and the Irish kids who held court with basketballs day and night, they had become mere spectators.

Occasionally he saw blacks running. He never saw a Jewish kid with sneakers. Oh, once in a while, he knew one would get in there on a basketball court, or become involved in baseball or football fraternity intra-murals. Some even turned professional, and he interviewed them all.

But he never knew a Jewish American runner. He never saw a kid with 'Jewish sneakers,' but maybe that was what was needed to wake up a new generation of Jewish kids. "Jews ran. They didn't just die in the crematoria. They were the fastest men on earth, and nobody even knows that anymore."

"Calm down," said Martha, helping him stretch his limbs and making sure he took his pills. Bobby had developed heart problems.

"Jews ran," he said, again, making a fist, whose bony protrusions would not scare anybody. "If we had won, what would those parks be like today?

"America loves its Olympic heroes. Two Jews that beat Hitler; how would that have played at the Albee. Cagney and Raft could have played us, dear. It would be two Jews beating the pants off Hitler. Jimmy grew up with Jews. He knew Yiddish.

'You dirty rats,' he'd say, but in Yiddish. What a movie that would be, and the world would have known Jews were tough.

"Martha, if we won, would that have stopped Hitler for one day? Would we have saved one Jew from the ovens? Would that have changed Hitler's timetable? "If only America stood tall against those Nazis, Bandage, and Dean. They both spoke at Nazi rallies until the war began, those bums, let them rot.

"What would Hitler have done? He was just a bully without American business. He wouldn't have had the time to rearm without help. If he saw that America wouldn't go along with the racial policy against the Jews, he may have stepped back. They may have traded their racial policy for guns and butter. They may have given the Jews one more day to breathe, one less ride on the transports to Auschwitz. Eichmann would've had to scratch off one name from the I.B.M. punch cards.

"If America had made that statement, of Jews and Blacks running together against fascism, the rest of the world may not have moved in lock-step with the Nazi timetable. The Jew wouldn't have been marginalized, not that fast, not in Europe.

"And maybe those Jewish kids would start standing up for their heritage. Maybe, they'd be running.

"I need to know if that can happen again-that we can run proud in this country, and not always be the victim? Somewhere in America, you know, there must be Jews left who are unafraid to compete and to win. I need to know if that still matters to any of them."

"I know, Bobby, I know, you do, and maybe we'll never know that answer, but I remember the day you and Joshua were supposed to run. How the neighborhoods came out in tank tops and running clothes. Williamsburg and Flatbush, Boro Park, the parents and the kids came out with cakes and flowers, and, Bobby; even an Italian accordion player serenaded your mother and father. They cheered your father who came out on the porch to make a speech.

"'We were going, Jews and Negroes, Italian, Irish and Protestant, we were going," he said, 'to smash the Nazis down. America was going to smash those Nazis down.'

"And the young, Bobby, they ran up and down the neighborhoods like the cars do today. They were like a squadron that worked in shorts and running shoes, tapping the pavement, turning the corners, lean and thin, a lot of them wearing skullcaps; always the same strong builds.

"Someone turned on the fire hoses. It was such a hot summer. That was one good thing Robert Moses did opening up pools for city kids. But not where we lived. There the kids laughed and they were lean and hearty. Those were the same children who would grow up to take on the whole Nazi army. Darn, Bobby, we were those strong sons and daughters.

"Some seemed as fast-well, almost as fast as you some shouted they were the fastest kid on the block and they raced each other between the sewers in the streets to prove it. A lot of laughter, a lot of good, honest American sweats, the day you were to run for glory," she said, but Bobby had fallen asleep.

Quietly, she changed the arrangements. They would have to catch a later flight to Washington. "The Medal of Freedom," she said aloud, her thoughts turning to Jesse. Looking at her husband, she marveled how when he slept, he didn't move a muscle, or take anything but quiet breaths. What pleasure she had known beside him.

The Medal of Freedom, she thought, thinking of the sacrifice of that generation, the hardships and struggle to overcome racism, the march to war and to defend our liberty, the indignities Jesse faced, always as a gentleman. He'd been a janitor, had even raced horses to earn a living. He was given awards, but couldn't eat in their dining rooms. His well-wishers had to find him in the servants' quarters. A grandson of slaves, but he was going to the White House, anyways.

"The Medal of Freedom," she said, choking back tears that were still bathing her husband's eyes with her own.

"It's not just Jesse's day, baby. We're going to Washington because it's our day as well. You were fighting the Nazis not just for your rights, baby, but for Jesse's as well."

She kissed her Olympian on the forehead one more time.

39

They weren't certain what the eighty-seven foot room would be used for, but Abigail Adams was able to hang her laundry there to dry. Later, Tad Lincoln got the idea to hitch his goats to a make-shift wagon and ride them on the luxurious carpets.

Union troops often stayed the night there. The Public Audience room, as it was called, was the largest room in the House. In Lincoln's time, the ceiling was frescoed in common ornaments. Flowers and cupids in a haphazard array watched the goings-on. More often than not, well- wishers of the popular President made off with parts of the lace curtains or the chords and the tassels and the damask drapery, leaving gaping holes the size of gold bars.

It was there that tragedy and history bore common witness. Abraham Lincoln lay in state on the catafalque platform made especially for him. Almost one hundred years later, John F. Kennedy, lay there as well. Both by assassination, never was the large room so honored, or so sad.

The Roosevelt kids thought roller skates would be ideal. The meetings, public receptions, awards ceremonies, recitals could not compete with the constant grinding of children's feet. Roosevelt had to renovate and put in the present motif that has been undisturbed since. Bronze electric light standards, a few Bohemian cut glass chandeliers, ornamented benches over an oak floor of Fontainebleau carpentry giving a somber tone to a place where great events occurred.

Between those walls came Heads of State or plain simple folk who had made their mark and were being honored by a grateful nation. Today another giant appeared. The White House,

Washington, D.C., Medal of Freedom Award, August 5, 1976. Jesse Owens:

"for especially meritorious contribution to (1) the security or national interests of the United States, or (2) world peace, or (3) cultural or other significant public or private endeavors.

He wore a white sport jacket, accompanied by his wife, Ruth, and was cheered by the entire United States Olympic team that had just competed at the summer games in Montreal, Quebec. Bruce Jenner, world record titlist in the Decathlon, Dorothy Hammil, World Figure Skating champion of the winter games, and Luann Ryon, Archery Gold Medalist were some of the athletes of that team.

The East Room shook with heartfelt emotion. Jesse Owens shook hands with everyone present. Bobby Gillman fell to tears and hugged him and would not let go. But nothing compared to the President of the United States. "Why did it take so long to honor this man?"

Gerald Ford didn't understand. He held the beautiful white starred medallion, an open palm with blue bordered bronze stars, emblematic of the original thirteen colonies. With the golden eagle carved above the pedestal of the design, the President then draped the blue ribbons around that great man of humility.

Not a dry eye was in the great house; not a heart that did not beat for that forgotten soul. It wouldn't be the last award for him. Like floodgates finally opened at the harbor, he would not be ignored again.

Six months later, Present Jimmy Carter would present him with the Living Legend Award. On that occasion, he said:, "A young man who possibly didn't even realize the superb nature of his own capabilities went to the Olympics and performed in a way that hasn't been equaled since...and since this superb achievement, he has continued in his own dedicated but modest way to inspire others to reach for greatness."

Posthumously, he would also be awarded The Congressional Medal of Honor, but why *did* it take so long?

Gerald Ford couldn't get that thought out of his mind as he anxiously scanned the crowd and stopped when he saw Bobby Gillman about to leave. For a moment he forgot he was president, and shouted across the wide expanse of the East Room. They talked briefly though passionately.

"Have you heard from him?"

"No."

"I know he tried the movies. That didn't work out."

"I didn't even know that. I saw him once in 1947. He was having dinner with a woman. I couldn't talk to him, then, about what happened."

"I still don't know why you didn't run, Bobby. I wish I could give something back to you and to him."

"Thank you, Mr. President, I appreciate that." "I understand there's talk about building some museum and an exhibit about those Olympic Games."

"Yes, Mr. President. I've heard about that, too. People should know the Holocaust didn't just begin with the killing of the Jews. It began when Hitler came to power."

"Yes, Bobby, even a president can take a lesson in American history."

"I'm sorry, Mr. President. I wasn't trying to be preachy today."

"Oh, Bobby, we go back a long ways. Call me Jerry, and don't tell anyone, but I think, after all that's happened in the county, I'm going to be just Jerry pretty soon. But I'd sure like to talk to him. He had so much speed, but he never ran again."

"I don't know if that really mattered to him."

"Oh, I saw him run. He used to lunge at that tape with his heart, Bobby. With his heart, not his head. He must've known he could walk into the White House without an invitation. He would always be welcome in my house. As long as he didn't wash dishes or started to sing."

"I've heard him sing, too, sir."

"Well, I just hope for him the music still goes round and round."

"Yes, Mr. President…Jerry. I appreciate your kind words."

He was telling Martha of that conversation as he headed to the airport. The television network had asked him to cover a Dodger game in Los Angeles that week. Martha didn't want to be in Los Angeles for three days with little to do but wait for the game. "How much shopping can one do in one lifetime?"

Bobby had an idea. "It's not always about being there. Sometimes the going is half the fun. Let's go by train out to L.A. We'll see America from the ground up. It's been awhile since I've been on the Super Chief.

Not since I started broadcasting, when I was wined and dined by the big boys and was afraid to fly."

"Okay," said Martha, buoyed at the idea, "but it's not the Chief, anymore. It's the Southwest Limited. All aboard?"

"All aboard," said Bobby, lost in memories of things still undefined.

40

There was a time long ago when the Super Chief pulled into Gallup, New Mexico, and its two wrought iron stallion figurines affixed to the gate at the entranceway, seemed to separate from the other, as the doors swung open to make room for the passengers that just got off the train. Those were the days when he lived in the old Harvey Hotel, later named the *Casa de Desierto*.

When dining cars were first introduced, the Harvey girls served fresh milk, brought by contract on special refrigerator cars to their roadside diners and then onto the train. They wore black and white uniforms whose skirts could be no more than six inches off the floor.

He came west with fine china and Irish linens on the Pullman cars, and more than once had a special conversation with a Harvey Girl, who were bound by ten o'clock curfews. He ate sumptuous meals on blue china plates served by one, and afterwards removed her 'Elsie' collar, stockings, and dull black shoes.

He told her that he was an athlete who was going to Los Angeles to make movies. And he may have actually made a few, though none were released and nobody knew his name. On his second trip out West, he sat between John Wayne and Frederick March and talked about running. They wanted to hear about Jesse Owens.

The farther west he traveled, the more he tried to forget the past while stepping out into the dust of Gallup. He made a phone call to his agent in Hollywood, but forgot who he was or why he came.

He imagined in the dust, the desert wasteland of Palestine, and as the news from his agent grew from bad to worse about work, he began to see that spot as his own holy land. When his agent told him there'd be no more auditions, he let the train leave without him. A perfect place, he thought.

Outside the railway depot, named for an old paymaster, he followed the flight of winged creatures toward the lonesome mountains. In nearby Church Rock, amidst the rise of sandstone cliffs, ravens flew among the dizzying beauty of red cliffs seeped with limestone and volcanic sand.

He liked being in the mountains; the elevation brought clean air into his lungs and he walked hills and valleys, avoiding snakes and prairie dogs, lizards, and coyotes, which were always starving and unashamed.

The dust settled on his clothes, in his hair, into his lungs. The agent was telling him about alternatives, and he tried to listen, but watched the swinging door of the galloping horses until he abandoned the phone to a Navajo man with a gleaming turquoise necklace and a wide-brimmed hat. When he heard the low mournful tune of the Super Chief departing, he knew he'd never be that singing cowboy his heart had imagined. He'd never be anything again. The American dream would never be his.

When the dust had cleared, and he had stopped feeling sorry for himself, he noticed a lot of poor people around him. Blacks were not segregated there, but moved freely among the white population. Men in cowboy boots, or the Indians, some in headdress – others wearing jeans and old checkered shirts-their hair braided, looked wild, but free.

The Natives wore caps of dark colors. They seemed colorless, their wear was for utility only; not caring to attract anyone. Dark jeans were cuffed, but the elders maintained their sense of dignity with clean, suede boots and white straw wide-brimmed hats. The patriarchs, though, weren't like their own children who came into town to greet the train. Rickety arms carried beads and bracelets and the earth tones of turquoise. The passengers bought some for a song.

But what he noticed was that many of the children were already bent and misshapen. Poverty and disease seemed to follow the Western train. Many walked bent with canes. Into Gallup came the opticians, who prescribed glasses for men, women, and children. Diabetes of the Dine, the Navajo people, was prevalent, and glasses were used as a precaution and as a necessity for the dimming of the diabetic light.

During the war years, New Mexico was a testing site for the Manhattan Project and the Atomic Bomb. To get the rich uranium, the Indians worked in the mines. Near Church Rock, the extraction of the precious ore caused residues to be embedded into the waters down the River Puerco, into the drinking water of the Pueblo, the Hopi, the Navajo, and the Zuni.

The Indian capital of the world began dying and birth defects were common. Incidences of cancer were greater than the general population from a people whom had had one of the lowest rates by race recorded. Yet they suffered alone, and their plight remained unrecorded.

He saw in the dust, a lone teenager in glasses, his hair braided under a white headdress, tapping a wooden cane. The boy was waving at the passengers that alighted from the train.

"My name is Barry," he said, but he pronounced it as the fruit, 'Berry'."

"I'm legally blind."

He said it as matter of fact, without trace of remorse or self-pity. Joshua wanted to cling to him for he knew that young man was already his teacher. Berry was artless and free from want or vanity. He didn't know shame or separation from his people, nor bitterness or regret. "Can I sing you a song?"

It was an irresistible offer.

For the next forty years, he stayed with the Dine, the Navajo people, and saw trains come and go. The Super Chief became the Southwest Limited, and when the Amtrak took over in 1971, the Southwest Chief was born. By then, he was a teacher and a coach at the Red Rock School. Berry was his sidekick, and they taught each other all they knew.

"You come from a concrete world," Berry once told him.

Berry liked baseball and John Wayne who came to New Mexico with the stars on the Super Chief and stayed at El Rancho, a hotel started by a brother of Cecil B. DeMille. As much as he tried, he couldn't get Berry to understand that Wayne had been destructive to his people. Berry couldn't understand that 'a lick,' because he didn't know anger or how to hate.

"I always wanted to be a cowboy, Pilgrim," Berry said, doing a lousy John Wayne.

He lived in accordance with simple needs. He didn't have to experience in order to enjoy the essence of things. One day he came to the teacher's home and asked him to teach him how to run.

"*Naatsédlózhii* , teach me, it looks like fun," he said, pushing his strong arms on the sides of the iron chair, a shawl around him and a woven blanket draped around his knees.

'*Naatsédlózhii*' was the name of a roadrunner, the state bird of New Mexico. It was also a perfect name for him. Capable of flight, the long legged creature preferred to walk. A member of the cuckoo family, it could run up to twenty miles an hour. Nevertheless, it was a bird that didn't choose to fly. The name fit, and he let the natives have their way.

He liked to teach sports other than running to lame children, or children who couldn't walk. They didn't believe him when he said he was a runner when he was younger. He'd even been on the Olympic squad during the 1936 Games.

"*Naatsedlozhii léi' chxóóh bił íísaal!*"

"The roadrunner is really speeding off, throwing up dust!"

It was easier to teach his small group the skills of basketball, baseball and volleyball because they could extend their arms and use upper body strength without the need for limbs.

"No, Pilgrim, I want to run," Berry said.

His living room had an odd assortment of useless items that held no meaning to anyone but him. Rummaging among the metal works, he searched for a book that could help him explain running as a concept to his friend.

Berry kept a cane under his arm so that he could be guided in dark spaces. His sunglasses followed the Coach, by some uncanny process, no matter where he walked.

"What are you searching for, teacher?" asked Berry.

There was an old punch card machine, some tangled electrical wire, a dead battery from an old model T Ford, a piece of aluminum. He stored early model phones, a tin of motor oil, a Fanta coke bottle, and in later years, vials of methadone. He had a Luger in a black holster, and an officer's pocket watch. During the war was the only time he left Gallup, and using his sparse knowledge of German interrogated prisoners.

What could he teach to Navajo children in wheelchairs? What did he know about the joy of running, or the whimsical journey of a long distance marathon run? To feel leaves crackling underfoot, or dust left on the side of a mountain trail. Kicking limbs and spreading the arms with only the afterthought of finishing. The marathoners had so much more fun. They had time to reflect about life, or about a lost love.

At the strangest times, he would think about Rachel. If she lived, she would write about running for she loved the sport in a way he could not. He was geared only for speed, for the electricity of the race, the burst from nothing to flight, to tear the lungs, to test the boundaries of heart and limbs.

Did she reach Palestine, or go into the ashes? He wondered, holding the old peace of tin, the electrical wires, the punch card machine, the jangled metal, and an old battery.

"Yes?" asked Berry, his head eager and to the side.

"Yes," he said, he would. He would teach him how to run.

And by degrees, lamed children, both Navajo and Caucasian, came to Red Rock School to be taught by the Coach, the master of the games. There were twenty wheelchairs and some assorted, wooden and, later, prosthetic limbs, crutches and orthopedic devices. Some couldn't afford even a cane, but he taught them how to make a solid walking stick.

He didn't have the love of the game anymore. He didn't feel what Berry did, what the twenty or thirty children did who came to him every day: how to love play. But he began to organize his children into combat troops, setting one team against the other until the smiles were no longer on their angelic faces, and they clawed at each other to win.

One day, a pupil came in with a flat stick that the Coach confiscated. He held the object firm in his hand, and his annoyance turned to a distant memory and to firm resolve.

"Line up in wide circles, three to each space. No, give yourselves a wide berth. The object of this game is to get the stick to your teammate and run to the next man. You want to run? We will run," he said.

That first race was a disaster. Wheels interlocked, and the runners toppled over each other as the third runner crashed into the other two, and the last racer ran off the course fearing for his life.

The stick-Coach insisted on calling it the baton- was dropped at the beginning. The pass, of course, was the hardest to master. It involved building momentum to release the grip of one hand to pass the baton to one's classmate.

Soon, everyone wanted a piece of the game - the lame, the blind, and the boy in crutches. As word spread in the far-reaching Dine community, healthy children in drab clothes flocked to school. Some even auditioned for a part. They raced in the dust high up along the sagebrush, scaring prairie dogs and rattlesnakes that came out of the brush, but the boys forgot to return to school.

As word spread in the Navajo way, children came from as far away as Flagstaff, Arizona. Charlie Glasses came from the Pimas; a desert tribe, their peaceful community were used to storing food. That was how they lived until the soldiers came and took their land away.

Modern man stripped the land around Scottsdale, raised rent and forced them out onto reservations. The Pimas still hoarded food, but instead of the healthier kind, it was MacDonald's and fries. One half of the Pima were obese and suffered from diabetes.

Charlie Glasses had trouble sitting in his wheelchair. He was a boy of twelve years old, and not so lucky. But he was their fiercest competitor. The coach was soon contacted by local news about the 'miracle in the desert.'

Children, the story went, who couldn't walk were running, and their diets reflected the change. When Charlie was caught putting two packs of chopped meat on the counter of Safeway, followed by eight, twenty-four pack, giant cans of Pepsi and Dr. Pepper, a *'Naatsédlózhii'*, as they were then called, ordered him to put the sodas back on the shelves or they wouldn't let him run.

"Coach's rules," said the counter boy as Charlie Glasses cried to his mother, holding his hands to hide his shame.

First the news spread from the local Dine newspaper. The Independent wrote about how an old white man was transforming the way their children lived. There were private sponsors that fielded the best of the lot for the finals in the Special Olympics in Albuquerque. He was called upon to meet with them, as it was going to be a televised national sporting event.

Stubbornly he called himself *'Naatsédlózhii,'* inside the ballroom of the Hotel Sheraton, when he finally arrived. It had been so many years that he'd been among his own people. He felt estranged, and still suffered from the humiliation he'd known years before.

He seemed more Native than white anyway. The sun had scorched his Semitic complexion, and his long, gray hair covered his head. His clothes were of modest dress, and Berry walked beside him, tapping a large circle that helped keep the reporters at bay.

"I have an open disability case," he said, struggling back into the wheelchair. Or out of it when he needed room to breathe.

The sponsors of the event were talking to him about foundation scholarships for Dine participants. Big business wanted a piece of the action-a few television spots- in clean, feel good commercials: Exxon, formerly Jersey Standard-always searching for clean fuels. The Rockefeller and Ford Foundations, Chase Bank, Boss Clothing, I.B.M., ALCOA, General Electric, International Telephone and Telegraph, DuPont, Ford, Coca Cola and the Alfred P. Sloan Foundation would be the biggest contributors to begin a network of special competitions broadcast around the world.

"Let's go, Berry. It's not for us," he said, walking away from a circling cordon of modern day initialed men.

"Why, Boss, it's good medicine," Berry said, but he still obeyed by tapping his cane like a whip, when the circle grew nearer. They were backing out the door, boys in wheelchairs and long-sleeved dark shirts and checkered vests, autistic kids in large red caps humming a tune, a microcephalic carrying a bouquet of flowers.

They were insulated from a vast network of American corporate might and separated by one man's thoughts, and his side-kick's silver tipped cane.

He took his group as far as valet parking. The area was cordoned off just outside the entranceway to the big downtown hotel, and away from the swinging doors, and formed a taut circle of wheelchairs, whose gleaming spokes shone in the hot sun. He tried to shield his students from the harsh glare of photographers, shooting their illuminated debris into their faces.

The Indians were trying to stave off the hostile, rabid band of paparazzi, a reverse Cowboys and Indians war, in the dry air surrounding the white peaks of the mountain city. Suddenly, someone broke through the barricade. He was quiet, but didn't make eye contact with the blue-eyed Navajo. "How do you get a corned beef sandwich out here?" asked Bobby Gillman to his teammate of long ago.

"You do not know me," said *'Naatsédlózhii.'* He tried to be fierce, though the heavy weight under his eyes gave him away like a signature.

"We were more than what we did or didn't do. We were men and we stood tall as Americans and as Jews."

"I don't understand. You have the wrong man."

"Those sponsors can help your students, Joshua, don't you understand? The past is the past."

"You work for them now, Bobby," he suddenly said, his anguish unleashed. "They worked for Hitler then, but they never paid the price for what they did. Those Olympics gave the blacks crumbs while it helped the Nazis prepare for war. The corporations gave them our know-how to build the crematoria, to identify the Jews for transport to the death house. They sold America out for money."

"You're not responsible for Rachel," Bobby answered, though wincing at the power of Joshua's words.

Bobby had heard bad news he needed to tell his unhappy friend who wilted under the weight he'd carried when he heard her name.

"Please, brace yourself, Joshua. During the War for Independence, Rachel died fighting for the land she cherished. She was buried with the honors of the Israeli State."

"She died? Rachel is dead? She cannot die. Her dreams are so alive within me," Joshua said, falling to his knees.

'She is home and she is free." He turned away from Joshua's tears.

"And now yours, Joshua, your dreams. What about your dreams?"

Joshua keeled over, unsupported, and suddenly older than his sixty one years. "I have no dreams, anymore."

"Run with me," Bobby begged, and he was crying too. And Joshua took his hand.

***

Later, in Gallup, the dust lifted like a veil with the comings and goings of passengers and trains. A magnet that both attracted and repelled the old Indian jewelry businesses scratched out meager livings in the dusty shops along the mother road, Route 66. Joshua didn't consciously make the connection or compare the genocide of the Natives to the Jewish people. But that desert of oppressed people gave him the solace he sought, his own Israel in the Diaspora, an outcast who couldn't leave America, though America had left him.

It had been a long time since he ran, and never that slowly. Time, he thought, had ravaged his Olympian body and mocked him every step of the way. But Bobby ran with him, and helped while Joshua faltered and stopped when his pal heaved for breath. Bobby carried something in his hands, a folded newspaper that he passed along to Joshua, as they rounded a clearing.

Joshua took it in the stance of the sprinter. The pass was certain. The paper was what they had. It used to be a baton. When he fielded it, cleanly, Bobby told him to open it, and read the headlines. Still running, Joshua saw the photograph first. It was of two dear friends, embracing. Gerald Ford was presenting Jesse Owens with the Medal of Freedom.

"I wanted to come. I was ... detained." And Joshua couldn't contain himself. He kneeled in sudden emotion. He loved Jerry Ford, and anguished when he heard Jesse's name.

"I worshipped Jesse," he said, kneeling. "But I was jealous, too. I wanted to beat him so bad. I was racist inside, where it really mattered, in a place I couldn't hide from myself. I would have turned him in to the *Gestapo* if I could. Steal that medal he won that I thought was mine. Inside, I never forgave him from running in my place. I believed what others had said. That Jesse angled to take my place, though I knew that was not true. Maybe, when he was already flush from victory, he wanted more. That was only natural. But he stood up for me at the meeting. You were there. You knew that was true."

"That's what Bandage did to us. To all of us, Jesse, too. They made us rivals, and tried to make us hate each other."

"I liked Davie Warren and Tom Grace. I really did. But they put us in a gladiator pit, and told us to fight each other with Olympic gold on the line. What wouldn't I do to make Jesse fall? I'm still ashamed."

"They did that to us, also. They did. They didn't let us become real friends. They put us under the microscope. I know it's not your fault. So does Jesse. He swears he's still ashamed they made him run in your place. So, let's run, Josh, let's run again. Each time we do, we beat them at their own game."

***

Joshua ran slowly, at first, then began gliding along the small stones leading downtown at the edge of the ephemeral streams. Near the River Puercos, he soon found at every turn, an entourage waiting for him.

The Indian Olympic team was threatened unless Joshua agreed to corporate help. The river today was as it usually was: dusty and barren, and not helpful for man, or the cattle that occasionally grazed.

But Joshua was an older man now. He'd have the children run whether lame or bound, with the unchallenged boys and girls who took note and ran around without guidance with their reservation dogs limping one-eyed or one legged beside them. Some raced quickly. He understood that burst of speed, the need to expend a heavy burden. Like a sack, his body had hurt him. Speed, he knew only then, existed in his mind, and not his legs. It had never deserted him.

The children followed the path of the river with fast hands and glad heart. Their legs carried them in ways his never did. The goal of the dash man was to drop the weight of the flesh. The marathon man wanted to remember, not forget. On Nizhoni Boulevard, a steep climb for the children, Joshua showed the ravages of time. He stopped to wipe his brow on a bench mercifully placed below the Navajo Indian hospital.

Officers in brown fatigues walked by. That was the first Federal health care system in America, given by treaty in the 1860's. In exchange for health care, the Natives agreed not to scalp white men.

He hadn't run in a long while. But he was also exhilarated in a way he couldn't explain. He could still do what he wanted except run fast. But he was able to enjoy the subtleties of the chase. He let visions come and go as he grappled with the dust above the waters. He could actually hear himself breathing.

Joshua reached the top of a sandstone cliff on a hill downtown. Down below, the children rested. They truly knew the joy of running.

Sometimes, a boulder could be the softest surface that can shelter the human body at rest. Joshua stretched his old bones there, and felt the energy that came from stone. He thought about the children whose infirmities were the result partly of diet and fast foods and corporate greed. It was greed that had made the waters contaminated and the mines diseased.

Bobby Gillman crouched nearby, watching his friend, hoping to reach the hardness within. Joshua, he thought, was still alone with his pain, even now. He wouldn't let go.

Joshua thought about what happened at school that day. He had to laugh at the children's zeal. They really wanted to win, no matter how badly they passed the baton, or wheeled their chairs. Some were naturals. Imagining the run, their hands did the heroic moves of their legs. Only Charlie Glasses couldn't keep up, but he was red-faced and angry, saying that he wanted to finish the relay race.

In the gymnasium, the children were screaming. They knew they could win in Albuquerque except for him. All eyes turned to Charlie, and Joshua had to agree. "Charlie, you're out *if* we go to Albuquerque."

And never did he hear more wails, or more fury from any other human being. "I want to run," Charlie said, "I want to run to the squiggly tape."

Charlie's face smudged with tears and his gaze turned inward. The flush was gone; not just the color, but dear life, itself, it seemed.

"Well, son," Joshua said, inhaling in a lone, deep breath. Suddenly, a memory remembered, he saw ghosts from the past.

In Charlie's sad eyes, Joshua was the Dean or Robertson, Bandage and the rest. Joshua had become the corporation. He was the beast that now made a crippled kid cry. Oh my G-d, he thought. Oh my G-d.

Saying nothing to Bobby, Joshua saw himself forty years younger in Berlin, his old body reacting to the slight shift of the earth.

He would rouse them again from hell to watch him run the first leg of the relay four hundred. With those thoughts, he began to breathe harder, reminded of that race for glory, the race that never was. He knew that race forever would be tainted by the betrayal of American blood.

But the zealots of business would never be hanged in America, nor would the initialed men who helped Nazis prepare for aggressive war. But if they would pay reparations to his children, who was he to say, 'no more?'

The alphabet soup of American business would never pay the price. They'd never be hanged in America for helping Nazi industry thrive. He'd take that scrap of gold medal in his room, and melt it back to dust, and spread it on the metal heap. Nothing from their hands, in that time past would be kept. That time it was not about the medal. It was for a slap and a death kiss to Nazis everywhere whom he'd drive to hell for their arrogance.

But what about his own arrogance, who was he while he alone had the power? His body bent, his breath short in the thin, mountainous air; he knew his time for glory was well past.

What about Charlie Glasses and the kids? They wanted the same dreams as his. What about Charlie Glasses and his American dream?

How many in the nation were given that same gift of greatness only to die penniless and in despair? Race prejudice had stopped generations of blacks from dreaming. How was his misery different from theirs?

Money was given for useless work. There were so many artists and scientists, brilliant mathematicians and inventors who were forgotten; perhaps never even known. Yet circumstance had made just one man, of those times, Jesse Owens, remembered.

Joshua, at best, would be like a fictional character in an unpublished novel, written by an unknown writer, tucked away in a manuscript lying dormant on a dusty shelf for thirty years.

In the end, he was another ghost runner, conceived by a ghost writer, ready to be placed into the category of forgotten dreams, as invisible as the shadows of the past. He was but another nameless victim, only to become nameless again and unremembered, but how fitting, he thought, that was. But so was Jesse Owens. They used him, too, to sell Nazi respect in the world view. He once said he wouldn't run in Germany unless Jews could, but his coaches, bug-eyed, told him that was a crazy view for his own future. Jesse was a real man who was used. He was the quintessential ghost runner, captain of the team.

But still there was a crack in time, a seam wide enough for sunflowers to pass through. Time also sometimes moved quickly, and life forgotten in a blur. A light though was shining through. He'd race again with Charlie's legs in a wheel-chaired dream just to see that face of hope and the screaming joy Charlie Glasses would feel even if just once. Not in the outcome, but in the race to the tape.

Papa, I understand, Joshua thought, the tears of joy suddenly lifting him back into a time when he could soar as high as an eagle. Suddenly, he was again, despite all that had happened to him, a true champion, and a true Olympic champion.

"Okay, Bobby. I'll take every fistful of dollars those American Nazis have for my kids."

Bobby smiled in his winsome way again. And he saw Joshua's face filled with that hope he showed over forty years before in Prospect Park. One last time the pair, on their hobbled legs, ran shouting into the dust of the high mountain air.

"Ray. Ray. U.S.A."

World War had come and gone, but he'd be a casualty no more. They ran soaring with wings, and Joshua heard his father's voice. It said how proud he was that Joshua had gone to the tape to beat Hitler and race hatred.

Above, a sudden squadron of cranes tipped their feathers in winged admiration. Somewhere in the clouds, Davie Warren made the skies safe once again. Joshua had never forgotten the American dream. Now he'd go the last mile to touch the tape with glory in his heart. To take his spot among the sons and daughters that rose to kill Hitler. Joshua knew he would never be, never was an also ran. His was the glory shared with the greatest generation.

Glory was also for others who dared. Glory would be for Charlie Glasses and the lame, Indian children who came to Albuquerque with hopes to follow the American dream.

And after that race in Albuquerque was run and the glory shared by every challenged Olympian there, Joshua gave Charlie a tearful hug.

"I'm sorry I doubted you, son," he said, presenting him a token of the team's appreciation though he came in dead last. It was a small oak tree, and the other kids decided, maybe because

Charlie's head was the only one that fit, that he would also wear the crown of laurels.

And Bobby Gillman, broadcasting the event for a national audience wept. It was the only time he couldn't finish the call of a sporting event.

EPILOGUE

He had been suffering those headaches, before the seizures came. Fugue is the Latin word for flight. The doctors at Gallup Indian Medical Hospital took his history. When did he begin to disappear within himself? To lose his identity? And obviously, he thought about Germany.

It started even before the pounding by the S.S. guards. They did their job with black truncheons on him. Or, maybe that little girl, on the pier at Cuxhaven who terrified him. What had he seen in those hateful eyes? No, he knew where it began, where he began to die. It was at the meeting of the American coaches. The day he became a ghost runner.

But he was too ashamed to tell the medicine men that. The years of training and denial. The forced competition until his guts hung loose. He had made promises to kids he couldn't keep, and back-stabbed his best friends to win. He had taken his papa's last five hundred dollars for Berlin. He had believed in his coaches, in his people, in his country. He gave something precious away to them. He gave them his youth, and his heart. Yet, when the race was run, he wasn't even an "also ran." Glory was not his. It never was *'bashert.'*

Then, he thought about Berry, and the Native children, running about the school with their "res dogs," their mangy mutts, on colored, bandaged stumps. He thought about Charlie Glasses and smiled.

Some years later, Joshua was walking in the mountains, when his hair was white, and his eyes had dimmed. A Native mother once told him she saw Navajo faces in those mountains. But he could see only hers.

The last laugh *was* for us, Rachel, he thought, speaking to a distant memory, of a conversation recorded in the city of hate, in the time of his nation's shame.

If only he could have told her how heroic she had been under the crooked cross. That whenever she thought about Berlin to be defiant. And as long as desire lived in the beating of hearts, both great and small, the human spirit could never be enslaved again.

He remembered Jesse Owens, and how he wanted to be his friend. But his pride had stepped between them. He could never share the light that came from Jesse's eyes. He could never feel the patter of rain, the sun drenched sky, or the cool air of autumn, seeping into his lungs, bursting with life.

Once, Jesse raced in a storm, under black clouds, lit with horizontal rain, in the crosswinds, when dust blew in his face. He welcomed the sure fire of white heat, the lightning that crashed about him like cymbals. It was music playing from flutes, from lyres, from songs of Olympus in a Grecian chorus, in the orchestra of the immortals. He never cared to win the race. Jesse ran for the joy of the chase, his soul yearned to touch the heels of paradise.

Soon, Joshua would go into the mountains, and not return. He would find Jesse, embrace him like a brother, and share another song. But, he'd never want to race him, never be his rival again. For whom had the American dream been betrayed, if not for him? Immortality was rightly given to Jesse Owens, history to exalt his name. The past was buried, and the future now was calling him. "Come on, come on," it seemed to say.

"I'm afraid the Nazis have succeeded with their propaganda. First, the Nazis have run the Games on a lavish scale never before experienced, and this has appealed to the athletes. Second, the Nazis have put up a very good front for the general visitors, especially the big businessmen."

Foreign correspondent William Shirer, Berlin, August 16, 1936.

ABOUT THE AUTHOR

Robert Rubenstein has been a teacher of special education for over thirty years. He has been working on this novel for thirty-five. Recently blessed with two grandchildren, he spends his time now teaching, swimming at Coney Island beaches, and making long treks to Maryland and Virginia. He brings presents, of course.

Comments welcome:
AriaTyger@ghostrunners.org

GHOST RUNNERS
an Olympic Dream Betrayed

A novel by
ROBERT RUBENSTEIN

Robert Rubenstein
Brooklyn, New York.

October 2015.

Made in the USA
Middletown, DE
04 November 2015